Legendary
TEXAS
Storytellers

Jim Gramon

Republic of Texas Press
Plano, Texas

Library of Congress Cataloging-in-Publication Data

Gramon, Jim.
  Legendary Texas storytellers / Jim Gramon.
     p. cm.
  Includes bibliographical references and index.
  ISBN 1-55622-939-9 (alk. paper)
  1. American wit and humor--Texas--History and criticism. 2.
Storytellers--Texas--Biography. 3. Storytelling--Texas. 4. Tall
tales--Texas. 5. Texas--Biography. I. Title.

PS266.T4 G69 2002
398.2'092'2764--dc21   2002011636

© 2003, Jim Gramon
All Rights Reserved

Printed in the United States of America

ISBN 1-55622-939-9
10 9 8 7 6 5 4 3 2 1
0209

All inquiries for volume purchases of this book should be addressed to Wordware
Publishing, Inc., at 2320 Los Rios Boulevard, Plano, Texas 75074. Telephone inquiries may be made by calling:

(972) 423-0090

To
the Texas Folklore Society
and
the Tejas Storytelling Association
and to all my storytellin' friends

Thanks for keepin' the stories alive!

Texas storytellers are always ready for a good time.
This sketch was drawn by Bill Erhard while sitting at the
Liars' Table at the Manchaca Fire Hall.

Texas is a state of mind,
not an accident of birth.
From the snows of Amarillo,
to the sunny Gulf Coast earth,
from the gators, pines and marshes,
to the Big Bend Mountain falls,
you've got to know that where you live
is the greatest state of all.

Song lyrics from
"Here Comes Another I Love Texas Song"
by Allen Damron, Tom Paxton, and Bob Gibson

Table of Contents

Contents

Acknowledgments

Thanks to my family and friends, for their continued support and encouragement (and for not throwing heavy things at me).

Thanks also to my subjects (my, that still sounds royal!), to the folks that are the subjects of this book and the folks that helped: Molly Ivins (Betsy Moon), Willie Nelson (Lisa Fletcher), Gayle Ross (Reed), Tim Henderson (Marian), Mike Blakely, Elizabeth Ellis, Aaron Allen, Bill Erhard (Tita), Hondo Crouch (Becky Crouch Barrales, Oscar Barrales, and VelAnne Howle), and Rusty Wier.

These are all wonderful, generous people who all took an incredible risk, allowing a prankster like me to write about them. When I called them about this project, they were there for me. They all gave generously of their time and granted me unprecedented access to their valuable archives. Thanx Gang.

A special prayer for all the wonderful folks in Luckenbach. As this book is going to press, much of the town has been washed away in the biggest flood the town has ever seen. But it only touched the buildings, not the spirit of the town!

A special thank you to Allen and Marie Damron. Their ideas contributed greatly to the overall composition of the book. In particular, Allen insisted that no book would be complete without two world class storytellers: Elizabeth Ellis and Gayle Ross. Also, congrats to Allen on his great new *Texas Spirit Live* CD.

A thank you to Cynthia Leal Massey, author of *Fire Lilies* and *The Caballeros of Ruby, Texas*; she suggested that I research Dr. Americo Paredes, whose biography is included in this book. Thanx Cyndi.

A big THANK YOU to Sue Ann Andrews for her always constructive editing. She's a rare editor. The poor lady thinks like I do. How strange is that? Thanx Beeps.

Thanks to music legend Segle Fry, for showing me some of the midnight back roads through the Texas Hill Country to avoid the donut denizens.

Thanks to Walter Proetzman, teacher, photographer, scientist, and fellow friend of Bill Erhard's. Thank you for allowing me access to your vast collection of Bill's wonderful drawings. And also, thanx for the Interferon.

Thanks to Linda Kay Anderson for her editing help, attention to details, and lots of encouragement.

Thanks to James and Anetta White, owners of the Broken Spoke Night Club in Austin, for all the pictures and wonderful stories.

Lastly, as always, thanx to my monthly storytellin' group, John "Guido" Bohac, Rick "The Kid" Pille, Ron Joseph, Heath Newburn, Calvin "Cajones" Jones, Jerry Heaney, Jimmy "The Hat," and, of course, Fred.

Liz Carpenter and Jim at a book signing.

Introduction

I've Been Lied to By the Best!

I still don't like book introductions! Most are boring enough to put your biggest insomniac fan to sleep. Actually, most seem written by someone asleep at the wheel (my apologies to Ray Benson and the band). But this one will be different.

Bob Cole and Sammy Allred, Austin radio personalities and long-time friends, decided sometime back that I have the best job in the world. They're right! When I'm not at home writing, I'm often listening to some storytellers at some Liars' Table or signing books for some nice folks.

Many of those folks bring more than just a request for an autograph. First, there are the wonderful, funny stories that they had collected from their lifetime and generously wanted to share with me.

Secondly, they often had the name of another storyteller that I should include in my next book. From whatever part of Texas they came from, they all know someone who has kept them amused with stories.

Those of you who have read my previous book on storytellers, *Famous Texas Folklorists and Their Stories*, know that I grew up hearing tales from legends like J. Frank Dobie, John Henry Faulk, Liz Carpenter, and Cactus Pryor. I'm proud to say I've been lied to by the best. In keeping with that theme, I'll be introducing you to some more of my wonderfully talented, legendary storytelling friends. Some you will already have heard of, others you will want to know more about. But, like always, they are all very interesting folks:

Aaron Allan	Molly Ivins
Mike Blakely	Willie Nelson
Hondo Crouch	Dr. Americo Parades
Elizabeth Ellis	Gayle Ross
Bill Erhard	Rusty Wier
Tim Henderson	

I didn't have the honor of knowing Walter Prescott Webb, Dr. Americo Parades, or Roy Bedichek personally. But I knew them through their wonderful stories that were shared with me by mutual friends like John Henry Faulk and Ben King Green.

Storytellers are a lot like Johnny Appleseed, spreading and planting their stories across the landscape. We then watch our stories sprout anew, watered by the imagination of other storytellers.

It is a compliment to a storyteller when other storytellers "steal" their stories, not their personal stories, but the stories they have told. "Stealing," in this context, is more like someone "stealing" a base in baseball, it is just part of storytelling.

Hondo Crouch once explained to me that, "the secret to genius is hiding the sources of your information." I cherished this nugget for many years. Then, about two years ago, I found that Hondo had gotten that quote from Albert Einstein!

One of the few rules in storytelling is, "The story belongs to the one that tells it best." This is just part of the sharing of the stories. I've been flattered that newspapers and magazines all over the Southwest, after giving my books a great review, have enjoyed them enough to "borrow" regularly for their columns. Some have even given my books credit for the loan!

As you read this book you will be stepping into a time machine of sorts that will be making stops all over the last 150 years. Stories will take you from Moravia in 1826 (ten years before the fall of the Alamo), all the way up to folklore festivals and storytelling events that are going on today.

Having said all of that, I must admit there is no way one book, or a shelf of books, can begin to cover this topic. I've already started another storytellers book to cover other legends that I couldn't fit into this book. Texas folklore is as vast and broad as the state. There are hundreds of years of history and thousands of talented individuals who have made contributions. My hope is that my efforts will introduce you to that world and give you the tools to learn more about it.

How a Texas Legend Was Born

or

What Happens When Austin Meets Boston?

Did you ever wonder how tall Texas stories get started? Often they are born out of everyday events that end up embarrassing non-Texans. Texas braggin' seems to get non-Texans' undies in a knot. (Actually, they're startin' off with a pretty big chip on their shoulders because they aren't Texans. It's hard for me to imagine the anguish they must feel.)

Anyhow, they say that Texans are always braggin' about their state. Although I can understand their reluctance to have their state compared with Texas, facts are facts and here is one:

It's not braggin' if it's true!

It's a bit like blamin' the weather bureau for the weather. Texas is great, and if some folks haven't figured that one out yet, then it's our job to give them the real skinny.

This first story shows how Texas "braggin'" stories get started. And it reiterates that sometimes the truth just truly annoys some folk.

It took me many years to realize how different the 267,000 square miles I call my home is from the rest of the world. It was only later in life that I realized most people can get out of their home state with less than an hour of driving. And, it doesn't seem to bother them a bit to do so.

Living in the Texas Hill Country, the quickest you could get out of the state would be about four hours of hard drivin'. Of course, I'm forced to ask, "Why would anyone want to get out of Texas?"

On a road map of Texas, an inch equals about half an hour of driving. For a lot of the other states and countries of the world, an inch equals about a foot of driving. Their road maps are damn near life-size; a half hour of hard drivin' and you're off that map and into another state!

Some years back I was a computer systems analyst at the orange and white university in Austin. I was putting some finishing touches on an investments and portfolio management system that I had designed for them.

At that time the "biggest" land grant college in the U.S. was Harvard University. I had gone up there to see how they handled some technical issues with their portfolio.

Harvard University's money is handled by an outfit called Harvard Management Company. So, I moseyed over to HMC and met with several really nice folks (these names are phony to protect the guilty and the innocent).

The first guy I met there was Bill. Now Bill is good folks. He and I went through a whole passel of stuff, and he was really a blast to work with (even if he did have a funny way of talkin'; of course, he said the same thing about me).

After a bit of visitin', Bill tells me that Reginald, the Grand Imperial Poo-Bah Muckety Muck that he works for, has heard that I was in town and he wants to meet me. So, we head off down one long hall, then turn down another long hall, all the time the paneling is gettin' darker and the carpet's gettin' deeper.

Bill and I shuffled into a large lobby occupied by a secretary who has clearly been on that new lemon-persimmon diet and does not appear to be having any fun in her life at all. Without speaking, she nods us toward a couple of chairs designed by the Spanish Inquisition and announces our arrival to Reginald.

After coolin' our heels in the lobby for the better part of half an hour, we are shown into Reginald's monster-sized office. (Bill told me later Reginald needed a biggun' to have room for his ego.)

One look and you know Jim's going to fit right in with Boston!

Reginald didn't even look up for about a full minute as we stood there in front of his ping-pong table-sized desk. He finally glanced up over his bifocals and, without a greeting, nodded us toward two straight-backed chairs that matched those in the lobby. By this point, I had already formed a good bit of a negative opinion about this yahoo. But I was representing THE University, so I gnawed on the corner of my tongue a bit.

Finally, Reginald spoke. "I understand you're from one of the universities in Texas."

More gnawing. "Yes sir, I am. I'd like to thank you for taking the time to see me."

"Well, it was a squeeze to get you in, my *shed-ule* is quite busy." (I always wondered where these folks thought the "c" in schedule went when they pronounce it shed-ule. Maybe the same place as the "h" in herbs?)

Then he started to seriously annoy me. "Harvard University has the largest endowment fund of any university in the world."

"Wow, that's somethin' really special." Even more gnawin'.

"You see Harvard University even has over seven thousand acres of land. How many acres does your university have?"

More gnawin' (serious raw spots were beginning to develop). Talk about playing the mine's-bigger-than-yours game! But things were lookin' up, because I was pretty sure he wasn't going to like my answer.

"Two and a quarter million," I replied.

Surprisingly, he looked pleased. "Is that the book value or par value of your land holdings?"

"Well it's neither; that's two and a quarter million acres."

Hearing that he had an involuntary reaction as his head jerked up, causing his bifocals to slide down to the end of his nose (had it not been so upturned, the glasses would have not been able to ride that buckin' beak).

"You must be mistaken," Reginald retorted, still trying to regain his superior demeanor, and glasses.

"Nope, we just had it resurveyed. It's about two and a quarter million acres, plus or minus about ten thousand acres." Truth be told, I was startin' to have a bit of fun, sittin' in a painful chair, chattin' with my old friend Reginald.

At this point, Reginald looked like he'd just eaten somethin' real nasty. He stuttered out, "Plus or minus TEN THOUSAND ACRES!"

"Yep, the old land grants had phrases in the deeds like, 'ride north for two days, on a good horse, till you reach the hill with a big oak tree, then ride west for a full day, till you reach the dry creek bed,' so you see, the horse, the tree, and maybe even the creek have been gone for a hundred years, so it's kinda tricky figurin' it out exact." (Notice that my language was quickly becoming more and more downhome Texas.)

Then I decided to add a zinger about his gigantic seven thousand acres, "But you know how it is, Reginald; plus or minus ten thousand acres is not that big a deal. So, what do ya'll do with all of your land?"

By this point his previously nonexistent stutter had taken a definite turn for the worse. "On, on, on your books, wha, wha, what's the value of your land per acre?"

"Oh, I don't know, somethin' like fifty bucks an acre."

"Fifty bucks! Er, I mean, fifty dollars per acre. That's quite low, surely it's worth more than that."

"You're right about that. But we still carry it on the books at what it was worth when the University got it."

"Wh, wh, when was that?"

"Late eighteen hundreds."

"Wha, wha, what do you think it's worth now?"

"Oh, now let me think. I did a report on that a few months back. I'm trying to recall exactly what it said." By this point it appeared that Reginald had started to sweat. (Actually, I'm not sure Reginald has ever done any sweatin'; I suspect he has only glistened. Either way, he was glistenin' like a racehorse.)

After an appropriate period of reflection, I said, "I reckon it's about five hundred dollars per acre."

I didn't think it was possible, but the upturned nose went quite limp. His glasses lost their grip and fell off on his desk. He grabbed his calculator, re-perched his glasses, and started to peckin' and mumblin'. A minute later he looked up like his pet high-tech stock had just died. "That means your endowment fund is more than twice the size of ours!"

"I'll take your word for it."

"Wh, wh, why don't you carry the whole value on your books?"

"We don't wanta be accused of braggin'."

He rose quickly and without even offering a handshake and said, "I've got some important business to take of."

Bill and I left Reginald's office, and I took off to catch my plane back to Texas. We chatted briefly before I had to leave, and I noticed that Bill seemed to be in much better spirits than Reginald. I was pretty sure I wasn't going to be invited back by my new buddy, Reginald.

When I got back to Austin, I sent Bill and Reginald notes thanking them for their time. I got a very nice reply from Bill. Didn't hear anything from Reginald though; kind of figured he was just too busy figurin' out some other way that they were the biggest university and tryin' to fit it into his *shed-ule.*

It's bout that
deep round here!

Sketch by Bill Erhard.

The Rest of That Story

About a year later, I was stopping over in Boston on my way to New York. I needed to ask Bill a couple questions about how they handled some accounting issues and to give him copies of some programs that I had designed to do stock performance graphing.

Bill said that's great but added that he was not going to be in his office. He asked that I meet him at another address at Gary Cooper Time (thanks Kinky), better known as High Noon.

When I arrived at the address he gave me, it was a large, stately building. As instructed, I punched the button for the top floor. The elevator doors open and I'm pretty sure this farm boy is in the wrong barn. You could smell the money, all the way from the gold lettering on the dark paneling that says, The Harvard Club, to the cut crystal collection sitting on a beautiful, century-old table. And this was just the damn lobby!

I could see the maitre d' glaring my way, over the top of his bifocals. His gold nametag read "Bogs."

Bogs had already spotted my boots and hat, and as I approached, I'm sure he was preparing to give me clear instructions to go anywhere but inside the club. As I approached him, I couldn't help but wonder if Bogs was short for something, like Bogswillie, or if he'd actually been named after swampland.

Bogs was about sixty, five foot ten, and possessing a huge mane of beautiful white hair, which came with a matching set of bushy white eyebrows. The scowl on his face pushed the eyebrows down till they nearly obscured his eyes and gave him the appearance of an Old-English sheepdog about to kill something (or at least give it a serious sniffin').

Planting my boots at right angles for a quick dash back to the elevator, I gave him my name, at which point Bogs' face changed completely. "Oh, of course, Mr. Gramon, how good to see you, sir. Your party is waiting for you. They are in our private dining room."

While trying to figure out what had come over Bogs, I was also thinking, *'hey a party, things are lookin' up!'*

My new friend Bogs and I strolled back through the dining room. I nodded and smiled at a few of the well-dressed locals as they picked at their lobster bisque and crème brulees. Several looked like they were ready to call security, then they probably decided I must have been allowed in on some sort of building maintenance call.

Like any good harbormaster, Bogs guided me past these treacherous shoals and up to a massive pair of dark oak doors. As the doors opened to the private dining room, a group of about ten folks, including Bill, stood and started to clap.

I, of course, stopped and looked behind me to see what had caught their attention. But there was nobody there. And confusion filled the land!

Bill jumped up and said, "And here's our guest of honor. Folks, this is Jim Gramon, a true Texas legend."

"Bill, I'm gettin' the feelin' you started this party some time ago, and I'm gonna hafta do some serious drinkin' to catch up. What's all this legend crap?" The group laughed.

"You are a legend around here, Jim. You are a walkin', talkin' Texas legend."

"What have you been drinkin', Bill? And can I have a couple?"

Bill maneuvered me up to the head of the table as he explained, "Jim, sit down and let me tell you a bit about what took place when you were here a year ago."

I was still confused, but they seemed to be a pretty amiable group. So, I pulled up to sit a spell.

"Jim, I'm sure you've noticed that your old friend Reginald is not here. You also couldn't help but notice that Reginald is one of the most pompous asses in the world."

"Well, I'll grant you, he did seem a tad puffed up." The group laughed again.

"Reginald got his job by cutting up everyone in the place. He is quite the backstabber. And everybody he climbed over was looking forward to the day when he got cut down to size. And you did it for us."

"Gee, I'm glad to have been of assistance. I've gotta tell you, he really didn't seem like he wanted to be buddies."

"Jim, the whole group wants to thank you for many days of relief from dealing with Reginald."

"Bill, I'm glad I could help ya'll. But exactly how did I manage to do all of that?"

"Well, every time Reginald becomes intolerably overbearing, we figure out some way to bring up The University of Texas, and he retires to his office with a headache!"

"Well, it was truly my pleasure. He worked hard for it didn't he? It just wouldn't have been right to not help him drop the air pressure in his ego a bit."

We had a wonderful lunch, and I made several more super friends. They all seemed to have a passel of stories about everybody's buddy Reginald. When I was leavin', my newest old buddy, Bogs, even told me a story about how condescending and demeaning Reginald was to him. He too wanted to thank me for deflating Reginald.

And so it was that another Texas braggin' story began. But, since all I did was tell the gospel (surveyor's) truth to Reginald, that wasn't really braggin', was it?

Sketch by Bill Earhard.

What is Storytelling?

Simple question. The simple answer is that storytelling is the ability to communicate a story. Well double-duh! But the answer becomes quite tricky when you start describing HOW those stories are told.

The first thing that comes to mind is verbal communication, yakkin'. Then there comes written communication, or written yakkin'. But then it becomes a tad more confusing. For example, you can get the story by merely watching actors or mimes that say nothing at all.

There are many ways to tell stories. You can learn invaluable stories about what the people and times were like by studying their music, humor, politics, styles of dress, mannerisms, and so on. The bottom line is, almost anything can be used to tell wonderful stories.

What Makes Texas Storytellers So Unique?
Lots of Diversity

There are a number of applicable answers. But I think the diversity of the people is one of the most important. The diversity of Texas is astounding. Most nations of the world don't begin to have that kind of diversity of people or terrain. The deserts of west Texas, the plains of the north, the semi-arid farmland of south Texas, the rich blacklands region of central Texas, the coastal plains bordering the Gulf of Mexico, and then there are the beautiful piney woods and Big Thicket of east Texas.

"Texans are a hearty combination of hard work and honesty, covered liberally with a desire to have a lot of fun. If you doubt that for a second, take a look at the list of festivals and events. Any group that will hold a festival for shrimp, mosquitoes, gators, or black-eyed peas is a group ready to party."

I wrote those words three years ago for *Famous Texas Folklorists and Their Stories*. I knew they were true. But I had no idea how true, until two years ago when I wrote *FUN Texas Festivals & Events*. In it I included 1,600 of my favorite events, many of which had their roots in other countries.

Few countries in the world have been populated with as many diverse cultures. From all over the world came groups looking for a place where they could express their individuality. And even many of the slaves chose to stay after their emancipation.

Throughout the state are towns that were started by various ethnic groups like Germans, Swedes, and Czechs. (Until just recently the town newspaper in West, Texas, was still written in Czech.) All of these groups bring their own centuries of history, but also they now have a shared history with all the other cultures.

The cultural influence of Mexico's occupation of Texas can still be seen. (I genuinely doubt that the Fourth of July is as big a holiday in Mexico as Cinco de Mayo is in Texas.) On a daily basis you can see the influence of the many Indian groups of Mexico on the current population of Texas.

But did you realize that Texas hosts two of the largest Celtic festivals in the world? The second largest is held in Dallas and the seventh largest is held in San Antonio (they dye the river green!). Cascarones and shamrocks, nowhere but Texas!

The festivals also are a reflection of the businesses in Texas, which are as diverse as the cultural influences. Some immediately come to mind, like farming, ranching, lumber, and of course, the oil "patch." But there were many others like mining, milling, and fishing.

I tease about Texans having always been in the chips. In the early days it was poker chips, then cow chips, and now computer chips. But whatever kind of chips, it was often a high-risk business. The rewards are high, but so are the risks. Texans are risk-takers, and that is one of the things that makes this state special.

All of these diverse cultures and job opportunities have blended in a variety of ways to create some very special towns. The populations vary as much as the landscapes. Many of the towns mentioned in this book are well known, like Dallas, Houston, San Antonio, Austin, and El Paso. But you will also get glimpses of several other towns that you may have never heard of, like Kopperl, Terlingua, Luckenbach, and Abbott.

You will meet a variety of wonderful folks who have put their own unique brand on how they convey a good Texas tale. You will meet some who are ink-slinging writers, and folks who use their voices to tell the tales through their stories, jokes, or songs.

You will meet many classic and some legendary Texas characters who are my friends. Through stories, songs, poems, and pictures they can become your friends too. Unlike most books on this subject, many of the folks I'm writing about are still alive and well. If you keep your eyes open, you can go see them at various events and meet some of these living legends.

The men and women who built Texas were special characters, almost without exception. The strength of character to make a living off the land also gave them the strength to speak their minds, whatever the cost, and here is some of what they had to say.

Storytelling is Alive and Well!

It has been said that when an old person dies, a library burns. So I decided to save lots of the stories before they are gone. In my books I always emphasize the point that storytelling is alive. There are lots of people telling the stories, and there is no reason you shouldn't be one of them.

Almost every place I stop I run into folks with wonderful stories. Often they begin with, "Have you heard the one about...?" Sounds like the start of a joke, and it often is. Sometimes they cross generations and circumstances to convey the essence of the story in just a couple of words.

I intentionally include a diverse group of storytellers. Here you will see the works of classic storytellers, songwriters, authors, musicians, a Cherokee storyteller, a political columnist, and even a DJ-singer-songwriter who is a member of the Texas Country Music Hall of Fame. So, let's get to the storytelling before everybody falls asleep.

Liars' Tables Across Texas

In the mornings, about an hour after sunrise, in thousands of small cafes, diners, and donut shops across Texas, people of the farming and ranching communities gather after performing some of their first chores of the day. In each of these places, normally in one of the corners, yet near the coffee pot, there is usually a Liars' Table. Around this oversized table, the locals gather to drink coffee, read the local fish wrap, discuss what's goin' on over at their places, and to swap stories and whoppers.

Ms. Tracy's Café
Terlingua/Study Butte, Texas

Ms. Tracy's Cafe.

I knew Tracy long before I met her. Don't know what it says about me, but somehow, without having been there in twenty years, I knew half the permanent population of Terlingua. Of course that only adds up to about a dozen folks!

Reicher "Rick the Kid" Pille and I worked together and sat in on some wonderful poker games together in Austin. When he decided to join Allen Damron and Steven Fromholz in Terlingua, he also decided that a phone wasn't really necessary.

Months after moving to Terlingua, Rick called to say that if we needed to reach him, to call Ms. Tracy's Cafe and leave a message with Tracy. In the next day or two, Rick would be in and get the message.

So on a regular basis Tracy and I chatted and swapped stories about Rick and Terlingua. In the fall of 2001 I went down to be a judge at the Terlingua World Championship Chili Cookoffs ("Behind the Store"), and I finally met Ms. Tracy. In a town full of characters, she and her cafe really stand out.

The cafe is actually in Study Butte (pronounced Stoodie Beaut, 'cause that was the guy's name, and that's how he pronounced it!). From the covered patio of Ms. Tracy's, you can look out across the flatlands that cross the small valley to the base of the beautiful mountains.

I pulled in late in the day, dusty, tired, and hungry. The minute I walked through the door, I knew this place was just like home, because a female voice echoed from the back, "You better get the hell outta my kitchen before you get hurt!"

Ahhh, home cookin'! However, it did occur to me that this might not be the best time to meet the proprietor.

When I mentioned this observation to a tall guy in a floppy hat, with one lens of his glasses tinted black, he told me, "Aww don't worry 'bout that, she's in a good mood today!"

That was my first introduction to cowboy poet, storyteller, and pretty nifty dancer Luke Dudley, "the One-Eyed Coyote."

The Liars' Table at Ms. Tracy's Cafe.

Not totally trusting Luke's assessment of the situation, I sat there, waiting for a better moment. Meanwhile, I looked around the combination cafe/antique store/curio shop. No available space was left unused in this neat place. Rocks, arrowheads, drawings, jewelry, and all sorts of other things that defy description lined the walls.

Soon a short, wiry, no-nonsense-looking little lady came out carrying a long butcher knife and asked me just what it was that I wanted. Knowing it was Ms. Tracy, I followed my instincts and growled back that I didn't have time to be jawin' with her, that I was there to do some business with Tracy herself, not the help.

She straightened up, glared at me over the point of the knife, tipped her head a little to one side, and said, "I know that voice. You're that guy from Austin that calls Rick all the time."

I smiled, confessed, and became friends with the sweetest little cactus in the Texas desert. Over the next few days Tracy and I shared several meals, several beers, and lots of stories. It's quite a story how this former British RAF (Royal Air Force) officer ended up throwing short orders, barbs, stories, and an occasional knife in what has been officially designated as "the most remote location in the United States."

Tracy and Jim share a laugh at the Terlingua Chili Cookoff.
Photo by Allen or Marie Damron.

So if you ever get down to Terlingua, tell Ms. Tracy that Jim sent you. Just be sure to ask her to put down her knife before giving you a hug.

Frank's Bait & Taco

Canyon Lake, Texas

A black cat greets me at the colorful front door of
Frank's Bait & Taco in Canyon Lake, Texas.

I nearly had a wreck trying to stop. Immediately when it came into
view, I knew the incredibly colorful place would require closer scrutiny. Bright yellows and pinks covered the rambling building that
carried a somewhat nautical theme.

19

Eddie Fonseca, the jovial owner of Frank's Bait & Taco in Canyon Lake, Texas.

Catch whoppers in the fishing tackle section of Frank's.

Whatever you need, it's in the produce section of Frank's Bait & Taco.

I wasn't sure exactly what it was, but it had to be interesting. Upon entering I found that this was Canyon Lake's answer to the town Co-Op. Just about anything you want can be bought there. Whether you need breakfast tacos, a sack of potatoes, rods and reels, fishing bait, pocket knives, a game of pool, or just some stories, Frank's is the place to stop.

The Liars' Table is actually the bar where they serve to a steady cast of characters, including lots of folks who like fishing. Some hobbies seem to attract more storytellers; golf, poker, hunting, and fishing head the list (but the competition for first place in Texas is fierce!).

In light of this, it should come as no surprise that Frank's is not owned or run by anyone named Frank. The owner is a gregarious guy named Eddie Fonseca. He's not named Frank, but he will occasionally answer to it.

You've gotta love a place that has the motto, "Our Bait Catches More Fish... Or Dies Trying!"

What's Cookin'?

Cumby, Texas

The What's Cookin' Cafe, in scenic downtown Cumby, Texas.

Between Greenville and Sulphur Springs, on I-30, is the quiet little town of Cumby. If you read my folklore book, you know that my family has deep roots in that neck of the woods. My earliest storytelling experiences took place along main street Cumby, as I listened to the likes of Ben King "Doc" Green and occasionally John Henry Faulk.

All of my life the building pictured above was the town post office. So I did a double-take when I noticed that it had become a cafe. It's not a big place, doesn't really need to be. But the coffee is always hot, and the cookin' is down-home good.

The Liars' Table stretches across the back wall of this friendly cafe. The Table is regularly staffed with some folks willing to pull your leg. Drop on by and tell 'em Jim sent you.

Heather Machen, Ashley Heer, Darlene Hammons, and Judy Machen hold down the fort at the Liars' Table at the What's Cookin' Cafe, in Cumby, Texas.

The walls of the What's Cookin' Cafe are decorated with a collection of saddles, ropes, bridles, and spurs.

Hitchin' Post

Ozona, Texas

The Hitchin' Post, in the West Texas town of Ozona, Texas.

Last November I was driving out to Terlingua. I had been driving for several hours when I hit the quiet little town of Ozona. After touring the town for a bit, I spotted a likely looking spot to get something to eat.

The gravel crunched as I pulled up in the parking lot of the Hitchin' Post. An ancient wooden wagon sat in the parking lot. Beside the rambling, multilevel building stood an old windmill and a raised water tank.

The Hitchin' Post on the inside had the feel of a classic Texas food-n-fun place. A brief look around told me this was one of the main gathering places in this historic town. The dark wood paneling is adorned with plaques from various organizations, announcing this

The decor is definitely western, and the furniture is
quite comfortable at the Hitchin' Post, in Ozona, Texas.

is their regular meeting place. The walls also have their fair share of
trophy mounts and other interesting items.

The place was in its post-Halloween celebration mode. Orange
streamers and spray-on spiderwebs adorned the place in a manner
that indicated the folks doing the decorating were having a good
time. That's important, you know.

Walking back, past the first dining room and Liars' Table, I
walked down a couple of steps into the sprawling multilevel back
section. Long groups of tables for luncheons were on the right. On
the left was the pool table.

There is even a pool table in the multilevel Hitchin' Post.

Luckenbach, Texas

As a collector of top quality Liars' Tables, I face a moral imperative to include Luckenbach. But there was a problem with getting Luckenbach organized, because that's an oxymoron. It'll never happen.

The problem was not so much with the town as with the pictures of the town. As you can see from the preceding profiles of other Liars' Tables, they have an identifiable, actual specific table or spot where the spinners spin.

The Luckenbach, Texas post office.

This is not so in Luckenbach. Nope, in Luckenbach, the whole town is one big Liars' Table! Oh, it starts at the bar, for sure. But then there is also the General Store, the dance hall, the sing-around fire pits in the back, the campgrounds, the tables out under the shade trees, and of course many a good story comes out of VelAnne Howle's office (she's the "Mare" [mayor] of Luckenbach).

As I write this, I can almost hear Hondo's chuckling laugh. I know he would be delighted with the problem he's given me. Hondo was never much on being fenced in or narrowed down to just one thing. (Be sure and check out the chapter about Hondo.)

So, here are some shots of some of my favorite storytellin' spots in Luckenbach.

The bar, "Everybody's Somebody in Luckenbach."
Oh, did I mention that Hondo liked to collect stuff?

Looking from the store into the bar at Luckenbach.
Becky Crouch Barrales, Hondo's daughter, produces the hats.

Broken Spoke Night Club

Austin, Texas

Owner James White in front of the Broken Spoke Night Club in Austin.

The "Spoke" has been a Texas legend for nearly forty years. It's hard to describe the Spoke, because it is quite a few different things. It's kind of like a gigantic Liars' Table, with great food, pool tables, a country music museum, and an incredible floor show.

About the Liars' Table, the Spoke is a little different from most of the others. They aren't open for morning coffee. But they stay open late to make up for it.

In 1964 Austin was a lot smaller town, but it was already a center for live music. James White felt like there were just not enough good, old fashioned country music nightclubs in the area. So he built one "out towards the edge of town" (it's practically downtown now). On November 10, 1964, the "Broken Spoke" opened.

The Liars' Table at the Broken Spoke. You'll always have some company.

James White is a gifted singer-songwriter and promoter. He was soon booking legends like Bob Wills, Ernest Tubbs, Roy Acuff, Hank Thompson, Tex Ritter, Ray Price, Kitty Wells, Grandpa Jones, George Strait, and Willie Nelson (who loves their chicken fried steak).

James wrote the "Broken Spoke Legend" song which is on the Alvin Crow album *Pure Country*. His love for country music has graduated from singing in the shower and writing songs while driving his pickup, to forming the Broken Spoke Company with Alvin Crow, and to singing at the Spoke with many of the Spoke's talented acts. Over the years he has performed with Willie Nelson, Kris Kristofferson, and Sons of the Pioneers to name a few.

The Spoke has featured some of Austin's very best local talent such as Alvin Crow, Gary P. Nunn, Sam and Son, better known as The Geezinslaw Brothers, Don Walser, Jerry Jeff Walker, The Derailers, Jimmie Dale Gilmore, Chris Wall, and Dale Watson.

For me, walking into the Spoke is like stepping into a wonderful past. From the front of the parking lot to the back door, the Spoke is a down-home, old-fashioned, hardcore country music dance hall. When you walk underneath that big old oak tree out front and you throw that front door open on this red rustic old building, you're at the Broken Spoke, the last of the true Texas dance halls.

The Broken Spoke is Texas's most definitive dance hall. It's not one of those fly-by-night, trendy newcomers you see springing up in out-of-business lumber yards or feed stores on every corner. You can't build a legend overnight. Owners James and Annetta White have been operating the Austin tradition for almost forty years, and its reputation for good country music and good Texas cooking has spread worldwide.

From the sixties through today, the Spoke has played host to countless country superstars. George Strait, Ernest Tubb, Roy Acuff, and even Bob Wills tipped their hats from the stage at the far end of this old dance hall.

Annetta and James White, owners of the Broken Spoke.

Willie Nelson started playing at the Spoke before he moved back from Nashville, when he still had a crew cut and a sport coat—before he brought braids and tennis shoes to the forefront of country fashion. In fact, it's not a bit unusual to stumble into the Spoke on a Friday or Saturday night and find the Red-Headed Stranger kicked back against an amp, picking with whatever band is the featured entertainment of the night. It's no secret that the Broken Spoke is one of Willie's favorite hangouts when he's home in Austin.

When I asked Steven (Fromholz) about performing at the Spoke, he said he had played there many times over the years. Then he laughed, "James White has one simple rule. If they ain't dancin' you ain't playin' there."

Through the years, James and Annetta have opened their doors and welcomed to the stage a pretty impressive list of aspiring musicians. George Strait and his Ace in the Hole Band cut their teeth in the music business playing by the neon lights of the beer signs in the Spoke. A wide variety of country superstars from Kris Kristofferson to Kitty Wells have jumped up on that stage and carried on the tradition of good country music that the Broken Spoke is famous for.

James White smiles a sad smile as he recalls one story about Willie. The IRS had seized almost everything Willie owned but his guitar, Trigger. James wanted to do something to help, so he took a gallon pickle jar and put it on the counter with a sign explaining that donations would be sent to Willie. Donations started coming in, then the media got hold of the story. Suddenly the Spoke was receiving donations from all over the world.

"A lot of folks love Willie. I'm glad we could help," said James.

The Spoke is a favorite hangout for most of Austin's "real" country musicians. Don't call 'em "hat acts," around here...the hats you see on stage at the Broken Spoke are as traditional as the music echoing off the walls.

When you are there, be sure to check out the Tourist Trap room, which is filled with photos, hats, and lots of other country music-related items. The Broken Spoke is a Texas treasure and an Austin tradition appreciated around the world and has been featured many times on *Austin City Limits*, a famous TV show on PBS.

About the Liars' Table, it's hard to identify "one" in the Spoke. There are actually about a hundred. From the pool tables to the dining tables, or the tables in the dance hall area, the whole place is a potential source of great stories.

Oh, did I mention that you need to watch for James himself? Well you better. How about this example:

James explains that Texas legend Davy Crockett stopped by the Spoke on his way to the Alamo. "Yep, old Davy came through here on his way to fight at the Alamo. Liked what he saw. He told me, 'James, don't change a thing 'til I get back.' And of course we haven't changed it, and we're not gonna change it."

Now that's a world class whopper!

One wall of the Tourist Trap room at the Broken Spoke.

I'll let James have the last word on the Spoke. "We ain't fancy, but we're damn sure country. Ya'll come!" You can check out the Spoke on the net at www.lone-star.net/bspoke.

Jim and James White enjoy a laugh and the music while the dancers twirl.

Galveston, Texas

I believe that the nature of people is often reflective of the nature of where they grew up. Often I include the history of the legend's hometown to provide perspective on that person's biography. The story of our first legend starts out in the beautiful island town of Galveston. There, lots of surf, sand, sailing, sunshine, a deepwater port, and a rich history all combined to shape Bill Erhard.

In 1785 José de Evia, who charted the Texas coast, named Galveston Bay in honor of Bernardo de Gálvez, the viceroy of Mexico. The bay sits between the mainland and Galveston Island, two miles out in the Gulf of Mexico. The island is a part of the string of sand barrier islands protecting part of the Texas coastline. On the eastern end of Galveston Island, where the city of Galveston stands, the currents of Galveston Bay maintain a natural harbor. Historically this harbor has always been significant, because it was the only deepwater port between New Orleans and Veracruz, Mexico.

Long before Evia charted the area, the Karankawa Indians had lived part of each year on Galveston Island. There, this tribe of six-foot-tall, often painted Indians hunted and fished. Europeans commented on their smell, until they realized that the Karankawas had rubbed themselves down with animal fat to protect their bodies from the swarms of insects. These critical Europeans soon started doing the same thing themselves.

Alvar Núñez Cabeza de Vaca, the Spanish explorer, became shipwrecked in 1528. Most historians believe this occurred on Galveston Island. His reports of the island and its occupants were duly noted back in Spain, and soon the word made its way to France also.

In 1816 Louis Aury established a naval base at the harbor to support the revolution in Mexico. From this base, Aury and others launched an unsuccessful attack against the Spanish in Mexico.

Galveston will still be
here when you come back!!!

Sketch by Bill Erhart.

Following their defeat, Aury returned to Galveston. To their surprise, they found it occupied by Jean Laffite. He had set up a pirate camp he called Campeachy, to dispose of their booty and provide supplies to the other pirates.

Laffite's fun ended in 1821, when the United States military forced him to vacate, and they departed. In their absence, Mexico designated Galveston as a port of entry in 1825 and five years later established a customs house.

Just a few years later, during the Texas Revolution, the harbor became the home port for the Texas navy. This site was designated as the last point of retreat of the Texas government.

At the end of the Texas Revolution, a group of investors, led by Michel B. Menard, acquired ownership of 4,605 acres on the harbor. There they founded the town of Galveston in 1838. The following year the Texas legislature granted incorporation to the city of Galveston.

The port grew steadily as immigrants and everything they needed and produced went back and forth across the docks. Ocean-going vessels and a wide variety of coastal ships transported cotton, grain, cattle, farming supplies, and coffee in and out of the port. All these activities contributed to the steady growth of the town.

Often these cargoes were offloaded then were shipped across Galveston Bay, through Buffalo Bayou to Houston. By 1860 there was enough business to justify construction of a bridge and railroad line from Galveston to Houston.

Business was booming until the Civil War started. Immediately, the Union navy dispatched forces to occupy Galveston. On New Year's Day, 1863, the Union army was forced out, but the blockade of the port remained in effect until the end of the war. Except for a small group of successful blockade runners, the port ceased to function, as did all the businesses in town.

On June 19, 1865, Major General Gordon Granger, of the Union army, led his troops into Galveston. There he officially announced the Emancipation Proclamation and freed the slaves. This event was the birth of the holiday now referred to as Juneteenth.

Despite losing the war, the port was quickly booming again, handling the demand for goods that had been blockaded during the war. However, only two years later, in 1867, three-fourths of the population of Galveston contracted yellow fever. Despite quarantines, the epidemic continued to be a problem for five years, with deaths averaging about twenty a day.

Amazingly, despite the yellow fever, Galveston had grown to be Texas's largest city by 1870, with 13,818 people. By 1880 Galveston had grown to 22,248 folks and was still the largest city in Texas.

Galveston was the home of numerous firsts. The *Galveston News*, founded in 1842, is the state's oldest continuing daily newspaper. Galveston had the first structure to use electric lighting, the Galveston Pavilion. The first telephone in Texas was in Galveston. Galveston was also the site of the first baseball game in the state.

It was soon passed in population as oil was struck in the other parts of the state and the new transcontinental rail lines went through other Texas towns. However, Galveston continued to thrive as a center for trade and commerce throughout the 1900s.

At a time when Houston, Beaumont, and Port Arthur benefited from the oil discoveries of the early twentieth century, Galveston had to put its energy into a recovery from the nation's worst natural disaster, the Galveston hurricane of 1900. The island lay in the pathway of hurricanes coursing across the Gulf of Mexico and suffered at least eleven times in the nineteenth century. The Galveston hurricane of 1900, with wind gusts of 120 miles per hour, flooded the city, battered homes and buildings with floating debris, and killed an estimated 6,000 people in the city.

On the mainland, another 4,000 to 6,000 people died from the hurricane. To protect itself from a reoccurrence, the city and county constructed a seventeen-foot seawall on the Gulf side of the island. Additionally, they brought in tons of soil, raising the level of the island. Then they built an all-weather bridge to the mainland. Their hopes were not only to protect their citizens but also their many businesses.

Unfortunately, despite their efforts, circumstances prevented Galveston from returning to its leadership role. Businesses were concerned about the possibility of more hurricane problems. That, combined with the new ability to dredge ship channels, sent businesses heading for more protected ports. In 1980 it had a population of 61,902 and ranked twenty-ninth in the state.

As it grew, Galveston acquired a reputation as a wide open town. Lots of money was being made and spent. Like the rest of America, Prohibition put Galveston on the fast track for organized crime. Liquor, gambling, nightclubs, brothels, and saloons soon opened and flourished around Galveston. Citizens not only tolerated these activities, they encouraged them! They took pride in living "in the free state of Galveston."

But publicity and politicians soon find each other. Although everyone had known about the activities in Galveston for many years, the articles about it created an embarrassing situation for some of the folks in Austin. In 1957 the Texas Rangers led a series of raids into Galveston that closed most of the major gambling and prostitution houses.

In an ironic twist, the citizens voted down legalizing casino gambling. But then the Texas legislature enacted a law that allows gambling on board cruise ships in international waters. A number of ships are now based out of Galveston.

Galveston had a significant role in all of my younger years. Whenever possible, my family would head out for a few days of fun on the beach in Galveston. The sun, sand, and surf made it a great place to get away and an even better place for a young man to grow up. And that is where our first legend did grow up.

A Galveston pelican
Sketch by Bill Erhard.

A Galveston "gal" pelican
Sketch by Bill Erhard.

Bill Erhard

Texas Cartoonist
8/4/32 - 7/7/01

Photo courtesy of Tita Erhard.

Several years ago I pulled up a chair at the Liars' Table at the Manchaca Fire Hall. The usual cast of characters were there and one new guy that I had never met. A glance at this wiry fellow told me he had done a lot of hard, outdoors work, probably down-on-the-farm work.

Clarence Vogel, the affable host of this down-home combination roadside café, fire hall, and town hall, asked me if I knew Bill. We did our howdys and Bill's slow easy drawl told me it was a Texas farm where he had done a lot of that work.

Even though he sat there saying little, I knew Bill was the classic example of the still waters runnin' very deep. The twinkle in his eyes told me this guy was not missing anything, and that he was having a lot of fun with it. That day we talked about contrary horses and contrary people and had a great chat, complete with plenty of laughs. We both like to laugh, a lot.

When Bill got up to leave, he tossed me a paper napkin. He said, "Here, Jim, this is for you." I laughed at his "gift," the seemingly blank napkin.

"Gosh, Bill, thanks a bunch. I hope I can do as much for you someday."

Bill laughed and walked out the door. Still chuckling, I picked up Bill's "gift" to me. There was nothing but coffee stains on the front of the napkin, and I tossed it back on the table. But as it landed, it turned over. Only then could I see that there was a drawing on the napkin. On the back was an incredible cartoon-like sketch of a horse. I have never seen such artistry, and here it was on the back of a plain coffee-stained paper napkin.

Picking up the napkin, I went to Clarence and showed it to him. He smiled and took me into his spacious fire hall office. There he produced a large notebook full of plastic sheet protectors, each containing two of Bill's sketches on napkins. I laughed till I cried at the wonderful cartoons.

I'm honored that Bill called me a friend, and I was even more honored when he said he would like to do some sketches for my first book. Unfortunately, Bill ran into some health problems and was unable to do the sketches. Fortunately for all of us, Bill gave me permission to use the original napkins. So, if the quality of a couple of the sketches is a little rough, you now know the rest of the story. And yes, those are real coffee stains on a couple of them!

This is the first sketch given to me by Bill Erhard.
Sketch by Bill Erhard.

That's the story about the source of these wonderful drawings that will appear throughout this book. But what about the man?

Well, Bill Erhard was a bigger character than any of those he sketched. The wiry guy with the friendly smile was born in Galveston, Texas, December 4, 1932.

He was a precocious kid, always "getting into things." Doctor and Mrs. Peter Erhard had their hands full with Bill's inquisitive nature. He made good grades and was quite athletic. He graduated from Galveston's Ball High School having competed in several sports, including track and football.

After high school, Bill headed off to SMU. He signed up for the pre-med program and was a defensive back on the football team. For the track team he ran the mile, 440, and the 880. (I couldn't help but chuckle when I learned the events Bill had competed in. Those were the same events I competed in while running track in high school.) After two years at SMU, family and financial obligations forced Bill to leave college.

Bill wasn't sure what he wanted to do, but he was sure it involved working with his hands. So he moved to Taft, Texas, and started farming some family land. Over the years he raised a lot of cotton

Bill at age 6. Photo courtesy of Tita Erhard.

and even raised carrots for Campbell's Soup Company.

In 1971 Bill moved to the quiet Texas Hill Country town of Bandera. On the other side of the fence lived a singer-songwriter that was trying to make his mark on the music world, Willie Nelson.

The ever-friendly Willie has always had an open-door policy at his place. Friends would drop by and sometimes were pretty slow to leave. During those times, when Willie needed to get away, he would walk out the back door and disappear. Unknown to his guests, Willie had become back fence buddies with Bill. Willie would come over and crash for hours; sometimes they would even load up in Bill's truck and go play a round of golf. All the while, the folks back at Willie's place were trying to figure out where he had disappeared to.

Bill used to laugh about Willie and his golfing. Not about Willie's technique, but rather about his coloring! Like Hondo Crouch, Willie regularly wears bandanas. Bill said that often, at the end of a round of golf, Willie's skin would be so red you couldn't tell where the bandana ended and his hide began.

Being a good friend to Willie, Bill never disclosed these frequent visits until after he moved. Most folks never did figure out where Willie would disappear to. Now you know the rest of that story.

In 1973 Bill married the love of his life, Tita. They had met in Bandera and there was an immediate attraction. It wasn't long before they were dating, and not too long after that they married.

Describing Tita is as big a challenge as it is to describe Bill. So, I'll let Bill do it. The first time I met Tita, Bill and I were sitting together having coffee, as usual. I knew Tita was coming over, and I kept thinking every woman that came in would be her. Bill noticed this and said, "Don't worry about it, Jim, you won't even have to look up to know when she arrives. She'll come a stormin' in here in a bit."

Sure enough, a few minutes later, echoing down the halls, came the words, "I can't believe that damn moron cut me off in the parking lot!"

Bill winked at me and said, "Tita's here."

Bill and Tita Erhard. Photo courtesy of Tita Erhard.

At first glance this fiery woman wouldn't seem to be the perfect match for the laid back Bill Erhard. But opposites do attract, and Tita's gregarious personality was the sparkplug that never seemed to stop amusing Bill (often to her annoyance). More than once he commented on things he had done that he was sure would "stir Tita up a bit," and then laugh. All the time, his love and respect for her was obvious.

Early in their marriage Bill got the opportunity to buy a used D-6 Caterpiller bulldozer. For those of you unfamiliar with their product line, let's just say that the D-6 is about the size of a small house.

Recalling these times, Bill alternated between pleasure and annoyance. He loved working where he could build and sculpt something. He did roads, building sites, tank ponds, and lots of drainage projects. Then, of course, there were the times when the D-6 wouldn't run and its size made it a real challenge to work on. He both loved and hated that D-6.

Drawing was one thing he loved all of his life. No matter what else was going on in his life, Bill was always drawing. I asked him if he had ever taken any art training in high school or college.

"None to speak of, Jim. It's just somethin' I've always done."

Doctor Erhard, Bill's dad, told me, "that boy was always doodling on something."

Important words, "on something." You see, the media that Bill chose was often as exceptional as his skill as an artist. He always did his drawings on whatever was handy. Often these masterpieces were done on everyday paper napkins. But some of his friends have a collection of Styrofoam cups, newspaper corners, and miscellaneous scraps of paper. Bill could draw on anything.

As if to prove that point, when the weather got so bad that Bill couldn't drive his D-6, he would make extra money painting "things." He painted things like denim shirts, blue jeans, and toilet seat lids. That's right, toilet seat lids!

Folks would come by and drop off their lid, and for $100 Bill would do one of his humorous cartoons on the lid. Tita once remarked that there were times, when Bill got behind on doing the lids, that she wondered if there was a toilet in the county with a lid on it!

Tita had an advantage that other wives don't have. On her way home from work, she could drive by the places Bill was likely to stop at on his way home. She wasn't trying to track him down. Nope, she would just stop in and ask to see the napkin that Bill had drawn on that afternoon. A quick glance at the napkin and Tita would know how Bill's day went and what kind of mood he was in.

On April 3, 1975, their adopted daughter Shannon was born. Shannon is, at times, just like both of her parents, smart, attractive, friendly, and yet fiery enough to make sure things don't get boring.

With both of us having beautiful daughters, Bill and I often talked about the joys and concerns that come with children. But the bottom line always got back to our pride in them and love for them. During

Bill Erhard and his daughter, Shannon.
Photo courtesy of Tita Erhard.

some of the darker days of his illness, I always knew that a smile would come to his face if I just asked about Shannon.

In 1978 Bill sold his D-6, and the family moved to Austin. They wanted Shannon to have the chance to attend a school in Austin. Once here, Bill went into carpentry, working for S.W. Smith. Bill was immediately put in charge of the toughest job in the business, making the customer happy. He would take care of anything that wasn't "just right." For many years Bill provided quality carpentry work to a wide variety of firms and individuals.

Sketch by Bill Erhard.

50

Sailing was another of Bill's lifelong passions, going all the way back to his growing up days in Galveston. His skills with woodworking and sailing meshed very nicely when he chose boats to rework.

Over the years Bill owned numerous boats. Some of my favorite stories about Bill had to do with "The Office." Tita had made the mistake of being out of town for a few days. Upon her return, Bill insisted that they drive up towards Lake Travis. There he introduced her to what she describes as, "the saddest looking junk heap of a boat" that she had ever seen.

Bill Erhard always loved sailing.
Photo courtesy of Tita Erhard.

Upon finding out that Bill had bought it, she took out the "hideous" cushions and burned them. Where Tita saw the boat as it was, Bill saw a ton of potential. It took several years for "The Office" to reach its full potential. But as Bill used to say, "It cleaned up all right!"

About the name, "The Office," Bill would chuckle. He always said, "If anybody calls, I just tell them I'm at The Office."

It ain't gona work as a boat — and it's too big for a lawn sprinkler...

Sketch by Bill Erhard.

In the spring of 2001 Bill told me he thought my Festivals book would be a lot of fun. He added that if I was interested, he would do some drawings for it. I was ecstatic. The honor of being able to include his art with my words was wonderful.

Unfortunately his cancer treatments made him too shaky to draw, so, with his permission, I made scans of the drawings on the table napkins. Fortunately they came out clear enough to be used in that book.

My collection of Bill's sketches numbers about 350. Walter Proetzman, a longtime friend of Bill's, has a collection of nearly a thousand. Out of our combined collections, we have about four that Bill has signed. When I asked him about it, Bill just gave me a cryptic smile.

Singer-songwriter Harry Chapin wrote a beautiful song, "Mr. Tanner," about a man who ran a cleaning shop but loved singing. In it he had some lines that I think might answer this question about Bill:

Music was his life,
but not his livelihood.
And, it made him feel so happy,
And, it made him feel so good.

And, he sang from his heart.
And, he sang from his soul.
He did not know how well he sang,
it just made him whole!

Bill's art made him happy and it made him whole. Nobody who knew him can picture him without it.

Why would he refuse to sign these magnificent drawings? He treated these mini-masterpieces as though he was embarrassed by the attention they attracted. So, when you look at the drawings below, take special note of the one that is signed.

Bill portrays himself in a diaper, greeting the new year, 1994.
Sketch by Bill Erhard.

A signed self-portrait of Bill sitting at McDonald's.
Sketch by Bill Erhard.

Bill loved the Dallas Cowboys (notice the cowboy hat-helmet-crown).
Sketch by Bill Erhard.

In June I told Bill that I was dedicating my book *FUN Texas Festivals and Events* to him. It was the only time I ever saw him with tears in his eyes. A few weeks later, on July 7, 2001, Bill Erhard passed away.

Hundreds of folks came to Bill's funeral. He would have liked it, because it didn't really seem like a funeral at all. It was a celebration of Bill's life, his love of life, and in particular, the humor that he could find, no matter how tough things got. (Bill never was big on sad.)

At the funeral, an elderly gentleman approached me and said, "I hear you are a storyteller. I've got a great story for you."

He recounted a brief story and then Tita walked up and said, "Dad, they're getting ready to start the funeral." That gentleman was Bill's dad, celebrating his son's life in the form Bill always appreciated, by tellin' a good story.

A young lady there told me that she regularly sat in the chair next to Bill's when they were receiving the long chemotherapy treatments. Laughing through her tears, she explained that she has a large collection of white foam cups that Bill had done drawings on. Like I said, he would, and could, draw on anything.

At the funeral I also saw a family friend I hadn't seen in years. I had no idea that he knew Bill. He said Bill had added a room onto his home a few years earlier. I asked if he knew about Bill's drawing. He smiled and said, "Jim, I came home one evening to see what Bill had done during the day. There I saw, on the raw, newly installed window sill, one of the most beautiful panoramic drawings with Bill's wonderful characters. Jim, I just took that window sill out and kept it. It annoyed him a bit, but I made Bill put in another window sill."

Following Bill's funeral, Tita told me, "Bill must have really liked you, Jim."

"I was honored to be his friend. I really cherished all of our time together. I really liked him too."

"No, Jim, I mean you must have been something very special to him, because he has never, ever, allowed any of his sketches to be published."

I had no response. I was stunned. What do you say when someone has allowed you access to a lifetime of magnificent work? Talk about pressure! I hope my words are adequate to have given you a glimpse of this wonderful and talented man.

Bill's sketches will be a part of every book I do. It's my way of keeping my friend close. To my friend Bill Erhard, I miss ya. Happy trails, Partner.

This sketch was among those in Walter Proetzman's collection.
Nobody ever knew exactly what Bill was thinking,
but this sketch sure seems appropriate here.

Luckenbach, Texas

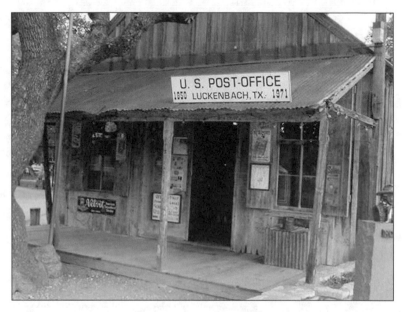

The post office at Luckenbach, Texas.

Legendary Luckenbach, Texas, is small in geography. It consists of only about ten acres between South Grape Creek and Snail Creek. But it is a gigantic presence in the minds of millions of folks.

The "town," located on Ranch Road 1376, 13½ miles from Fredericksburg in southeastern Gillespie County, consists of only a few buildings. The oldest is the post office/general store/bar, opened in 1849 by Minna Engel, whose father was an itinerant preacher from Germany. The community, first named Grape Creek, was later named after Minna's husband, Carl Albert Luckenbach.

It was first established as a community trading post and was one of the few that never broke a peace treaty with the Comanche

Indians with whom they traded. One year later a community hall was built, which is now known as the world famous Luckenbach Dance Hall. Still standing are the blacksmith shop and steam-operated cotton gin that were constructed in 1879.

Have you ever rented a whole town? Most folks never even think about it. Well, for a few hundred dollars, you can rent the whole town of Luckenbach for your event. For generations families came to Luckenbach for reunions, weddings, or just to have fun.

In 1970 a local rancher, Hondo Crouch, responded to an ad he saw in the local paper. It read, "town - pop. 3 - for sale." For thirty thousand dollars, Hondo bought Luckenbach, and the rest is legendary Texas history.

HISTORICAL FACT: According to Hondo, "We have discovered that Luckenbach, on the globe, is right in the middle of the world. And we figure that if God hadn't intended for us to be the center of the world he wouldn't have put us here."

Hondo Crouch's bust greets visitors to Luckenbach, Texas.

Luckenbach's motto was, "Everybody is Somebody in Luckenbach." This attitude attracted a wonderfully talented group of folks, including lots of Texas storytellers and musicians. Sitting around the campfire, telling stories, and pickin' became a wonderful tradition.

In 1976 Hondo died. His music-making friends penned the song "Luckenbach Texas," which was recorded by Waylon Jennings and Willie Nelson in 1978. The song, now a classic, became a number one smash hit all across the nation and beyond, putting Luckenbach on the map for good.

Today Luckenbach is still a social center. Many consider the Luckenbach Dance Hall the "Best Dance Hall in Texas." The bar is the regular gathering place for folks from all over the world. I've never been there when I didn't meet somebody interesting. Why? Because the clocks run slower in Luckenbach. Things slow down in Luckenbach. People take the time to speak to others in Luckenbach. Everybody is somebody in Luckenbach!

An armadillo knocks back a longneck in the Luckenbach General Store.

Jalapeno Sam Lewis runs the armadillo races at Luckenbach along with one of his armadillo wranglers, Benny Howell, and his lovely bride, Nick. Sam owns an armadillo ranch just down the road a piece.

Willie and VelAnne Howle, the "Mare" of Luckenbach.
Photo courtesy of VelAnne Howle.

Hondo

Peter Cedarstacker
John Russell Crouch (1916-1976)

Photo courtesy of Becky Crouch Barrales.

The thousands of us who knew Hondo will all agree. Nobody knew Hondo! Often I don't even think Hondo knew what he was going to do next. The mercurial man approached life like a treasure hunt, excited by life's joys, big and small. In his quest for fun, Hondo brought joy and confusion to all those around him.

We can all also agree that Hondo touched this world. He grabbed hold of everything within reach. Pieces of wood and flint, ignored by others, were worked into spoons and arrowheads by Hondo's weathered hands. He had an amazing talent for making something useful, or humorous, out of the everyday items ignored by others.

But, more importantly, Hondo did the same thing with the people he met. He checked them out. What's the texture of this new friend? Do they have a sense of humor? Can they laugh at themselves, or are they full of themselves?

No matter what their station in life, or whatever their texture, Hondo held them up to the light, examined them, and made them feel like they were important to him. And they were. Everybody IS somebody in Luckenbach.

Out West we have an expression that goes, "God created man, but Sam Colt made all men equal." Well, so did Hondo Crouch. Whether you needed some buildin' up or some whittlin' down, Hondo was the man for the job. If you were the Grand Imperial Poo Bah back in your hometown, you were surely disappointed if you expected Hondo to make any big hoopty-do over you.

As we sat around the campfire one night, a particularly noisy Yankee feller had just finished explaining how important he was, claiming his company would close without his valuable presence. When the guy got up to get another beer, Hondo asked me, "Jim, what do you do with a gas bag?"

I played along, "I don't know, Hondo. What do you do with a gas bag?"

"You stick a pin in 'em!" and then he chuckled.

With that I knew the stage was set. Hondo had picked his target. It was now just a question of what would he do, and when?

Hondo performs a rope trick for Jerry Jeff Walker. Photo courtesy of Becky Crouch Barrales.

Well, the windy one returned with his beer and started to sit back down. He had gotten to about mid-squat, when Hondo said, "Hold on there! You can't just sit back down at a tribal campfire like this 'un without first honorin' the spirits! That's downright disrespectful."

The Yankee, still in mid-squat, said, "Oh, I'm sorry. How do I honor the spirits?"

"You have to check the perimeter for evil spirits, of course!"

"Uh, how do I do that?"

"By slowly walking all the way around the camp, of course!"

Duly admonished, the Yankee headed out to walk around the city block sized town of Luckenbach, looking for "evil spirits."

When he was out of earshot, Hondo winked at me and said, "While he's gone I'll have time to run get another beer! I'll bring you another, Jim."

Somewhere, about halfway around the town, the light went on for the Yankee. To his credit, he did come back laughing. As he came back he couldn't help but notice that Hondo and I had fresh beers. We didn't hear another word about how great he was, because everyone around that campfire already knew who the greatest one there was. Hondo was the master. He had again stuck a pin in the gas bag.

Writing about my friend Hondo Crouch is difficult. I would like to think we were friends, though I don't know if anybody could ever say they really knew him. But just like the coyote and the roadrunner, we keep trying to share him with a world that truly needs his wonderful brand of humor.

One night by the campfire in Luckenbach, after several bottles of what some Germans call "liquid bread," I asked him why life was so exciting for him.

Hondo said, "Well, Jim, I love to get up in the morning, just to see what I'm gonna get into that day!"

Hondo loved the startled look that people get when something unexpected has just happened. I'm sure if he ever thought he was on the verge of being describable, or predictable, he would have immediately changed his direction and headed straight for Totally Unpredictable.

Hondo was one with the world, not the other way round. He found a way to enjoy everything this world has to offer. No thing, and certainly no person, was ignored by Hondo.

With a childlike excitement and curiosity, he examined everything he came in contact with. The earth, trees, plants, critters with four legs or two were of interest to him. Where did this remarkable man come from?

John Russell Crouch was born on December 4, 1916, in Hondo, Texas, to Ione and Harry Crouch, a telegraph operator for the Southern Pacific Railroad. In a Texas filled with characters, Hondo stood tall above the rest from the beginning.

He grew up loving the outdoors. Hunting, fishing, and trapping were his favorite pastimes. But he also developed a love for swimming. Years later he told me he had to learn to swim in a wet wagon wheel rut. He would laugh and say, "That's how I learned to swim so straight."

Straight, yes, but also very fast. He was an outstanding swimmer in high school and soon caught statewide attention. After he had won everything and left, folks would ask, "Who was the Hondo guy?"

John Russell "Hondo" Crouch at the age of 21.
Photo courtesy of Becky Crouch Barrales.

The town of Hondo had a great group of swimmers at the time. They all had a great time and loved to sing the Hondo team song:

We come from Hondo, good ole town,
Where broncos buck and coyotes howl.
We're wild and woolly and full o' pep!
So look out, buddy, and watch your step!

Crouch became an All-American swimmer at the University of Texas. It was while making swimming headlines in high school and college that Hondo picked up his nickname.

After each win the newspapers would run headlines like "John Russell Crouch from Hondo Wins." Well that was a bit of a mouthful, so it wasn't long before they had shortened it all down to, "Hondo Crouch Wins." And by the end of a stellar college career it was, "Hondo Wins."

There was another reason Hondo was loved by the newspapers. He was always doing something just odd enough to be interesting. Some newspapers dubbed him the "Swimming Cowboy." Other headlines read, "Boot Wearing Cowboy Crouch, acclaimed by some as the best form swimmer at the national last year."

Ralph "Alligator Boy" Flanagan, a great swimmer from Florida, brought a foot-and-a-half-long alligator (Apalachicola, "Appie") with him when he came to swim at UT. Who else would he room with but Hondo?

Ralph and Hondo would take Appie down to Greg Pool when they had swim practice. Ralph left UT after a year, and he left Appie with Hondo. The pair became such campus celebrities, that when Appie died, it made front page headlines in the campus newspaper, the *Daily Texan*.

Swimming was the first thing Hondo did that brought a small Texas town to the attention of the entire state. But it would not be the last.

In 1941 Hondo was awarded a degree in physical education from UT. But it was just a few months before World War II broke out.

Hondo trained as a navigator in the Air Corps at Garner Field in 1942.

Hondo married Helen Ruth (Shatzie) Stieler, daughter of the 1945 "Goat King of the World," Adolf Stieler of Comfort.

Following his time in the service he settled down to raise sheep, goats, and cattle near Fredericksburg. He never stopped enjoying swimming and was swimming coach at various Texas children's camps from the 1930s until the 1970s. In 1964 he was president of the Hall of Fame for UT athletes and in 1975 was influential in persuading the university to build the Texas Swim Center.

From 1963 to 1975, under the pen name Peter Cedarstacker, Hondo wrote several hundred "Cedar Creek Clippings" for the *Comfort News*. Through his characters from the mythical town of Cedar

Hondo writes another Peter Cedarstacker story.
Photo courtesy of Becky Crouch Barrales.

Creek, he satirized politics, government, ecology, deer hunters, social life, and everyday country problems and celebrations.

In 1971 Hondo bought Luckenbach. There are a couple of stories about why Hondo bought Luckenbach. What he told me was, "I had two farms, and Luckenbach was right in between 'em. I got used to stopping by and having a beer when I was going from one farm to the other. Then one day the store was closed. I decided to buy the whole town. That way I can always get a cold one if I need it!"

In Luckenbach, Hondo presided as mayor over a population of three plus a single parking meter. As "clown prince" he brought to life the town's motto, "Everybody's Somebody in Luckenbach."

Over the years, Hondo held an endless string of zany celebrations, such as the Luckenbach World's Fair, the first Texas "Women Only" Chili Cookoff (the Chili Bust), Return of the Mud Daubers, Valentine's Hug-In, and no-talent contests. Crouch participated in a Folklife Festival for Texas at the Smithsonian Institution in 1964. On July 4, 1976, Luckenbach received national attention for celebrating

Hondo plays with a chicken on the window ledge.
Photo courtesy of Becky Crouch Barrales.

the Non-Buy Centennial, protesting the commercialization of the bicentennial of the Declaration of Independence.

While researching this book, I had the opportunity to visit Hondo's daughter, Becky Crouch Barrales, and her husband, Hector, on their ranch south of Fredricksburg. Becky authored *Hondo, My Father*, one of the most enjoyable, sensitive, biographies I've ever read. It is both biography and autobiography. Here is an excerpt that will give you an insight into the Hondo she knew:

As a youth Hondo had always carved on wood — beautiful bas-relief Mexican or Southwestern scenes on boards used for free-standing pictures or doorstops.

At the age of fourteen Kerry [Crouch] revitalized the whittling and carving art in our home. Clyde Cook, Fredericksburg's furniture and woodcraftsman, came out to the Ranch to show Kerry some of his techniques of chiseling bowls and smoothing spoons. Kerry also was a natural in a class of Lynn Ford, expert woodcarver and designer. Kerry would whittle a pair of pliers out of one piece of wood or a chain whose links had no seams.

The way some people smoke cigarettes and chew gum, Hondo was always carving on a wooden spoon. He and Kerry together carved Pennsylvania Dutch style wall sconces, boxes, spoons, bread boards, bowls, and crosses.

Hondo didn't work a spoon into shape, he loved it into shape. After each chip was carved, he felt with his fingers. Cut. Feel. Cut. Touch. Cut. Rub. The spoons were patiently sanded, stained, mellowed with worm holes or deliberate scratches. Stains varied from shoe polish, water colors, oil paints to agarita root dye. He rubbed them on his nose for oil.

"You have to hold your knife blade real flat to the whetrock, Kerry, to get a good blade. A good sharp blade is the most important part of whittling. You have to sharpen it about every fifteen minutes. You are constantly shaping the blade as well as the thing you are whittlin' on."

Sometimes Hondo didn't whittle wood but flint. Protecting his palm with a thick piece of leather, he'd shape a piece of already "worked" flint into an arrowhead by snapping and flaking the edges with the point of a deer antler or a nail. He even tried dipping a blade of grass in cold water and stroking the hot flint with it, popping off surface pieces. He especially delighted in making thin bird-point arrowheads because they were small and easy to perfect. Kerry cherished Hondo's whittled arrowheads, wrapping them in cotton to bed in tiny oiled boxes under his pillow. "They are symmetrical," he said, "tiny pieces of sculpture you can put into your pocket."

From whittling wood, shaping, holding arrowheads, Hondo made us aware of the art of touching.

"Hondo carried the sensitivity of the things he touched to other people," Kerry said.

"The best feeling," Kerry once said, "is to walk barefooted through a freshly plowed field."

And it was barefooted through plowed fields that we often hunted arrowheads. We revered arrowheads in our family. The best times to hunt were after a rain or at sunset. When the sun glinted off flint from a certain angle the flint was easy to see.

Hondo taught us to hunt arrowheads "in a place where you think an Indian might have lived — near water, or on the south side of a hill protected from a norther. Or you look for a midden," he'd say, "land changes, evidences that a culture has once lived there. It's usually a mound made by debris with small squarish rocks, broken from campfire burns."

Hondo could always spot a mound. As we approached the square limestone rocks, sure enough, flint was abundant. If we didn't find perfect bird points or drills, sometimes an axe head or scraper. Most exciting to me were the "unfinished" points. I'd always wonder why it wasn't finished. Was it imperfect? Was the tribe moving on? Maybe I picked it up joyfully after an Indian threw it down in discouragement.

Hondo usually broke in a "city slicker" guest with an arrowhead hunt. One particular time it was a big-city guy who wanted to hunt on Hondo's land. He and Hondo strolled the caliche ground with Juan and Kerry, searching for arrowheads while terms were being discussed. Hondo stayed close to the man's side, telling him to step carefully. The city man's eyes were dull, Hondo knew. Suddenly Hondo stopped. The boys knew that Hondo had spotted an arrowhead, but they remained silent.

"His boot toe must be pointing to it," Kerry thought. "He's just waiting for that city guy to see it."

Unaware of Hondo's boot tip hint, the man finally saw it and enthusiastically picked up the genuine artifact.

"By gosh! Here's one!" He shook with excitement.

Kerry saw that the arrowhead, perfectly formed, had mud stuck to it as if it were freshly pried out of its dirt tomb.

Fondling his new treasure from the earth, the man rubbed the dirt off. Turning it in his palm, he glanced again at something written on the back of the arrowhead.

"A dollar seventy-five! Plus tax!" he shouted.

Juan and Kerry were about to explode with laughter. Kerry winked at Hondo.

"Hmmmm." Hondo casually shrugged. "They've gone up."

Like lots of my friends, Hondo had no trouble going against the grain. So in a state that hadn't had a Republican in its legislature since Civil War Reconstruction, Hondo was a Republican.

Hondo Crouch died of a heart attack on September 27, 1976, in Blanco. Flags across the state were lowered to honor his loss.

Upon hearing of Hondo's death, Bobby Emmons and Chips Moman penned a beautiful tribute to Hondo. Everyone who heard it, loved it, particularly two Texas boys named Willie and Waylon.

Some dubbed Hondo the "Clown Prince of Luckenbach." Others called him a "Comic Cowboy Philosopher." Whatever name you choose, you won't be able to fully describe this poet, rancher, philosopher, comic genius, woodsman, father, husband, and friend. Whatever he was, Hondo Crouch was a true Texas folk hero.

The Cookoff Kickoff
as told by Hondo to Jim Gramon

One evening Hondo and I were talking about one of the major pastimes in Texas, the chili cookoff. Having found out that most cookoffs didn't allow women to enter, Hondo put together a women only cookoff that has continued to be a fun event to this day.

As we talked, I mentioned the Terlingua cookoff. Hondo laughed and told me he had been kicked out of their cookoff. I assured him that I didn't think that was possible. He assured me it was.

"Well, that year I nursed my old truck the whole way down there, carryin' a half-bed full of fine dry Hill Country oak and mesquite wood. You see, I could cover my gas money sellin' some of the wood to the new folks that didn't know to bring some. Anyhow, I got there and cooked up a pretty damn fine pot o' red. And all them judges mmmmm'd and smacked as they tasted on it. They thought it was right special tastin'. But, they couldn't figure out just what all I'd put in there, and they asked what that secret ingredient was."

Hondo chuckled as he took another sip of his beer. He then winked at me and said, "I told 'em that I didn't think they'd want to know what my secret ingredient was. And they said, 'Oh Hondo, but we do, we really do.' So, I says alrighty then, if you insist, and I flipped back the tarp I had over the bed of my pickup, and there lay a roadkill armadillo that I had picked up on the way to Terlingua!"

"Geez, Hondo, I'll bet they were hacked. What happened next?"

"Well Jim, you shoulda seen their faces! I actually thought the fat'un on the end was gonna have a hissy fit! The tall'un with the beard looked like he was havin' a heartastroke. They sure was a touchy bunch. For the life of me I can't figure out why they threw me right out of the contest."

"Hondo! You didn't really tell them that, did ya?"

"God's honest truth, boy. I laughed my butt off the whole way back home. Gotta tell ya, that was a really good time!"

Looking across the creek at the large fire pit where folks gather
to tell stories and play music most every evening in Luckenbach.

Dr. America Paredes

(1915-1999)

Photo courtesy Arte Publico Press, Houston, Texas.

As a writer you want to capture the reader's attention in your first lines. I've started this chapter four times. Each attempt carried significant concepts. Each lacked significant aspects about the position Americo Paredes holds as a writer and storyteller.

Americo Paredes was the John Steinbeck of Texas literature. His work was ethnocentric and primarily focused on the use, and abuse, of Mexican American laborers at the hands of a wide variety of people.

The settling of the Texas territories was often an unpleasant, challenging endeavor. Physical, mental, and social challenges have continued to this day.

Part of the charm and complexity of Texas is that it is a true melting pot of cultures. While researching my last book, *FUN Texas Festivals and Events*, I was astounded at the dozens of cultures that still retain a strong influence in Texas. How did this come to be? Well, it first started with the land. The rich soil, plenty of water, and moderate climate began attracting folks thousands of years ago. Numerous Indian tribes throughout northern Mexico and the American Southwest called the "Texas territory" their home.

Some believe things were peaceful in Texas until the Anglos arrived. Not true. Indian tribes warred, off and on, for centuries prior to the arrival of other races. Several tribes were defeated and absorbed by other tribes.

The melting pot was boiling and has seldom rested since.

In the 1500s and 1600s the French and Spanish established their colonies in Texas. Sometimes these colonies were able to get along with their neighbors. Often they didn't.

Settlement was encouraged by most of the parties. So the word went out around the world that there was land to be had in Texas. And the people came from all over the world, looking for new starts in this new land.

Each group, Mexican, French, Spanish, native Indians, and dozens of Anglo groups all battled for their piece of Texas. Right or wrong, the battles took place on many fronts. Some of the vestiges of those battles still remain today. Cinco de Mayo is widely celebrated in Texas, despite the fact that Texas really wasn't involved on either side of the battle (aside from being the birthplace of General

Zaragoza, who led the Mexican army that defeated the French on May 5).

Spaniards and the Mexicans

As a nation, Texas threw open its doors and invited everyone to come and settle. These settlements were normally about fifteen to twenty miles apart, about a day's ride by wagon. This space provided each culture the space to develop and grow, while still maintaining much from their original cultural heritage.

While working on my first book, *Famous Texas Folklorists and Their Stories*, I sought to identify storytellers from all the cultures that have influenced Texas. In particular, I was interested in finding representatives of the Texas-Mexican culture. At that time I was told by several sources that The University of Texas - Pan American, in Edinburg, Texas, was the best place to research the topic. Unfortunately, I was unable to go there at that time.

Since then I've learned a great deal about one of the original folklorists in this genre, Americo Paredes. He pioneered what is often referred to as the Chicano tradition in the folkloric study of Texas-Mexican culture.

Paredes believed in the use of folklore to bring about what he referred to as, "a feeling of unity that enhances the dignity of the group and gives them the confidence to face their challenges." This approach stood out in stark contrast from many of his fellow folklorists at that time. Anglo folklorists were generally collectors and distributors of the tales that they encountered. These stories were often reflective of the frictions and prejudices of the groups that told them the stories. Paredes became one of the earliest to focus on stories that reflected the Texas-Mexican point of view.

In 1958 Paredes captured the essence of the frictions between the Anglo and Texas-Mexican cultures with the publication of *With His Pistol in His Hand: A Border Ballad and Its Hero*. This book reconstructed the story of Gregorio Cortez Lira, a Mexican

American who killed an Anglo sheriff in a misunderstanding over the ownership of a horse. The story then follows Cortez's flight from a posse of Texas Rangers. His flight inspired *corridos*, songs celebrating his courage and tenacity in outwitting the posse, while attacking the rangers for their racist attitudes.

Paredes had studied with J. Frank Dobie and Walter Prescott Webb. He felt that their works had properly lauded the Texas Rangers for their heroic actions but had failed to also include an accurate picture of some of the rangers' attitudes towards minorities.

The publication of Paredes' book was a significant event in the Texas-Mexican community. In the opinion of many, it was the first time many of their issues had found a voice, and it was hailed as a pioneering breakthrough.

Paredes' resentment of Dobie was so deep that in the late 1930s he wrote *George Washington Gómez*. In it he satirized the figure of Dobie as a garrulous racist named K. Hank Harvey, the "Historical Oracle of the State." However, Paredes did not publish this book until 1990, twenty-six years after Dobie's death.

Part of the irony of this was that Paredes' use of fictionalized accounts of actual historical events came in stark contrast to the strict historians in the folklore community. The same ones who Dobie also disagreed with regularly on the same topic. Disagreement over that very issue caused Dobie to separate the Texas Folklore Society from the American Folklore Society. (This is discussed in detail in my biography of J. Frank Dobie in *Famous Texas Folklorists and Their Stories*.)

Dr. Americo Parades, Cultural Translator

All people who write have "filters" through which they view the world. The filters are comprised of a complex combination of training, ability to observe, life experiences, and many other things, which form "our view" of the world around us. Americo Paredes recognized early that his "filters" were different from those of his contemporaries in much of the storytelling community.

Early on Paredes couldn't understand why others did not see what was obvious to him. But then he realized that part of his function, as a folklorist, would have to be more than a recorder of events. He would also have to serve as a translator, not so much of the language as of the culture. As a cultural translator, he needed to explain not just the events, but also the underlying circumstances behind the events that made them significant in the lives of the people. Paredes soon became a strong voice for the Texas-Mexican community.

I often encounter a lack of ability to relate in audiences that have never lived in a small community or on a farm. They have nothing in their experience to help them relate to things like a barn raising. They have never lived in a community where the people always come together when one of their members has a problem.

So I try to educate them about how things are in those places and times. Too often it seems groups are angered that others don't understand them. Often it's just that nobody took the time to explain the situation. They aren't necessarily rejecting the group, just not understanding.

Paredes recognized this. Through his classes, speaking engagements, and publications, he set in motion the learning that has led to better enlightenment, understanding, and greater acceptance. He is considered by many to be the father of Mexican-American studies.

A true scholar, he never stopped learning himself. He marveled at the diversity of cultures that had merged in Texas and in Texas folklore. In *Folktales of Mexico*, Paredes wrote that folklore in Mexico and the United States is a blend of "imported, indigenous and American-historical traditions," molded by a combination of "colonization, the westward movement, Negro slavery, immigration, regionalism, the rhetoric of democracy, and the technology of the mass media."

Animal folktales, such as "The Ram in the Chile Patch" and "Perez the Mouse," are among the stories he collected for the book.

"Folktales of wonder and adventure still are told in Mexican villages and towns with all the old embellishments," he observed.

The Life of Dr. Americo Parades

Americo Paredes was born September 3, 1915, to Justo and Clotilde Paredes in Brownsville, Texas. At that time the area was still dealing with the events of the Mexican Revolution. He grew up listening to the corridos and stories told by his fellow Tejanos.

His thirst for knowledge was evident early, because he maintained a good school record, despite working regularly to help support his large family, which included seven brothers and sisters. While in high school he even won first place in a statewide poetry contest.

Upon graduation from high school, Paredes attended Brownsville Junior College. He was fortunate to find instructors who encouraged and nurtured his growing interest in all forms of writing. His talent was obvious, and he was soon employed by the local newspaper as a writer, proofreader, and translator for the *Brownsville Herald*.

Paredes was first published when he came out with his first book of poetry, *Cantos de adolescencia*, the songs of youth. He married Consuelo Silva in 1939. Everything was going well for Paredes but not for the world.

World War II broke out and Paredes volunteered for the army. He served the duration of the war as an infantryman and, at the end of hostilities, was asked to become a writer and editor for the publication *Stars and Stripes*, the official publication of the U.S. Military. In that capacity he helped cover the war crimes trials in Japan that followed the war.

Paredes returned to college after receiving his discharge from the army. In a fortunate decision, he chose to return to college at The University of Texas at Austin. I say this was fortuitous because UT Austin had become the center of folklore activity in the state at that time. Cornerstones for Texas folklore were being laid by folks like Roy Bedichek, Walter Prescott Webb, John Henry Faulk, and J. Frank Dobie.

Unfortunately his marriage to Consuelo did not survive the long separation during the war, and they divorced. But in 1948 he wed Amelia Sidzu Naeamine. They had four children, Julia, Americo Jr., Alan, and Vicente. Paredes was quite proud of his children, and many of his books were dedicated to them.

In 1951 Paredes finished his bachelor's degree in English and graduated *summa cum laude*. He completed his master's degree there in 1953, with a focus on English and folklore studies.

In 1956 Paredes completed his doctorate in English (folklore) and Spanish. At this point he was asked by the University to teach, and over the years he taught many students about the issues surrounding the Mexican-American way of life.

In 1957 Paredes organized the Folklore Archives at the University of Texas and served as the archivist. He was also elected president of the Texas Folklore Society in 1961-1962 and was the vice president of the American Folklore Society in 1964-1965.

He became a full professor of English at UT in 1965 and professor of Anthropology in 1966. During that time he was serving on the folklore program faculty. He was later named the Ashbel Smith Professor of English and Anthropology and the Anderson Centennial Professor. After retirement, Paredes was honored again when he was named Professor Emeritus of English and Anthropology.

This literate, articulate man began to document much of what had been passed along orally for generations. His writings were often the first documentation of stories that existed along the Rio Grande. These seminal texts were praised by the academic community and provided him with the teaching materials necessary to get Mexican-American studies added to the curricula offered by colleges and universities.

He founded the University's Mexican American Studies Program in 1972 and directed the Center for Intercultural Studies in Folklore and Oral History.

He also earned a lifetime achievement award at the 1998 Texas Book Festival, hosted by Laura Bush when she was First Lady of Texas. It was at this event that I met Americo Paredes. I was working as a volunteer for the Book Festival and ended up in a long line greeting Mr. Paredes and a couple of other featured authors. I regret that there was no time to talk, beyond a brief hello.

Honors

Americo Paredes was rightfully proud of having a middle school in Austin named in his honor.

In 1989 Dr. Paredes was honored by the National Endowment for the Humanities with the Charles Frankel Prize for his lifelong contributions to the humanities. The government of Mexico in 1990 awarded him the Order of the Aztec Eagle, the highest award to non-citizens, for preserving Mexican culture. Paredes died on May 5, 1999, at the age of eighty-three.

At the time of his death, the Office of Public Affairs at The University of Texas at Austin observed that by learning the songs and the lore of the Rio Grande region, he "set in motion a revolutionary approach to writing about the way things and people had been in early Texas. In doing so, he helped to shape a positive cultural identity among Mexican-Americans and influenced a whole new generation of Texas scholars."

UT Austin president Larry R. Faulkner said, "Américo Paredes was a great part of the soul of The University of Texas and the Austin community for many decades. He will be sorely missed. And on this occasion, the entire University community reaches out with fond regards to the members of his family."

Molly Ivins

Contrarian

I seem to be drawn to folks who have something to say. Wow, did I ever hit a liberal-minded gold mine when I met Molly (in Texas all you have to say is "Molly," and they know who you are talking about). As Molly puts it, "I write about Texas politics and other bizarre happenings."

I first met Molly several years ago, at the Texas Book Festival. A fiery redhead was explaining to a questioner about what being a Texan means. It was obvious that she is a keen and often critical observer of the political landscape. At our first meeting we had laughed when I joked that finding humor in Texas politics and politicians was not nearly as hard as it ought to be.

Molly Ivins flashes her trademark smile while playing with her dog Athena.

Molly said, "You're exactly right. It is often quite funny. But it is all too often quite sad, the incompetence and waste that takes place. It all too often hurts those who can least afford it."

And that is typical Molly. In many ways Molly reminds me of my old friend John Henry Faulk. Both are fiery patriots, ready to do battle with those who they think threaten individual freedoms or the well-being of the less fortunate in our society. (In one of those serendipitous circumstances, Mrs. Elizabeth Peake Faulk, "Lizzie," John Henry's widow, has worked with Molly for many years.)

Molly has often reminded me of my neighbor, another fiery patriot, Barbara Jordan. She was the first black woman in the Texas Senate and the first black woman in the U.S. Congress. (In one article Molly observed that often Barbara's official title seemed to be "The First Black Woman To _____ " then you would fill in the blank with her most recent accomplishments.)

I've often imagined what wonderful conversations about the constitution, freedom, and government would have taken place if Barbara, John Henry, and Molly could have spent some time together discussing the constitution. I also marvel at how blessed I have been to have known all three of these wonderful folks.

Molly and I related to each other right away. She has the casual, soft-spoken style of someone who grew up in rural Texas. She doesn't need to raise her voice; her words carry the weight of her argument.

Ah, but when she laughs, it's the full, rich, booming laugh of someone who is comfortable with themselves and not self-conscious at all. I must amuse Molly, because she laughs quite a bit when we are together (frankly I'm not sure if that is good or bad).

Two years ago, while working on my first folklore book, I asked Molly if I could include her. It was obvious to me that politics, Texans, and storytellers are always a strange mix. And I always enjoyed the humor that she regularly uses while making her point, right or wrong.

I once told her that I will defend, to the death, her right to be wrong.

To which she responded, "Ditto."

Which is a wonderful example of Molly's sense of humor.

Jim and Molly at her south Austin home. That's right, she's a Bubbette!

At that time, Molly wasn't interested in being included in my book. She said, in one of her more emphatic tones, "I'm no story-teller and certainly not a folklorist!"

I assured her that she most certainly was a great storyteller about the tumultuous contemporary political scene in Texas, and in particular the goings on in the "Lege," her term for the Texas Legis-lature. I asked her to think about it and assured her that I would be back. I then retreated to put on bandages.

Fast forward a couple of years, to the Authors' Party at the 2001 Texas Book Festival. I was the envy of many of the men at the party, because on my arm that night was my lovely daughter, Nicole. As

Nicole and I chatted, a tall blonde walked up and swung an arm around my shoulders and said, "Hi Jim, it's good to see you again."

I responded with, "Great to see you again. How have you been?" I would have introduced her to Nicole, but I was temporarily stumped as to who she was.

As she responded to my question, my electrical circuits finally connected, the light came on, and I realized it was Molly. Finally in possession of a name, I introduced her to Nicole and asked Molly, "Well, is it true, do blondes have more fun?"

"Oh Jim, you know I always have fun."

I then told her I was working on a new Texas storytellers book and asked her if she had thought about being in it. Then I held my breath.

"Yes I have thought about it, and yes I would be honored to be included."

That very evening I started on this section of the book. One of my goals with my books is to convey that storytelling is an art that crosses all the boundaries. No matter what century or location or business or language, good storytellers are wonderful to find. Storytelling is alive and well today, and Molly is a great practitioner.

I like Molly because I like people who make humor a big part of their life. Some people act funny. Molly is naturally funny and uses humor in many different formats. Long stories, short stories, anecdotes, vocabulary, and all sorts of gags are all part of her arsenal.

An example occurred on my first visit to her lovely, secluded south Austin home. I was greeted by her beautiful dog, Athena, a tall, proud, standard French poodle. Molly introduced us, and as I was petting Athena, Molly explained that she gave Athena a classy name to make up for her previous dog.

So, I bit, "What was your previous dog's name?"

"Her name was Shit."

"You're kidding!"

"Nope, that was her name. Sure did rile up the neighbors when I would wander through the neighborhood at night shouting for her."

Nobody could possibly let that one pass without the obvious follow-up question, "How did your dog get that name?"

Well, after investigating it carefully, it seems there are two different answers to that question. Molly says she named the pup Shit because she was so incredibly uncoordinated that she stumbled around like she was shit-faced drunk.

The story possessed a certain level of credibility. However, I found another version. I publish a monthly column in *Texas Co-Op Power Magazine*, one of the most widely distributed magazines in Texas. Each month my column features some Texas festival.

My editor at the magazine is a wonderful lady named Kaye Northcott. (Please note how rare this is for a writer to use the words wonderful and editor in the same sentence, without sarcasm.) It seems that Kaye was the original source of the, uh, er dog in question. Kaye's dog had a litter of "purebred mongrel mutts." As she explains it, "They were all about three generations away from being bright."

According to Kaye, all the dogs looked about the same, except for the one that had a small bit of "stuff" on top of her head. Instead of cleaning it off, Kaye used the small "item" as a way to distinguish that dog from the others.

One of the pups ended up with Governor Ann Richards, and the pup with the spot on her head ended up with Molly. Glad we cleaned up that dog name "mess."

Anyone who would name her dog like that is obviously a practicing contrarian. I asked her if she had been contrary all of her life.

"Oh yes, Jim; my mother always said that reverse psychology always worked best on me."

"OK," I said, "what would you do if you woke up one day and organizations were in agreement with your views on how things should be run?"

"Well, I would be quite surprised. But, although I am a contrarian, I try not to be a knee-jerk type of anything. Of course, no matter what the circumstances, I'm sure there would be something that I felt was wrong and should be brought out."

As such Molly has an incredibly interesting and impressive life.

The facts contained in Molly's biography are most impressive. Mary Tyler "Molly" Ivins was born August 30, 1944, in Monterey, California, the daughter of Jim and Margot Milne Ivins. As the old joke goes, she wasn't born in Texas but got here as fast as she could. She grew up in Houston (frankly Molly's like me, she'll probably never grow up).

She has an older sister, Sara, who is a schoolteacher in New Mexico. She also has a younger brother, Andy, who is an attorney in Boerne.

Molly has a B.A. from Smith College and a master's degree in journalism from Columbia University. Then she studied for a year at the Institute of Political Science in Paris.

She served for three years on the board of the National News Council and is active in the Amnesty International's Journalism Network. She is also on the Reporters Committee for Freedom of the Press. Molly writes about press issues for the American Civil Liberties Union and for several journalism reviews.

She began her career in journalism as the Complaint Department of the *Houston Chronicle*. She rapidly worked her way up to the position of sewer editor, from whence she wrote a number of gripping articles about street closings.

For some hazardous duty pay, she also handled some weddings. "Trust me, Jim; you've really got to get everything just exactly right on weddings, because there is no more dangerous creature on earth than an enraged mother-of-the-bride!"

She next went to work for the *Minneapolis Tribune*, first as a police reporter and later on a beat called Movements for Social Change. She covered militant blacks, angry Indians, radical students, uppity women, and a motley assortment of other misfits and troublemakers.

In 1970 Molly returned to Texas as coeditor of *The Texas Observer*, an ever vigilant, muck-raking publication devoted to the coverage of Texas political and social events. Her specialty was covering the Texas Legislature, which doubtless accounts for her frequent fits of hysterical laughter in those years. When the Lege was not in session, Ivins roamed the state in search of truth, justice, and good lead stories for the magazine.

Now let's talk 'bout politics!

Sketch by Bill Erhard.

In 1976 the Columbia University's School of Journalism named Ivins Outstanding Alumna. That same year, demonstrating that she fears nothing, Molly joined *The New York Times* as a political reporter. He first assignment was at City Hall. Within a year she had impressed and annoyed enough folks that the *Times* sent her to keep watch over the legislators at the statehouse in Albany.

Only one year later, probably at the request of some of the Albany politicos, she was named Rocky Mountain Bureau Chief for the *New York Times*. Impressive title indeed, considering that she was the only one in the bureau! Must have made for some very short staff meetings.

For three years she buzzed around the nine mountain states by herself. Since sleep was not an option, she assures me that she just gave it up entirely.

In February 1982, in an attack of common sense or masochism, Molly returned to Texas. She insists that it was masochism. I speculate that it could have appealed to her sense of humor, because she already knew that the Texas Legislature would keep her in incredible material for as long as she is willing to take notes.

Texas is full
of spooky
Politicians!

Sketch by Bill Erhard.

Molly's freelance work has appeared in *Esquire, Atlantic, The Nation, Harper's, TV Guide,* and numerous other publications. She also does occasional commentary for National Public Radio and the McNeil/Lehrer program.

She speaks both French and Spanish, loves to camp, canoe, and run rivers, and is a semi-famous storyteller and beer-drinker.

She is author of two best-selling books, *Molly Ivins Can't Say That, Can She?* and *Nothin' But Good Times Ahead,* both collections of essays on politics and journalism. She has been a finalist for the Pulitzer Prize three times and was the winner of the 1992 Headliners Award for best column in Texas.

Molly is a widely syndicated political columnist for the *Fort Worth Star-Telegram.* Her column appears in 200 newspapers besides the *Star-Telegram.* She often says that Texas politics, "is better than the zoo, better than going to the circus, rougher than football, and more aesthetically satisfying than baseball."

Which brings me to the definition of contrarian. Every so often, when the usual occupants of the dictionary don't measure up, I'm forced to dig deeper to find a new word. And that's what I had to do with Molly. Having gathered a pile of info on Molly, and a long list of things that partially describe her, I found the word contrarian.

That is a person who goes against the flow, the grain, rubs the fur the wrong way, goes against the accepted norm, and generally is never found in the big crowd. That's Molly. Molly is in pretty good company on this. Roy Bedichek, John Henry Faulk, and Ben King Green were all contrarians. All of these independent thinkers were generally uncomfortable as a member of the majority. Experience failed to prepare them for that unusual event.

But these folks aren't contrary just to be contrary. They have their reasons for their positions, but if you disagree and have a reasoned argument for your position, they will listen. Which separates these intellectuals from the common garden variety idgit, because these folks regularly reassess their positions.

Molly and I get along well because we are both constantly inquiring about practically everything around us. She reads an average of about two books each week. Subjects vary all over the map, but for pure relaxation she loves a good mystery.

For a contrarian example, when I asked what her greatest honors have been, Molly made no mention of her three Pulitzer nominations or her numerous other awards. Instead she said, "the first was when the Minneapolis police force named their mascot pig Molly, after me. The other high water mark was when I was banned from the campus of Texas A&M for possessing views they did not share. It was wonderful." (She certainly seems to be taking it well, doesn't she?)

In her very funny, best-selling book *Molly Ivins Can't Say That, Can She?* Molly tells it like she sees it. If you are uncomfortable with her observations, that's your problem.

Over the last few years, Molly has had some health problems. When I asked her about it in the spring of 2002 she said, "I am doing just great. Thank you for asking. I had a second surgery last November and had a little infection following that. But now I am feeling wonderful!"

We then proceeded to compare the pros and cons of the various chemotherapy programs that we had participated in. Molly is now strong, vibrant, and lookin' great and lookin' for fun.

What does Molly have going on right now? Well, besides her regular column and public speaking engagements, Molly and her brother, Andy, have purchased some land together. "We are refusing to do that trite old weekend ranching thing. So, we've decided we are going to become vintners. You know, raising grapes and all" (contrarian).

I gave Molly copies of my books and asked her if she knew what a Liars' Table is.

Predictably she said, "Not exactly, but I'm sure it has something to do with the Texas Legislature!"

I told her that was close enough! The concept is the same, just a lot more expensive.

Here is one of Molly's political observations;

She referred to Dolph Briscoe, a 1970s-era governor, as the most boring leader Texas ever had. "He was the pet rock of governors," she recalled. "Never bothered anyone with charisma or ideas. He was given to appointing dead people to various boards and commissions and they, too, were restful and caused no trouble at all. However, he did create a good highway system, and today we are like Mississippi, but with good roads."

With ideas like that, perhaps contrarian, should be spelled "contrary 'un."

To keep up with Molly and her columns, check out www.workingforchange.com and www.dfw.com/mld/startelegram.

My platform is anything I can sleep on.

Sketch by Bill Erhard.

Terlingua

Brewster County, Texas

Welcome to Terlingua, population 30.

Most folks have heard of the Terlingua chili cookoffs. However, most of these folks couldn't put a pin in a map within five hundred miles of where it is located. As I said before, when there is no well-known landmark nearby, you tell folks that it is located in Brewster County, in the Big Bend region of West Texas, along the Rio Grande.

Now that you've found it on the map, you still probably aren't aware that there have been three different sites called Terlingua.

Which is ironic, since most sources agree that the name Terlingua evolved from the Spanish term *tres lenguas* (three tongues), referring to the three Indian languages used there at the time, which were Apache, Comanche, and Shawnee.

In the mid-1880s quicksilver (mercury) was discovered and mining camps sprang up in the area. The camp in Mariposa and Marfa also became known as Terlingua. To keep them straight, the original village came to be called Terlingua Abaja, or lower Terlingua.

This new Terlingua began to grow quickly, with the addition of a new mining complex. By 1905 the population had grown to around 1,000 folks, even though there were still very few buildings present.

Ten miles to the north, the Chisos Mining Company camp had also opened and was doing well. When the Marfa and Mariposa mine closed in 1910, the Terlingua post office and name were moved there and prospered. By 1913 Terlingua was a company-owned town, and the 1,000 inhabitants had some mail and phone service, a company-owned commissary and hotel, and even a company doctor.

Most of the folks in town lived in some variation of a tent city, with one exception. Mine owner Howard E. Perry's mansion, erected about 1908-1910, was the showplace of the region.

Old Town Terlingua, where memories
of the past share space with a theater and store.

95

Terlingua's high point as a mining town came in the early 1920s, because of the high demand for quicksilver production during World War I. By 1922, 40 percent of the quicksilver mined in the United States came from Terlingua.

Production declined over the next twenty years, until the Chisos Mining Company filed for bankruptcy in 1942. The operations were purchased by another firm that ceased operations at the end of World War II, in 1946, and Terlingua became a ghost town.

The jail in Old Town Terlingua.

In the late 1960s folks looking for the wide open spaces started having their annual chili cookoffs in Terlingua, and it was somewhat reborn.

In 1967 Terlingua was dubbed the "Chili Capital of the World" by the Chili Appreciation Society International, better known by chili-heads as CASI. The former company store reopened as a gift and art shop, river float trips are scheduled in the former cantina, and a dinner theater occupies the former motion picture theater.

In 1994 Terlingua had thirteen businesses and a population of twenty-five. Now there are about thirty people living in Terlingua. I'm not really sure what it says about me, but I was friends with about twenty percent of the permanent population, even though I hadn't been there in forty years.

Well I corrected that last year. My friend Buffalo Chuck Cudd invited me to come down and be a judge at the Terlingua World Championship Chili Cookoff. I accepted and, like always, did some research. I had wondered why Buff had emphasized that this was the "Behind the Store" cookoff. I soon found out.

Camp
Cook

My cookin'
is like whiskey,
the older it gets,
the tastier it gets.

Sketch by Bill Erhard.

Seems that many years ago, famed chili-maker Wick Fowler had a disagreement with the CASI folks, and they decided to have their own cookoff. Not only were they going to have their own, they were going to have it in the same place AND at the same time!

So when I pulled into town in November of 2001, I was in a town of 25 permanent residents that had grown to a population of near 30,000! But my fears of overcrowding were quickly calmed. These folks had been hosting these events for over thirty years. Everybody was prepared, and everybody had a great time.

The people come from all over the world each November to celebrate chili, Texas, music, the beautiful high mountain plains, and TO HAVE FUN. These cookoffs are a blast.

In just a couple of days, a barren section of land is converted into a sea of campsites, RVs, and vehicles of every description. Everywhere there are campfires where the folks gather to share music and stories. You can't go without making new friends. The whole thing is a bit like an adult, fall version of Spring Break. It's lots of fun, be sure and go.

The Rio Grande winds through a deep gorge in the beautiful, rugged, mountains surrounding Terlingua.

The Rio Grande that flows through the area has sustained not only the farms in the region, but also a thriving rafting industry. Unfortunately, the volume of water has been reduced to dangerously low levels. The gallows humor joke now goes that if someone falls out of a tour boat, "we just dust 'em off and help 'em get back in the boat."

Kopperl

Bosque County, Texas

Mainstreet in Kopperl.

If you live in the "country," away from the big buildings, you give your location relative to something people might recognize. For me, I live in San Leanna, Texas, just south of Austin, off I-35. Most folks either know where Austin is or are too embarrassed to admit that they don't. Either way, you don't get any more questions about where you live.

But when you get a bit farther out, into areas where there aren't large towns nearby, you go for what name recognition you can find. And so, let me introduce you to Kopperl, Bosque County, Texas.

To help those of you diving for a map, Kopperl is about twenty miles west of Hillsboro, which is on I-35 between Dallas and Waco. The town is located near Farm Road 56, fourteen miles northeast of Meridian and forty miles northwest of Waco, in northeastern Bosque County.

Kopperl was one of the many stations on the Gulf, Colorado and Santa Fe Railway. The rural community flourished for many years. Farming, ranching, and even some light manufacturing took place in Kopperl, in part because of the ready access to the railroad.

In 1953, after the construction of the Lake Whitney dam, a levee was erected around the town to protect citizens from possible flooding. In 1904 the estimated population was 329. The population in 1974 was 225. In 1990 the population was still reported as 225.

The post office in "downtown" Kopperl.

Why is Kopperl being featured here? Two reasons. First, because it is the type of small Texas farm community that I love to write about. Secondly, because Kopperl was the subject of a song by Steven Fromholz, the "Texas Trilogy."

The history of this quiet town is similar to that of a hundred other Texas towns. It was founded in 1883 by the railroad as a junction station. It was named Kopperl to honor Moritz Kopperl, a Galveston banker and railroad director.

Mr. Kopperl was born in Moravia in 1826. At twenty-two he was invited to immigrate to the United States, living with his uncle Charles, in Carroll County, Mississippi.

He lived for nine years with Major Kopperl. But he was increasingly intrigued by the new land of opportunity, Texas. So, in 1857, he set out with his friend, known only as A. Lipman, for Texas.

They settled in Galveston and started the dry-goods firm of Lipman and Kopperl. Things went smoothly and their business grew. But political storm clouds were gathering over the nation. By 1860 the Civil War had begun, and one of the first things the North did was blockade the Southern ports, including Galveston. With nothing to sell, the store soon closed.

Kopperl made out as best he could until the end of the Civil War. During that time of reconstruction, he became a cotton broker. He was successful and expanded into importing coffee. With his connections and business skills, Galveston soon became one of the largest coffee-importing ports in the world.

But he wasn't all business, and in 1866 he married Isabella Dyer from Baltimore. Over the next couple of years they had two children.

Investing money from his other successful ventures, in 1868 Kopperl became president of Texas National Bank. It was a shrewd investment. The bank was on the verge of failure, and he quickly brought it back to sound financial condition.

With his importing experience, Moritz Kopperl was a natural to help the city of Galveston improve their harbor's shipping facilities. So in 1871 Moritz Kopperl was elected to the Galveston City Council.

In 1876, after helping get Galveston out of debt, he was elected to the Texas Legislature, where he served as chairman of the Committee on Finance and Revenue. In that role he played a significant part in getting the state's finances into better shape.

Restless for another challenge, he then took over the Gulf, Colorado and Santa Fe Railway in 1877. Like the bank, this railroad was in financial trouble. And like the bank, Moritz Kopperl got it back into a sound financial condition. He served as its president from 1877 to 1879.

Four years later, in failing health, he sailed back to Europe. He died in Bayreuth, Bavaria, on July 3, 1883.

Inspiring story, Jim, but what does that have to do with the Texas town?

Well, upon hearing of his death, the folks at the Santa Fe Railroad decided to honor him by naming their newest station Kopperl.

So, now you know that the town was named to honor someone who never set foot in it. What does that have to do with legendary Texas storytellers? Well, that will become clear just a little further into the story.

Meanwhile, back in Kopperl, things are clickin' along pretty well. Farming and ranching are doing well. Folks are coming and going through town, much of their business has to do, in some way, with the presence of the railroad station.

But eventually the railroad decided it was no longer necessary to maintain a station in Kopperl. The glory days of Kopperl had passed. Many businesses closed and many folks moved away.

It's a painful thing to watch. Like watching a loved one, once active and vital, now no longer able to care for themselves.

Less people in town meant less money in town. Less money meant it was tougher to make a living. Many folks were forced to either give up their land or constantly scramble to pay the bills.

Lives become simpler. You don't have to worry about your budget when there is no money. You find ways to make what you've got last longer, and you work to figure out how to "make do" with what you have.

It was in this town, at this time, that the man was born who wrote what is considered by many to be the best song ever written about what it's like growing up dirt poor on a Texas farm. He wrote, "No, the train just don't stop here no more."

The deserted train depot in Kopperl.

Steven Fromholz

Livin' on the Fringe

The clear blue cyes take it all in, just as they always have. But they are much clearer now than thirty-five years ago (that was the nature of the sixties). The twinkle carries a few more answers, a few less questions, lots of smiles and miles.

Steven Fromholz, legendary singer-songwriter and entertainer.
Photo courtesy of Steven Fromholz.

It started at a tiny table in the corner of a live music club in Austin, the Chequered Flag. Long gone now, it used to be on 15th Street. The room was very dark—they called it atmosphere then and still do in some Italian restaurants. The tiny table seemed even smaller because I was sharing it with Bill Moss, the brilliant and often ebullient guitarist and very, very large guy.

We were catching Allen Damron's act when a lean cowboy in well-worn everything wandered in. Having spent a lot of my growing up on my uncle's ranch-farm, I knew the look. This wasn't a drugstore cowboy. The wear on the boots was from farm work, not city doings.

Bill's large arm went up, "Hey, Steve, over here," he motioned at the cowboy making his way through the crowd by the door.

My first thought was I couldn't believe Bill was giving away another part the tiny table that barely accommodated our two beers and an ashtray. Management had it all figured out. Smaller tables left room for more tables. More tables allowed for more people. More people brought in more money. So, on a normal crowded night, one person never moved without getting several others involved.

"Who is it, Bill?" I inquired.

"You mean you don't know Steven? Why this is Steven Fromholz. He's put down some pretty good ink. Some of his stuff is going to hit it big. Mark my words!"

The big, handsome, and incredibly young guy with clear blue eyes and lots of hair pulled up a chair. I liked his open smile and ready laugh. He had plenty of jokes to tell as he and Bill caught up on who was performing where.

My time with Steven that night was brief; he was on his way to somewhere new to check out something different. For most of Steven's life this seems to have been the case.

I was impressed with Steven as a nice guy, but what impressed me the most was that Bill was impressed. When Bill, a Julliard-trained, brilliant musician and singer, was impressed by someone's talent, it was unusual.

I was awed by Bill's talent. While I struggled to flog out a few chords on my old guitar, Bill could play brilliantly WITH JUST ONE HAND!

It truly did annoy me! Bill could fret the string with his massive fingers so hard that the string would vibrate to the point that he wouldn't even have to strum the strings with his other hand. In the pickin' business it's called "downing the strings." It takes talent and years of practice to do it well.

So when Bill was impressed with someone's talent, I took notice. Bill was right about Steven. Over the years he's become a legend because his work touches people. During his forty-year career he has done 125 songs, and 75 of his songs have been recorded. Oh, did I mention that he also has had five movie roles and is a river guide in Terlingua and Lajitas, taking folks on tours down the Rio Grande? He also has done numerous stage roles, ranging from Ebeneezer Scrooge in *A Christmas Carol* to Tevye in *Fiddler on the Roof.*

As you might have guessed, Steven is quite an entertainer. But even more than that, I believe he could have made a living as a stand-up comedian. What else can you say when he sings one of his classics like "I Gave Her a Ring."

Then, while the smile is lingering on your face, he can sing something serious, like the "Texas Trilogy." These three songs are considered by most to be the best, most unflinching look at the hard life on small farms and ranches in Texas.

Yet, even when we are laughing at the lyrics, we can still feel the emotion behind the songs. His phrasings sometime make you feel that you have had the experience yourself.

How does Steven do it? Well, it comes from a whole lot of talent and a whole lot of livin'. Here's the whole story....

Steven was born in Temple, Texas, on June 8, 1945. His father, Al, from Wisconsin originally, was stationed at Fort Hood. His mom, Georgia (better known as Skippy), was from Bosque County, Texas. During World War II she had worked at a war plant near Fort Hood, and that's how they met and married.

Steven grew up with an older sister, Angela, and a younger brother, Jimmy. His dad was in the automobile business and spent most of his time on the road. Meanwhile his mom worked in the fashion industry as a coordinator and even as a model.

Home for his heart seems to have been at his granny's place in Kopperl, Texas. But home with his parents was all over the Midwest. In a succession of positions with Ford Motor Company, they lived in Des Moines, North Platte, Memphis, and various other towns stretching from Canada to Mexico.

He put off his singing career till, at the ripe old age of ten, he sang "The Yellow Rose of Texas" in the Kopperl school auditorium. Church choirs were a regular part of his routine wherever he traveled. After high school Steven started playing guitar and writing some of his own songs.

In 1963 he entered North Texas State University in Denton. It was a very special time for Steven, for music, and for Steve's music. Rock and country music were firmly established, but the newest sound around was folk music, and it resonated within Steven's soul. He became the president of the North Texas State University Folk Music Club.

It was there that Steven met lifelong influences like Segle Fry, Don Brooks, and Michael Murphey (before he could afford the middle name, Martin). His early "professional" performances were with Michael Murphey and Patty Loman, in "The Michael Murphey Trio." Together they hit many of the Rotary, Optimist, and Lions Clubs in the area, in return for a questionable meal.

Michael worked on developing his unique sound, with Patty and Steven doing backup. Meanwhile Steven learned how to fingerpick a guitar by watching Michael.

In 1965 the Dallas County Jug Band was formed. Besides Steven and Michael, it included Travis Holland, Segle Fry, Johnny Vandiver, Don Brooks, and Ted Cack. They occasionally played at the legendary Rubaiyat, in Dallas, but most of their gigs were in Austin at the ID Coffee House, just off the UT campus.

Rod Kennedy knew that folk music was going to be popular, he just wasn't exactly sure how that popularity could be harnessed. But he was sure radio had to be part of the equation. So Rod went in with KHFI and put together the Zilker Park Folk Festival. (Years later Rod put this experience to work when he, Allen Damron, and some others put together one of Texas's longest running and most beloved events, the Kerrville Folk Festival.)

I'LL BET YOU DIDN'T KNOW THAT: The regulars at the Kerrville Folk Festival are proudly known as Kerrverts. Oh, you knew that. Well then, who created the term Kerrvert? Gotcha! Well, it was Steven Fromholz who captured the essence of the activities with the term Kerrverts. The festival has run for thirty years, and Steven has played there twenty-five times.

Meanwhile, back in Austin, 1965 was the first year of the Zilker Park Folk Festival. Steven and the Dallas County Jug Band was on the bill with Tom Paxton and Segle Fry. That summer, and those events, were a marvelous, magical time in the life of the twenty-year-old developing musician with an "evolving" musical sound.

Actually, at that time, the "sound" was so early in its evolution, it was generally just referred to as "really interesting music." Today "doing your own thing" and "developing a new sound" are everyday goals for a musician. But in 1965 it was an untested concept. Back then music was handed down in families. You played your daddy's music.

But in the sixties, thousands of musicians took Daddy's music places that Daddy didn't really want it to go. Country, jazz, rock-and-roll, soul, and even bluegrass were being blended together. We said it was being "fused." Many of the daddys just said we were "con-fused."

Whatever it was, in Austin we all felt much lighter, not carrying generations of musical expectations. It was wonderful. We could hit a bad note and claim it was intentional. A poorly tuned guitar was "what you wanted to do" because you were "developing your own sound," a "new sound." As you can imagine, many of those "sounds" were better left in the sixties.

But some of the sounds were magic, and we mirrored our love of the music back and forth, sharing ideas with others and getting encouragement in return. Today we look back on those times and it's amazing all the "musical legends" who came and went through Austin. Janis Joplin, Roy Orbison, Willie Nelson, Jerry Jeff Walker, Allen Damron, Kinky Friedman, and the legendary singing group Peter, Paul, and Mary to name just a few.

Steven Fromholz at the Kerrville Folk Festival.
Photo courtesy of Steven Fromholz.

But there were storm clouds on the horizon for many of us young musicians. The United States was involved in a confusing "conflict" in some place called Vietnam. Imagine our disappointment when the military informed us young musicians that they were interested in adding a new title to our resumes, soldier. Imagine our further disappointment when we found that they weren't interested in a military folk band.

It was 1965 when Steven got his draft notice from the army. As he put it, "I didn't want to go to Fort Hood or Fort Polk or Fort Anything!" So he enlisted in the navy and they sent him to Electronic Technician's School at Treasure Island, in San Francisco.

[Author's Note: Have you ever noticed the wonderful names of some of the military bases. Treasure Island sounds like it might be a pretty cool place. Steven assured me that wasn't the case. Me, I did some time at the world's biggest misnomer, Fort Bliss in El Paso. As a writer, lots of words come to mind when I think of that base, BLISS is NOT one of them!]

Nam was a conflicting time for young musicians. Steven was caught between his "artistic urges" whispering in one ear and good ol' Uncle Sam whispering in the other. As he puts it, "Thank God I'm a Gemini!"

It was in San Francisco that Steven got his first really good guitar, a Gibson J-50, and it inspired Steven to write a bunch of great new music. On his first off-base liberty, Steven went up to Grant Street. He did have a cool guitar. But he didn't have any hair!

He wandered into a popular cafe called Coffee and Confusion. It was hoot night, where anybody could get up and try a few tunes. The music was right and they offered him a job for Thursdays, playing at the owner's other place, The Coffee Gallery, located in a funky little part of San Francisco right off North Beach.

He was working there for ten bucks a night. It seems that most of the wonderful things that have to do with music, writing, or songwriting have absolutely nothing to do with money! Actually artists and money seldom cross paths! There's a handful that made a lot, but most of that often disappeared as a result of creative account-ing on the part of promoters, agents, and studios.

It was at Tamalpais that Steven met some Texas folk, including Sally Ann Mitchell, Jamie Spence, Mike Lowe, and Judy Caldwell. He started singing regularly with Judy, naming their duo "The Buffalo Chips." Every Thursday night they played at The Drinking Gourd on Union Street, where they quickly became a favorite.

For most songwriters, large amounts of mental energy is required to create something new. You can't make yourself be cre-ative; it's not like physical labor. You can encourage, nurture, nudge, and scream. But if you are mentally drained, it probably won't happen.

Texas musician

Sketch by Bill Erhard.

Life was being good to Steven in 1967. He married Judy, and on October 21 along came their daughter Darcie. On the music front, audiences loved his tunes and the way he and Judy performed them. All this encouraged him to write more, and more. And that's when he wrote the legendary three-song "Texas Trilogy."

It's hard to overestimate the impact of the "Trilogy" on Texas and music. In *Book of Texas Best* (Taylor Pub., 1988), Kirk Dooley names Steven's "Texas Trilogy" as the best song ever written about Texas.

Many say this is the best song about rural Texas life ever written. Steven wrote it about Kopperl, where he did some of his growin' up (he swears he never really did).

How significant was the "Texas Trilogy"? Well, if you check out the history of Kopperl in The Handbook of Texas Online (www.tsha.utexas.edu/handbook/online), you will find this line: "Kopperl was the subject of a song by Steven Fromholz, the 'Texas Trilogy.'"

Amazingly, he wrote the "Texas Trilogy" in just three hours, all at one sitting. A few hours after that, he had worked out all the chord changes, memorized the lyrics, and was ready to perform it that night at The Drinking Gourd. The house was packed that night, and they were really into each song. That's when Steven decided to try the "Trilogy" out for the first time. I'll let him describe what happened;

> "I thought I sang it very well, but when I finished, the room was total quiet and I thought, 'Oh Jesus, I really screwed up this time!' But then after about fifteen very long seconds the room exploded and everybody just went nuts! I figured at that point that I might really be onto something good. That was a great night for me because I had never written a song, much less three songs, in such a short time, and I had never ever experienced such immediate approval for my work. It's very rare in this business to have that happen."

Artists of every type often talk about the feeling that they are just some sort of a pipeline for something they have created that just seemed to flow out of them. I've always used the restaurant analogy to describe it to folks. You are going through your day, doing all sorts of things, then all of a sudden, it's like someone hollers, "Order Up!" and it's there.

For me, I often don't know where it came from. Didn't know I was working on it. As I'm writing it down, I often don't know if it's a song, a poem, a short story, or a novel. But by golly, when you hear "Order Up!" you drop what you are doing and start writing it down. At times I almost feel like a stenographer, writing down a letter from who knows where.

Steven is the same way. He was scribbling it down frantically, afraid he would lose it. It was like he couldn't write it down fast enough. All the time wondering where it was coming from then realizing it came from all those memories and experiences stored in him that were all busting out at once.

Having said all that, anyone who knows Steven also knows the "Texas Trilogy" is from his soul and his roots. He is a gifted lyricist, musician, and composer, and it all shows. The phrasing, rhyming, and stories are all true to what it was really like, not just in Kopperl, but in thousands of small towns.

It's not a bouncy little ditty. But it is all true and captured a part of the lives of millions of folks who grew up, dirt poor, on farms and ranches.

As Steven puts it, "Things moved pretty slow in Kopperl. Not a lot ever happened. But when something did happen, it had a lot of feelings attached to it. I don't know about other folks' lives, but that's the way it was for me when I grew up."

Here are the lyrics to the "Texas Trilogy":

Texas Trilogy 1: Daybreak

Six o'clock silence of a new day beginning
Is heard in the small Texas town.
Like a signal from nowhere the people who live there
Are up and moving around.
'Cause there's bacon to fry and there's biscuits to bake
On the stove that the Salvation Army won't take.
And you open the windows and you turn on the fan
'Cause it's hotter than hell when the sun hits the land.

Walter and Fanny, well, they own the grocery
That sells most all that you need.
They've been up and working since early this morning —
They've got the whole village to feed.
Well, they put out fresh eggs and throw bad ones away
That rotted because of the heat yesterday.
The store is all dark so you can't see the flies
That settle on round steak and last Monday's pies.

Sleepy Hill's drugstore and the cafe are open —
The coffee is bubbling hot.
'Cause the folks that ain't working gonna sit there 'til sundown
And talk about what they ain't got.
Someone just threw a clutch in the old pickup truck.
It seems like they're riding on a streak of bad luck.
The doctor bills came and the well has gone dry.
Seems their grown kids don't care whether they live or die.

Texas Trilogy 2: Train Ride

Well, the last time I remember that train stopping at the depot
Was when me and my Aunt Veta came riding back from Waco.
I remember I was wearing my long pants and we was sharing
Conversation with a man who sold ball-point pens and paper.
And the train stopped once in Clifton where my aunt

bought me some ice cream.
And my mom was there to meet us when the train pulled into Kopperl.

release

But now kids at night break window lights
And the sound of trains only remains
In the memory of the ones like me.
Who have turned their backs on the splintered cracks
In the walls that stand on the railroad land
Where we used to play and then run away
From the depot man.

I remember me and brother used to run down to the depot
Just to listen to the whistle when the train pulled into Kopperl.
And the engine big and shiny, black as coal that fed the fire
And the engineer would smile and say, "Howdy, how ya fellows?"
And the people by the windows playing cards and reading papers
Looked as far away to us as next summer's school vacation.

release

Texas Trilogy 3: Bosque County Romance

Mary Martin was a schoolgirl just seventeen or so
When she married Billy Archer about fourteen years ago.
Not even out of high school, folks said it wouldn't last.
But when you grow up in the country, you grow up mighty fast.

They married in a hurry in March before school was out.
Folks said that she was pregnant, "Just wait and you'll find out."
It came about that winter, one gray November morn,
The first of many more to come — a baby boy was born.

chorus

And cattle is their game.
And Archer is the name

They give to the acres that they own.
If the Brazos don't run dry
And the newborn calves, they don't die,
Another year from Mary will have flown.
Another year from Mary will have flown.

Now Billy kept what cattle his father could afford,
Bouncing across the cactus in a 1950 Ford.
The cows were sick and skinny and the weed was all that grew.
But Billy kept the place alive, the only thing he knew.

And Mary cooked the supper and Mary scrubbed the clothes.
And Mary busted horses and blew the baby's nose.
And Mary and a shotgun kept the rattlesnakes away.
How she kept on smiling no one could ever say.

chorus

Now the drought of '57 was a curse upon the land.
No one in Bosque County could give Bill a helping hand.
The ground was cracked and broken and the truck was out of gas.
And cows can't feed on prickly pear instead of growing grass.

Well, the weather got the water and a snake bite took a child.
And a fire in the old barn took the hay that Bill had piled.
The mortgage got the money and the screw worm got the cows.
The years have come for Mary — she's waiting for them now.

chorus

Writers work to capture "what it was like to be there for an event." Once in a while we even do. But this song changed songwriting for many of us who heard it. Why? Because it was true and it wasn't funny. Oh, we had all written that broken-hearted-love-gone-wrong song. (Some of us several times. You write what you know best, darn it!)

But we had been reluctant to write about the other sad times in life. "Nobody wants to hear a song that's not fun," were the words of advice from record producers. Then came the Trilogy, and another musical door flew open.

Shortly after writing the Trilogy, Steven met Mike Williams, a twelve-string guitar player. Soon he joined Steven and Judy, becoming the third "Chip."

Musically things were clicking along in 1968, but the combination of doing his Navy Electronic Technician's School training all day and playing music most nights was beginning to take its toll physically and mentally. So Steven went to visit the navy psychiatrist.

I would love to meet this guy! He told Steven, *"Fromholz, you could exist best on the fringe of society."* Now that was one smart shrink, and the navy must have thought so too, because they gave Steven an honorable discharge and sent him on his way.

Fresh out of the navy, Steven loaded up Judy and Darcie and they headed to Cave Creek, Arizona, a tourist town just outside of Phoenix. Steven's mom was the social director at the Care Free Inn there. She set him up to be a bellhop.

After a brief stay in Cave Creek, Mike Williams showed up and the group was soon off to try their music in Denver. They settled into the Denver Folk Center, where Steven and Michael started learning how to back each other up on their individual songs. It was "hippie heaven" back in the summer of '68.

Harry Tuft was the unlikely name of the wizard who ran this magical land. He took the wanderers in, like the lost children they were. Harry was a slight fellow, balding blonde hair, a very, very nice man.

But at the Folk Center, the sound was good and the people came to listen. When the popular folkies played somewhere in Denver they would often stop by and visit Harry. They bought strings and guitar picks and often did a special show for Harry. The folkies included Judy Collins, Joan Baez, Ramblin' Jack Elliott, Doc Watson, and even Reverend Gary Davis. It was a listener's paradise.

The night they moved into town, Michael and Steven grabbed their guitars and went out on Colfax Street, looking for a job. Now they were known as Frummox, a nickname given Steven by Judy. She had said it fit him, a cross between Fromholz and a big clumsy lummox.

More Texans entered Steven's life at this time. Michael had a friend, Dow Patterson, who was married to Becky, Hondo Crouch's daughter. Dow was a picker from San Antonio, and Becky was from the Fredricksburg-Luckenbach area. Dow was in the air force stationed up in Denver.

Steven recalled the Christmas of 1968 when Hondo and his wife, Shatzie, came up to visit Dow and Becky. "One night they all ended up at our house, the 'hippie house' right around the corner from the Folklore Center, and spent the night singing songs and swapping stories and having an incredible time."

That was the first time Steven met Hondo and, not unexpectedly, it was an amazing experience. Hondo was busy being Hondo, and Steven recalls that he really liked Steven's song "The Man with the Big Hat."

It was through Dow Patterson and Michael that Steven met Dan McCrimmon. Dan was a folk singer and harmonica player. Around the end of '68, Michael got his draft notice. They still had gigs booked for Frummox, so McCrimmon and Steven became Frummox.

Frummox was soon booking more events back in Texas. Back at my favorite Austin haunt, the Chequered Flag, Segle Fry had invited them to play. Steven, like myself, loved playing at "The Flag." Segle, Allen Damron, and Rod Kennedy had done a wonderful job of creating a great venue for both performers and the audience.

Frummox was a big hit at The Flag. Fans quickly spread the word about this new kind of music, and soon Steven and Dan were appearing there regularly. The word was definitely out when *Time* magazine listed two folk duos that should be watched, Brewer & Shipley and Frummox.

Meanwhile, back in Denver, Frummox did a live recording at Harry Tuft's Folklore Center. The producer must have liked what he heard, because he hooked Frummox up with ABC Probe Records. At that time Probe was the progressive arm of ABC Records.

In the summer of '69, the producer came back out to Denver, and they started to get the details of their musical and business arrangements finalized. Travis Holland was playing some guitar and mandolin with Frummox, and when Dick came out he liked what he heard. Steven, Dan, and Travis rehearsed with Dick in Denver then went to New York in August of that year to begin work on the Frummox record.

Steven describes the two weeks he spent in New York, working on his very first album, as "a really amazing experience. At that time we were still blessed with ignorance. One of the worst things that can happen to you in the music business is to make your first record, because by the time you make your second one you think you know what you're doing. If you could just make your second one first, you'd be a lot better off. But being blessed with ignorance really helped us get through our first album. We just sat in the studio, did what Dick told us to do, and tried to sing our songs as well as we could."

Two weeks after they arrived, the Frummox album was completed. They didn't know it then, but it would soon be a classic. All they knew for sure was that they had their record company checks and had to decide whether to come back home that weekend, or go to a music festival in upstate New York. They were a little homesick, so they headed back, missing their chance to attend Woodstock.

By 1974 the musical life had taken its toll, and Steven and Judy had split up. Later that year he began dating his new sweetheart, Janey Lake.

Frummox sold well but not well enough to keep ABC Probe Records from folding. So Steven and Dan just took their show, and their record, back out on the road. They had already gotten enough feedback to know they had something special; they just needed to get the word out to more folks. And so, with just the two of them promoting the record, it's all the more amazing that Frummox became a classic.

In the summer of '71 Dan went off to teach school and do his own music. Meanwhile Steven showed his diversity by hooking up with Stephen Stills for his first solo tour.

Personally, Steven has been able to live a full and happy life with Janey and the kids. He has even found time to do some acting and whitewater river rafting in the Big Bend region around Terlingua and Lajitas. He still enjoys taking tours down the Rio Grande when the water is flowing.

Steven Fromholz relaxes in Terlingua.
Photo courtesy of Steven Fromholz.

Over the years Steven has played almost every venue in the Southwest. In a single day he has performed in a place with nearly ten thousand fans, then later for a crowd of fifty. He enjoys them both. But his favorite venue is "on a riverbank, in a quiet canyon

somewhere, sittin' on a beer cooler and singin' for a few happy camp-
ers sittin' around a campfire."

Professionally, ever since that magical summer, Steven has continued to write music and perform regularly. "That's what I do." And
he does it well.

Over the years Steven has written songs recorded by many other
songwriters. Hoyt Axton, John Denver, Lyle Lovett, Michael Martin
Murphy, Willie Nelson, Jerry Jeff Walker, and Rusty Wier have all cut
his tunes. Willie Nelson's recording of Steven's "I'd Have To Be
Crazy" earned the writer two platinum records.

Steven sings his songs in a rich, smooth baritone voice with just
enough edge on it to sound like honey and tequila. He can be big and
boisterous on one tune and tender and touching on the next. He has
the heart for the ballads, but when asked, Steven describes his music
as *"sort of a free-form, country-folk rock, gospel-gum, bluegrass opera,
with a bit of cowjazz thrown in for good measure."*

One of my favorites of Steven's is the classic "The Man with the
Big Hat," which was recorded by Jerry Jeff Walker.

The Man with the Big Hat

In a bar in Arizona on a sultry summer day,
A cowboy came in off the road just to pass the time away.
He pulled a stool to the bar and pushed his hat back on his head.
I listened to the stories told, to the words the cowboy said. He said,

"I could tell you stories 'bout the Indians on the plains,
Talk about Wells Fargo and the comin' of the trains.
Talk about the slaughter of the buffalo that roamed.
Sing a song of settlers come out lookin' for a home."

> *chorus*
> *And THE MAN WITH THE BIG HAT is buyin'.*
> *Drink up while the drinkin' is free.*

> *Drink up to the cowboys a-dead or a-dyin'.*
> *Drink to my compadres and me.*
> *Drink to my compadres and me.*

His shirt was brown and faded and his hat was wide and black.
The pants that once were blue, were gray with a pocket gone in back.
He had a finger missin' from the hand that rolled a smoke.
As he smiled and talked of cowboys, but you knew it weren't no joke.
He said,

"I seen a day so hot your pony could not stand,
And if your water bag was dry don't ya count upon the land.
And winters, I've seen winters when your boots froze in the snow,
And your only thought was leavin' but you had no place to go."

   chorus

He rested easy at the bar, his foot upon the rail,
And laughed and talked of times he'd had out livin' on the trail.
The silence never broken as the words poured from his lips,
As quiet as the .45 he carried on his hip. He said,

"I rode the cattle drives from here to San Antone,
Ten days in the saddle and weary to the bone.
I've rode from here to Wichita without a woman's smile,
And the camp fire where I cooked my beans was the only light for miles."

   chorus

He rolled one more cigarette as he walked toward the door.
I could hear his spurs a-jinglin' as his boot heels hit the floor.
He loosened up his belt a notch and pulled his hat down on his head,
And he turned to say good-by to me and this is what he said. He said,

"Now the highlines chase the hiway and the fences close the range,
And to see a workin' cowboy is a sight that's mighty strange.
A cowboy's life was lonely and his lot was not the best,

But if it hadn't been for men like me wouldn't a-been no wild,
wild west."

   chorus

Now you've seen the lyrics to a couple of Steven's songs. And you've read my words about how he writes from the heart. Now let me introduce you to the "other" Steven Fromholz, the one who wrote songs like "I Gave Her a Ring"...

I Gave Her a Ring

A chip of a diamond in ten-carat gold,
I hocked all my dreams. All my secrets I sold.
I brought all the love this poor boy could bring her.
I GAVE HER A RING.
She gave me "the finger."

We had talked to the preacher and to her mom and dad.
We talked of the future; Oh, the plans that we had.
I sang all the love songs this poor boy could sing.
Must not of liked what she heard 'cause she gave me "the bird"
When I gave her my ring.

   I GAVE HER A RING.
   She gave me "the finger."
   I said, "Babe, that's the wrong one,"
   When she showed me the long one.

The look in her eyes said I need not linger.
I heard the fat lady sing when I gave her my ring
And she gave me "the finger."

   She flipped off our love.
   There ain't nothin' crueler.
   So I carried that ring
   On back to the jeweler.

He said, "This ring is like love, son. There's no guarantee.
Like when you gave it to her, I'm gonna give it to you
When you give it to me."

I heard the fat lady sing when I gave her my ring
And she gave me "the finger."

Now doesn't that bring a tear to your eye?

In January 2001 Steven released his first studio recordings in many years, a fourteen-song Felicity Records collection entitled *A Guest in Your Heart*. The CD features "a bunch of new tunes and a few old friends and some pleasant surprises." Some of those "few old friends" include the last session recordings by the late pedal steel legend Jimmy Day, appearing with old friend Johnny Gimble. Lyle Lovett sings some background vocals, and Butch Hancock added some harmonica! This is a wonderful CD. I've just about worn mine out!

You can check out what Steven is up to at www.Steven-Fromholz.com.

Gayle Ross

Cherokee Storyteller

Photo courtesy of Gayle Ross.

Her demeanor is one of a calm inner peace, meanwhile her dark eyes take in all that is going on around her. She's an island of tranquility in the sea of frantic backstage activity at the Kerrville Folk Festival. As I approach the woman she says, "You're Jim?"

"Yep. You Gayle?"

That evening we didn't talk storytelling, just about the beautiful music coming from the stage of this legendary folk festival. This was the last night of the 2002 version. But, just as significant, this was Rod Kennedy's last night in charge of the festival. Rod is a good friend of Gayle's; she was going to miss him.

Rod Kennedy and Gayle Ross on stage his
last night at the Kerrville Folk Festival.

That night Gayle and I discussed the music and the people that had created the magical Kerrville Folk Festival. One of those folks was Allen Wayne Damron, a friend to us both for many years, the reason Gayle and I were meeting and the closing act for Rod's last show. Allen was there with his lovely wife, Marie. He had been the opening act at the very first KFF, and he had been a critical part of keeping it going during the hard times.

Marie Damron, Allen Damron, and Gayle Ross
backstage at the Kerrville Folk Festival.

It was Allen who suggested that Gayle and I meet. We had a wonderful evening, and I'm forever grateful to Allen and Marie for introducing me to Gayle.

Gayle Ross is a descendant of John Ross, the principal chief of the Cherokee Nation during the infamous "Trail of Tears." Her grandmother was a storyteller, and she grew up listening and learning about the Cherokee and their rich heritage. This was the wellspring from which Gayle's storytelling comes.

Over the last two decades, Gayle Ross has become one of the best-loved and most respected storytellers to emerge from the current surge of interest in this timeless art form. She has appeared at almost every major storytelling and folk festival in the United States and Canada, as well as performing at arts halls and theaters through-out the U.S. and Europe, often appearing with some of today's finest Native American musicians and dancers. She is in great demand as a lecture artist at college campuses, and she continues to mesmerize children at countless schools and libraries across the country.

Whether she is provoking laughter with a trickster tale or moving her many listeners to tears with a haunting Cherokee creation myth, Gayle is truly a master of the age-old craft of storytelling. The National Council of Traditional Arts has included Gayle in two of their touring shows, "The Master Storytellers" and the all-Indian show, "From the Plains to the Pueblos."

Gayle Ross talks about storytelling.

She was invited by Vice President Al Gore to perform at a gala at his residence entitled "A Taste of Tennessee" and was chosen by the White House to appear in the giant Millennium on the Mall celebration in Washington, D.C. As an author, Gayle has been asked to speak at the American Library Association, the International Board of Books for Young People, and the International Reading Association.

"Gayle Ross will weave a spell and take you away.
She makes a child's eyes big with wonder and an adult
laugh...I could listen to Gayle all night."
— Tom Chapin

In 1995 Gayle was featured in two hour-long segments of the award-winning documentary "How the West Was Lost" on the Discovery Channel, and her stories have been heard often on National Public Radio on such shows as "Living on the Earth" and "Mountain Stages." From the kindergarten classroom to the Kennedy Center, Gayle's stories have enthralled audiences of all ages.

She got into storytelling after a successful early career in television. In an ironic twist, when Gayle went back to college to get her degree, she found that it would have required her to give up the job all of the folks in her classes were dreaming of. So she passed on that "opportunity," deciding to keep her TV job.

It was through her association with Elizabeth Ellis that Gayle realized she possessed a gift as a storyteller. She also came to realize how important it is to her that the stories be nurtured and protected. She lives with her husband, Reed Holt, and their two children on a ranch a few miles south of Fredricksburg, Texas. Her son, Alan, is a high school senior and her daughter, Sarah, is in ninth grade. Gayle has cut back on her travel somewhat, so that she can spend more time with her family. But we are lucky that she does events in Texas because travel doesn't take so long.

One of the marvelous things about many Native American stories is their sense of the passage and continuity of time. While most Texas folklore stories take place within a day or so, many of the Native American stories take seasons to reach an end. Some stories actually never end, like the story of the creation of the mosquito. These stories are ongoing like the circular passage of time, seasons, and lives.

Gayle and I have had some wonderful discussions about storytelling and the differences between contemporary American storytellers and Native American storytellers. Stories are the coin of the realm within contemporary storytelling groups. Expressions like, "The story belongs to the one who tells it best" convey the sentiment of sharing.

In this environment the stories are often distributed all over the countryside and back again. However, within the Cherokee and many other Native American cultures, it is an insult to tell someone else's story without them giving you their permission to tell the story. Stories are not given without due consideration. A Cherokee story is a trust. The story is to be protected by the holder and won't be passed on to anyone who won't treat it with the same respect.

This creates a dichotomy. On one hand, if the stories aren't shared, people won't have a chance to learn any of the wonderfully educational and entertaining stories. On the other hand, there is the risk of the integrity of the stories not being protected if they are passed on by people who do not understand the history and responsibility of the storyteller.

I am honored that Gayle has entrusted two of her wonderful stories with me.

Why Buzzard's Head Is Bald

by Gayle Ross

This is what the old people told me when I was a child, about those days when the world was new and all creatures spoke the same language.

Now at first the middle world was nothing but water, a great ocean that covered everything. And all creatures that lived, lived in Ga'lunlati, The World Above. Then Beaver's grandchild, the little shiny backed water beetle flew down from the world above, swam to the bottom of the sea, scooped up one tiny handful of mud, and left it floating on top of the water. That tiny handful of mud stretched and grew to become this land that is our home. But the earth was still soft, soft mud; you could not walk upon the land. So Buzzard flew down from the world above. Flying very close to the earth, and making a great wind with his wings, he dryed out the land. When he reached the homeland of the Ani Yun Wiya, he was tired and he flew too close to the earth. His wings began to strike the ground and there the valleys were carved. Where his wings rose, the tall mountains grew. Fearful that Buzzard would make the whole world mountains, the others called him home. But if you have seen the Smokey Mountain homeland of the Cherokee people, you have seen the beauty that Buzzard created for us there on that day.

But Buzzard became very proud of himself for what he had done. He gave himself a new name. He insisted that everyone now call him "Earthshaper." And he was vain as well because he was so handsome. In the beginning days, Buzzard was very good looking. Creator gave him a shiny suit of black feathers that flashed in the sun whenever he flew. Buzzard began spending all his time circling in the air, so the others would notice his feathers flashing like sparks in the sky. Creator also gave Buzzard a gorgeous white topknot of feathers that curled just so over his forehead. Buzzard took to holding his head very high, tilting his head this way and that; so that everyone could admire his fine looks.

Buzzard became so proud and so vain that he refused to help the other big birds with one of their most important jobs. Creator had given everyone their work to do, and it is true that the job given to the bigger birds is not one of the most pleasant. They must eat dead meat. When an animal died in the beginning days, Crow, Raven, Eagle, and Hawk would come down and eat up the dead meat. That helps clean up the earth. But Buzzard would never help. He would say things like "Oooo, it's got little crawly things in it. It smells bad. You eat it. It's just not good enough for me."

When the other birds had had enough of Buzzard's attitude, they went to see Rabbit. Rabbit is the leader of them all in mischief, and no one can think up better tricks. Even though Rabbit behaves every bit as badly himself, when he heard how Buzzard was acting, he said "Oh no one should think so highly of themselves as that. We will teach Buzzard a lesson." Rabbit thought about it and after a while he had what he thought was a pretty good idea.

Rabbit went to Buffalo and told him exactly what he wanted Buffalo to do. Then he explained his plan to the other birds. Buffalo climbed to the top of a mountain to a clearing where he could be seen from the air for many miles. He came staggering out into that clearing; slobbering all over himself as though he was very sick. Swaying back and forth like he was very dizzy. When he reached the center of the clearing, he rolled his eyes up into his head, dropped to his knees, fell over on his side, and held real still.

The other birds gathered in the treetops, and Buzzard began circling lower and lower to see what was going on down there. They began to call up to him, "Buzzard, Buffalo has died. Buzzard, Buffalo is sooo big. It will take all of us to eat him. You have to help!" Buzzard circled a time or two longer, looking at that Buffalo. It didn't look like he had been dead very long. The meat was probably still pretty fresh and would taste very good. Maybe just this once he would help the others eat dead meat!

He landed in the clearing and told all the other birds, "You must let me eat first." Now this was an honor he was asking for. Whenever Cherokee people come together and it involves a meal (and whenever Cherokee people come together, it involves a meal!) it is always the elders, the honored ones, who are served first. Eagle, Hawk, Crow, and Raven backed up and said, "Buzzard, you go right ahead!"

Now Buffalo has a strip of fat that runs up the back of his leg. It is very tasty and since he wanted the best for himself, that is where Buzzard went first. With his strong beak, he began to tear big chunks from the back of Buffalo's leg. Buffalo held just as still as he could, while Buzzard pecked higher...and higher. When Buffalo decided that Buzzard was in just the right place...he opened up his butt, leaped backward, and slammed it shut on Buzzard's head! Then he jumped up and began to run, dragging Buzzard along the ground behind him.

He ran up and down the hills, jumping over fallen trees and big piles of brush, with poor Buzzard bouncing in the dirt and crashing into tree limbs and branches. Buzzard's wing feathers became ragged and torn; his shiny feathers coated with dirt and dust. He was screaming for Buffalo to turn loose, but Buffalo just held on tighter and ran faster!

Finally, Rabbit told the others, "I bet he has learned his lesson." So when Buffalo dashed by, Rabbit reached out, grabbed Buzzard's feet, and POPPED him right out. And that pulled every white feather from the top of Buzzard's head! He no longer has that beautiful white topknot, just an ugly red naked head. With his ugly head and his dirty battered suit of feathers, he is not nearly so good looking. Buzzard certainly learned his lesson. Today, dead meat is all he does eat. And he waits till it's rotten; he wants to make sure it's really dead! And that whole experience is why Buzzards everywhere stink so bad, to this very day!

The First Vigil

by Gayle Ross

This is what the elders told me when I was a child. In the beginning, everything here was water. There was nothing but a great ocean. Then Water Beetle dove to the bottom of the sea and brought up a handful of mud which grew to become this land.

Buzzard came down from the world above and flew across this world. Making a wind with his wings, he dried the earth; carving the valleys, shaping the mountains.

Grandmother Sun began following the path through the heavens that she follows to this day, and Uncle Moon smiled at night. And all creatures came down from the World Above to make of this middle world a home.

At that time, Creator spoke to all his children, plants and animals alike, "It is my wish that you all fast and pray for wisdom, for strength. Keep watch and stay awake. This you must do for seven days and seven nights."

Throughout that first night, almost all Creator's children were true to his charge. When the sun rose, only the littlest people, the insects had fallen asleep. But as day followed night and night followed day, more and more creatures succumbed to their weariness and drifted into dreams.

When the seventh night had ended, of the animal people, only the panther and the owl remained awake. Along with the wisdom and strength they had gained through their vigil, they were given the power to see in the dark and to prey on those who must sleep at night.

Among the standing people, the trees, only the cedar, the pine, the spruce, the laurel, and the holly had remained true to Creator's instructions. To these Creator gave the gift of remaining evergreen, while their brothers and sisters shed their leaves in the fall and stand bare during the cold months of winter. It was given to them also to be the greatest for medicine. They were given the most sacred of all powers, the power to heal.

Gayle has three award-winning books in print, along with two critically acclaimed audio tapes. The self-produced tapes are *To This Day — Native American Stories* and *Live at the National Storytelling Festival. How Rabbit Tricked Otter* is an audio tape on Harper Children's Audio.

The three books are *How Turtle's Back Was Cracked* and *The Story of the Milky Way* (coauthored with Joe Bruchac), both on Dial Books for Young Readers, and *The Girl Who Married the Moon* coauthored with Joe Bruchac on Bridgewater Books.

For bookings and information on tapes contact Gayle Ross: P.O. Box 761, Fredericksburg, TX 78624 (830) 997-3661, her email address is grrh@fbg.net.

Gayle's delivery of these wonderful stories is just as powerful as the stories themselves. Great storytellers suspend your disbelief and transport you to another place, time, and emotion. Gayle Ross does this and more. Don't miss an opportunity to hear her speak.

Aaron "Double A" Allan

(Allan Aaron Crenwelge)
It's All About the Music!

Photo courtesy of Aaron Allan.

The man's full rich baritone voice says, "Good afternoon, you're lis-
tening to KCTI in beautiful Gonzales, Texas. Where the Fight for
Texas Liberty Began. Birthplace of Texas and the Cradle of Texas
Independence. This is Double A, Aaron Allan, bringing you all the

music worth listening to. Today we're going to have a whole lot of fun, because my old friend Jim Gramon is my very special guest."

And so starts another day at the microphone for Aaron "Double A" Allan. For over fifty years he has been bringing great music to listeners.

Aaron Allan was born Allan Aaron Crenwelge on a cold snowy January 28, 1929, in Fredericksburg, Texas. A few years later his family moved to the quiet little German town of New Braunfels.

He wanted to be an astronomer as a kid. He was and still is interested in the heavens. As he explained it, "I even built my own telescope. A Newtonian design, with a six-inch lens. Unfortunately, my math just wasn't strong enough for the astronomy gig."

His mother was one of four sisters. Two of his aunts had sung professionally in a variety of venues in Fredericksburg and around Gillespie County. Aunt Tootie taught him a few chords on the guitar when he was about fourteen.

"I was so excited, particularly when I found out I could play an entire song after having learned only three chords! The first song I learned, I'll never forget it, was 'Be Honest With Me,' an old Gene Autry song."

Folks seemed to like what he was doing, and he decided that playin' the guitar was what he wanted to do from then on. At that time TV was still several years away. The heart of the music industry was being on the radio.

Aaron spent his youth listening to Red River Dave on WOAI in San Antonio, Del Dunbar on KTSA, and Big Bill Lister on KABC (which became KENS, which became KBAT, which is now KKYX. Aaron's life has been filled with four-letter words!).

"Those guys were stars! Everybody that didn't want to be them, wanted to at least meet them!"

While still just a sophomore in high school, Aaron decided he wanted to be in the music business and figured deejaying was a good way to achieve that. With that goal in sight, Aaron called the program director at KTSA, Bob White, and announced that he wanted to audition. Aaron must have had a good line, because Mr. White agreed to have him come in to audition.

So Aaron loaded up his guitar, hopped on the Greyhound bus, and went to San Antonio. He laughs as he explains that, "I was a country boy, and not as hip as kids are today."

Allan Aaron Crenwelge, age 21.
Photo courtesy of Aaron Allan.

Arriving at the bus terminal, he walked a couple of blocks then decided to take a cab to the Gunter Hotel. The cab driver looked at him blankly then smiled and told him to get in. The cab driver then drove around the block and stopped to let Aaron out at the exact spot he had gotten in!

As Aaron put it, "Then it got worse, because the cabby even charged me full fare for the ride! Oh well, you gotta learn sometime, and I'm sure it gave the cabby some good laughs!"

Aaron went upstairs to the studio, and Mr. White took him back to a sound booth. Aaron played him about five songs, including some Burl Ives tunes. "I was really into Burl Ives back then."

When he finished his songs, Mr. White asked him, "What does your repertoire consist of?"

"Well, I had no idea what a repertoire was. But I thought it had something to do with clothes. So I told him I had about six pair of pants and three sports coats. Mr. White looked at me funny, smiled a little for a minute, then asked me how many songs I could play. I told him I had about fifteen, and he suggested I come back after I graduated from high school."

Skip forward two years. It's 1948 and Aaron has graduated from New Braunfels High School and is ready to start his radio career. He got an interview at KITE in San Antonio. "I met two wonderful people there who have been lifelong friends. Charles Balthrope was the owner of KITE. Alex Chester was the programming director for the station."

And Aaron adds, "They were nice, but they were also very bright people, because they gave me my start in radio, and they appreciated what I was doing. Why they even gave me my own daily fifteen-minute show singing folk songs at one every afternoon. We got Comal Cottons, out of New Braunfels, to sponsor the show. Obviously our theme song was the original version of 'Cotton-Eyed Joe.'"

Having gained their confidence, Aaron now had to do the show. He said, "I was totally scared to death! Now during that time you didn't sit down while you did your part of the show. They used those old standup microphones. Well I was standin' there, and my legs were shakin' so bad that Alex Chester noticed. He came to my rescue and surprised me a bit when I suddenly felt him slippin' a stool up under my butt! He saved my life with that stool!"

With the new name Aaron Allan in 1957. Photo courtesy of Aaron Allan.

It was Alex Chester who told Allan Aaron Crenwelge that he needed a new name, a radio name. After some discussion, a name was picked. And that was the birth of Aaron Allan (Double A).

To give you a perspective on the significance of Aaron having his own show, the local New Braunfels newspaper, the

Herald Zeitung, ran a front page story announcing, "Local Boy, Aaron Allan, Gets His Own Radio Show." Another indication of Aaron's popularity in the community came when the local high school would suspend classes each day at one so that everyone could listen to Aaron's show in their classrooms.

The Korean War started a couple of years later, and Aaron enlisted in the army. He had been in about three months when they realized he is legally blind without his glasses and gave him a medical discharge.

Returning to KITE, he completed his contract and then went to a new station, KGNB, which was opening in New Braunfels. Aaron and Howard Edwards were the original on-air talent for the station.

After KGNB Aaron went to KWED in Seguin, east of New Braunfels. Then in 1953 he went to KBOP in Pleasanton, south of San Antonio.

Perhaps this would be a good time to give you an overview of the radio business. It is an industry that is in constant change. Stations are bought and sold every day. New owners want new formats and new on-air talent. Now you see 'em, now you don't! Stories are rampant in the industry about folks coming in to do their show and finding that the ownership, locks, call letters, and format had all changed overnight.

KBOP has evolved into a legendary station because of the skinny kid that was hired after Aaron left to go to WOAI (both radio and TV) in San Antonio. Like Aaron, the new kid had deep Texas roots and was wanting badly to get into the "business."

Like Aaron, the new kid loved the music and wanted to be a DJ—wanted to be close to music in any way he could. After a few years of changing stations, the kid finally broke into the music world as a songwriter. I've heard that sometime later, after his DJ career ended, Willie Nelson even did some singing (but that's another story).

Aaron and Willie have been friends since 1954. A few years back, a group of folks, including Aaron and Willie, were sitting in a motel

Aaron Allan and Willie at one of Willie's 4th of July Picnics
that Aaron emcees for Willie. Photo courtesy of Aaron Allan.

room. Willie started telling a story: "You know that guy sittin' right there (pointing at Aaron) is the first guy I used to listen to on the radio every day. When I was a kid I used to listen to WOAI every chance I got. My favorite guy on the radio was this guy right here, Aaron Allan. I decided years ago that I wanted to be singing and announcing on the radio, just like Double A."

Aaron told me, "I was completely shocked and humbled that a legend like Willie Nelson had enjoyed my work, and even had looked up to me. It's a sign of the type of man Willie is, that he would tell folks that story today."

At WOAI Aaron did lots of live commercials for radio and TV. During the days he did shows like the *TODAY Show* with Dave Garroway. Sometimes he would do evenings and the original *TONIGHT Show* with Steve Allen.

In 1959 Aaron went to KLEN in Killeen. A few years later it was KMAC, then KCUL in Fort Worth. Next was WLBN in Nashville, with another legend in the music business, Neal Merritt.

Aaron was on the air in Nashville in late November 1963. He was doing a remote broadcast. For the remote Aaron had taken copies of the top thirty songs of the day. Suddenly the producer broke in and said, "We are going to have to take it back to the studio for a moment. We have a news bulletin from Dallas. The president of the United States has been shot!"

Aaron was in shock, just like everyone else. But he had a very immediate problem. As soon as they finished the news break, they would be returning the show to him. What, out of the top thirty, could he possibly play that would be appropriate.

The record on top of the stack was the incredibly inappropriate Hank Williams song "I'll Never Get Out of This World Alive." Frantically Aaron dug through the stack. To this day he has no idea how the record got there. But in the middle of the stack was a copy of "The Bells of Saint Mary's" played by Mother Maybelle Carter on the autoharp.

Years later, after Mother Maybelle had passed away, Aaron happened to be going by The House of Cash (Johnny Cash's publishing company in Nashville). Amazingly they were having a yard sale! June Carter-Cash and her sisters, Anita and Helen, were out closing deals on items. Aaron told June how her mother's record had saved him on that terrible day.

"Jim, I'll never forget her standing there in that yard sale with tears running down her face."

By this time Aaron's songwriting career was starting to roll. Charlie Walker had recorded "Bow Down Your Head and Cry" on Columbia with the Jordanaires.

In San Antonio, now with KBER radio, Aaron was on another remote with the KBER Bandwagon. Willie Nelson's steel guitarist, Jimmy Day, had dropped by to give Aaron a couple of records and do

Tom T. Hall and Aaron.
Photo courtesy of Aaron Allan.

an interview. When they got off the air, Aaron told Jimmy that he had just written a song, and he played "Truth #1" for him.

Well, Jimmy loved it and said, "You've got to play that for Willie. He's over in the motel room sleepin'. Let's go wake him up."

And they did! Willie must wake up in a better mood than most musicians I've known, because he failed to harm either Aaron or Jimmy. And so Aaron sat on the floor and played "Truth # 1," while Willie sat on the edge of the bed in his underwear.

Willie liked the song, despite them waking him up.

Truth # 1

by Aaron Allan

I don't really want your bed,
Just a place to lay my head
as I contemplate this troubled way of life
I don't want your vintage wine
Just a minute of your time
and a crumb, or two, from the staff of life.

Now the staff of life for me
is in your good company

Could I share just a moment with you.
Let us talk about some things.
Let us make the music ring.
While we're not yet old enough to know the truth.

For in the metaphysical world
you'll find the answer furled
never to be played by human hands.
But if you'll just await the high
the truth will come in time
unfurling like the flowers in the sand.

Now I'm outside the sphere
of the influenced ear
as I look around for a sister soul.
And if honesty transcends
all the love and dangling ends
then the finding of the truth is my goal.

If you're on the left or right
you're still in for the fight
that's one thing I don't have to glamorize.
And if the middle you are in,
you can always be my friend,
just as long as you never compromise!

There is nothing really lewd
If you prefer the nude.
It's just a state of mind that we are in.
But while some people's minds
are thinkin' dirty most of the time,
we'll make rags to cover up God's skin.

If you think my thoughts are crude,
I'll try not to be rude,
after all, you are free to criticize.
But, if you think you can refine,

vinegar to vintage wine,
the Grapes of Wrath will curse you all your life.

We could sit here all the night,
trying' to make the wrong to right.
But you're thinkin' it's my philosophy,
But I'm thinkin' all the while
so much rather see your smile,
which is Truth # 1 for me !!

Within a few weeks Willie recorded the song at the RCA Studios. When they finished the recording, Willie and the band called Aaron and played their version of it over the phone. Unfortunately, they got disconnected shortly after the first verse. It was a full year before the record came out and Aaron was finally able to hear the whole song.

Sometime later Willie was doing a concert and had invited Aaron to sit down front. Well, always dependable, Willie gets halfway through "Truth #1" and forgets the words. So Willie stops the music and tells the audience that the songwriter is there, and he invites Aaron up to sing the song with him.

They start the song over again, and of course, Aaron is a nervous wreck, hoping he doesn't hit any clinkers. Well, Murphy's Law was in full force that special night. Willie and Aaron got halfway through the song and they BOTH forgot the lyrics.

The audience roared with laughter. They all assumed it was part of the act. Far be it for Willie and Aaron to spoil the joke. But now you know the truth about their version of "Truth #1."

After leaving K-Bear, Aaron spent a couple of years writing music and jingles for a wide variety of stations.

Amazingly, after years of rambling, Aaron has found a home. He has been with KCTI in Gonzales for fourteen years now. "They have great and stable ownership. There's not all the politics and constant shuffling that is so common in the radio industry."

Gonzales has been good for Aaron's music writing also. He has been writing both music and memoirs. Aaron Allan has written about nine hundred songs. Twenty of his songs have been recorded by other artists.

Chet McIntyre Sings Aaron Allan, Full Spectrum was released in June 2002. All of the songs on the CD were written or co-written by Aaron. Like so much of Aaron's life, this CD is a little bit different. You see Double A is pretty much country, all the way down to his yellow boots. But Chet McIntyre has done all of these songs using jazz arrangements!

But it really does work. The songs translated from country to jazz very well. As Aaron explains, "Jim, I like the album. Love what Chet has done with the songs. But that sure isn't the sound I was hearing in my mind when I wrote them!"

Aaron has been inducted into the Country Music Association of Texas Hall of Fame, and he is a nominee for the DJ Hall of Fame in Nashville. He has also received a "Humbie" from the outstanding Humble Time radio syndication.

Aaron is the emcee at most of Willie Nelson's 4th of July Picnics.

So what does Double A have going on? Well, like always, he's writing the music.

Aaron has asked me to help him write a book about his tumultuous life in the music industry. I'm just doing some editing for him. Biographies of celebrities and characters are my specialty. But of all of those I've done, there hasn't been anyone who was more willing to take an unblinking look at his life, even the less flattering aspects.

You've seen some examples of Double A's lyrics, but you should also know that he is a very talented author, with an inimitable style. Aaron's writing carries an honesty about himself and the events of his life that is seldom seen.

Aaron and I are going to be collaborating on his biography, which should be out in the fall of 2003. Each chapter of the book will be about Aaron's experiences with one of his friends. You readers will have the first peek at Aaron's writing, with this excerpt from the chapter about Aaron's experiences with the legendary Neal Merritt.

Jim and Aaron enjoy the music and good cigars at Rob Robinson's Hill Country Humidor, on the square in San Marcos. Photo courtesy of Rob Robinson.

Neal and Me

by
Aaron Allan

I had made up my mind that I wasn't going to write about Neal Merritt, until now. I'm still not sure I will, but now that I've begun, I can't submit this paper to the trash basket. At least not yet, because Neal Merritt was my friend. He was my best buddy, my worst enemy, my peer, and one of the greatest disk jockeys who ever lived. Neal was also one of the greatest dreamers who ever lived, one of the greatest country song writers who ever lived, one of the worst hus-bands who ever lived, one of the heaviest drinkers who ever lived, one of the foulest tongues that ever wagged, one of the most depend-ent people who ever lived, and possibly the loneliest man I've ever known.

Now, all these years later, I realize how much I love Neal, and the memory. I listened to Neal Merritt on the radio when I was dreaming of being a radio personality. He was broadcasting on KONO Radio in San Antonio, Texas, with a country record show of his own before the music was called country.

The late forties and fifties was the time, back in the days when radio stations still "block programmed." This simply means radio did not specialize so much, but mostly played a variety of music. Stations then would devote a couple of hours to the "pop" music of the day, a couple of hours to "hillbilly," religious, and for God's sake, remember "twilight time?" A must on every evening show. Great theme music!

Of course, Sunday was church and a couple or three hours for "classical" music. Those were the days the disk jockeys had their own theme songs, used not only to open, but to close each show, the days when the ever-present telephone was answered by the disk jockey personally, in order to accept those requests that were con-stantly pouring in.

Those were the days too, when every radio show had a name. Names like, "Saddle Pals," "Saturday Afternoon Jamboree," or maybe "Western Caravan." Now it's the "Joe Blow Show," and the "show" is not even a show anymore. Now the "on air" creativity is gone. Everything is so pre-programmed, that nothing is new and spontaneous. The DJ today is more than likely doing two or three jobs at the same time, with log keeping, meter reading, and trying to save the station's ratings by adhering to the formula.

The formula: that which does not allow for anything beyond a certain point, depending of course, on the time of day, the speed of the beat, and the length of the tune. Oh yes, and usually the mood of the boss, or his wife. The formula, the bane of every great disk jockey. The trick is to live with the formula as much as possible, and be so damn good, you can afford to bend the rules; but only because you have proved yourself in the ratings.

These are some of the reasons why Neal Merritt isn't disk jockeying anymore. That and the fact that he is dead. KONG Radio in San Antonio was where I first heard Neal. KONG is the same station where Ernest Tubb got his start in the middle thirties. Come to think of it, I heard the late T. Texas Tyler on KONG radio in the fifties. This station featured two of the greatest country request shows that ever aired. One was "Saddle Pals" and the other was an afternoon show called "The Cowboy Roundup." Two great old announcers, as they were called in that era, were Stan Cox and Ray Hunt. Hunt ran the Roundup show and Cox, the morning Saddle Pals. Later Neal Merritt came in and did a nighttime all-request program.

Neal had an "on air" way of his own. He was very personable and personal. He was one of those rare jocks who talked with his listeners, rather than to them. There was always a song for his "shut-in" friends, records for people falling in and out of love, anniversaries, birthdays, or a song for "old so-and-so" who caught the biggest fish over the weekend or at least "claimed" he had; all the while, playing records current at the time by people like Red Foley, a young Ernest Tubb, Roy Acuff, Riders of the Purple Sage, a young Merle Travis, the great Bob Wills, Ted Daffan, Al Dexter (remember "Pistol Packin' Mama"?). There's more from that period, the late forties and the fifties, but I've got to stop.

I listened to Neal Merritt when radio was exciting and unrehearsed; when you didn't know what you'd hear next, simply because the radio man had hundreds to pick from rather than the top thirty or forty; when you knew a hit was made by the people, instead of having been hyped by big bucks, big ads, and big favors.

It's well worth remembering all the good that has happened to country music since that time. The obvious fact of its general acceptance now, and the fact that the ladies have made it...

It wasn't until 1962 that Neal's and my paths finally crossed. In three years time, I worked with Neal Merritt for a lifetime, at no less than four different radio stations, from Texas, to Kansas, to Nashville, and back to Texas.

I will never forget the first time I saw him. It was from the rear. At that time, 1962, Radio KENS in San Antonio had some great names on its DJ roster; 50,000 watts worth of country music presided over by the likes of Charlie Walker, Bill Mack, Paul Morgan, Ray Baker, Neal Merritt, and I had just been added.

KENS Radio was upstairs and I was going to work, my first day, up the short stairway, and he was in front of me. Now Neal was one of those fellows with no seat. You could have taken a carpenter's level and placed it along his backside and the bubble would have evened out. No matter how well his pants fit, they were always baggy in the back. Somehow, this characteristic made him look regular. You know what I mean. Like a regular fellow. Those were the kind of friends I looked for. They usually had hangovers, and so did Neal that morning, and almost every other morning of his life.

When it came to booze, I was no slouch myself, but there seems to be a pattern of some kind, with a just barely discernable demarcation line between a serious boozer and a person who is the accepted norm for an alcoholic.

Oh, I drank hard, but Neal was so sincere with his drinking. I could tell by the way he held his beer can or bottle in front of him. Have you ever noticed a waiter, the proud kind, who walks straight, his eyes straight with arm crooked at the elbow, hand stuck straight out before him with a towel hanging over his forearm. A regal sight, you know. That's Neal. That's the way he carried his drink at all times, as if he were following it.

Roy Bedichek

Naturalist - Philosopher - Storyteller - Author
1878 - 1959

Philosopher's Rock in Barton Springs in Austin. The statue portrays Roy Bedichek, J. Frank Dobie, and Walter Prescott Webb.

Roy Bedichek was one of the most complex individuals Texas has ever adopted. Considering the cast of characters that have passed through, that's quite a statement! As you can see from the string of titles below his name, he was quite talented in a variety of areas. He also could be contrary as hell.

There were few folks that Roy Bedichek didn't find fault with. But part of his complexity was that he was drawn to the folks he could disagree with. When asked why he had so many friends with such a wide variety of political views, former Texas State Comptroller Bob Bullock once told me, "If you have two people that feel exactly the same, one of them is not needed."

Roy Bedichek didn't go quite that far, but he got pretty close at times. For example, he ridiculed patriots, while his actions were consistently those of a patriot. He believed in the individual. Individual rights and individual responsibilities. He believed in evaluating folks individually, and he was skeptical of most activities involving large groups.

Suffice it to say that Roy Bedichek was a man who often disagreed with himself. While he acknowledged the need for government and patriots, his own basic instincts made him untrusting of those very things.

This driving curiosity to explore all aspects of our world and himself was manifested in his long relationship with J. Frank Dobie and Walter Prescott Webb. The three men formed what is now known as the Texas Triumvirate, the cornerstone of documenting Texas. The land, the people, the events, and the philosophies behind them were all considered and documented by these three thinkers.

No, they certainly were not the first storytellers in Texas. But all three took the time to record what they had learned, basically transcribing stories that had previously only been shared orally. They took this information from the campfire to the classroom, and in so doing, allowed all the rest of us to share their campfire.

Dobie, Webb, and Bedichek wrote about the Texas they knew. They all tried to acknowledge the complexity of the state's heritage and never claimed to have the definitive view of the state. They could only write of what they saw. They never presumed to speak for any group other than themselves and left it to others to write from different, non-Anglo, perspectives.

I was delighted the only time I ever met Roy Bedichek. Starting out, it had nothing to do with him. I had no idea who he was, but he was speaking to an assembly at Porter Junior High, and it was getting me out of an algebra class that I had, once again, not properly studied for.

They had said he was a naturalist. Back then I wondered if naturalists were the folks who wander around in the woods with no clothes on.

Well he did have clothes, but he started talking about nature, wildlife, plants and such. I had been raised in the country and had figured out that there wasn't going to be anything in this for me. I was hunkering down to get some shuteye when Mr. Bedichek started talking about the mating habits of rattlesnakes. When you are in junior high school, the mating habits of anything but plants is interesting.

An hour later I realized I had learned a great deal about the world that was already familiar to me. I also realized that he loved the land and everything about it, good and bad. From then on, I was a Roy Bedichek fan.

About four years later, I was sitting on the front porch of the Mercantile Co-Op in Cumby, Texas. Sitting beside me was my irascible cohort in storytelling, Ben King "Doc" Green. (Both Cumby and Ben Green are described in my book *Famous Texas Folklorists and Their Stories*.)

Ben commenced to tell me the story about...

Upon completion of his story, when the laughing died down, Ben said, "Stole that 'un from Roy."

The name didn't ring any bells with me, so I asked, "Roy who?"

"Bedichek. You know him."

"Name rings a faint bell, Ben. But I can't remember from where."

"Well ring that bell harder, Jim. Every Texan has to know about Roy Bedichek. He wrote the best book ever written about Texas, *Adventures With a Texas Naturalist*."

I remember being impressed that Ben was impressed. Generally speaking, he didn't have a lot of respect for ink slingers, no matter what they wrote. OK, I'll admit it, Ben didn't have a lot of respect for most of the population. So it really stood out when he spoke highly of somebody.

Maybe they got along well because they both viewed the world through cynical eyes. They were both naturalists and loved the study of nature and the creatures around them, including the human animal.

Like Kinky Friedman and Ben, you didn't want to ask Roy Bedichek a question unless you were prepared for a direct answer. The term "politically correct" hadn't been coined when Roy was alive. But the concept had been in place for a couple of thousand years. There were things "you just shouldn't say." Those admonishments meant very little to Roy.

The friends of Roy's that I've known have all been bright, quick-witted, and outspoken. People like John Henry Faulk, J. Frank Dobie, Cactus Pryor, and Ben King Green. None of whom would back away from an intellectual debate.

Roy Bedichek.

The Life of Roy Bedichek

As the old joke goes, Roy wasn't born in Texas, but he got here as quick as he could, which only took six years. He was born in Cass County, Illinois, on June 27, 1878. His parents were James Madison and Lucretia Ellen (Craven) Bedichek.

In 1884 the family corrected their error and moved to Falls County, Texas. Roy grew up living in that rural area, attending several local schools, including the Bedichek Academy, which had been established by his father in the small town of Eddy.

He entered The University of Texas at Austin in 1898. There he got a job working in the registrar's office for John A. Lomax. In 1903 he received a B.S. degree. (Later, in 1925, he would receive an M.A.)

Following graduation Roy Bedichek worked at a wide variety of positions. First he was a reporter for the *Fort Worth Record* for a year. He taught high school in Houston during the 1904-05 school year. The following three years he taught high school in San Angelo.

He left teaching to become the secretary of the Deming, New Mexico Chamber of Commerce (1908-13). He also edited the local newspaper, the *Deming Headlight* (1910-12). While living in Deming, Roy married Lillian Lee Greer. Lillian and Roy had three children.

In 1913 he and Lillian returned to Austin. Based on his Deming Chamber of Commerce experience, he became the secretary of the Young Men's Business League, which later merged with the chamber of commerce.

In 1915 Roy was hired by Will C. Hogg as the secretary for the Organization for Promoting Interest in Higher Education in Texas.

From mid-1916 to mid-1917, he was the city editor of the *San Antonio Express.*

Returning to Austin in the fall of 1917, he began work in Austin with the University Interscholastic League. This was one of the passions of Bedichek's life. As the League's director, he helped shape its policies and growth for over thirty years. He retired as director in 1948, at the age of seventy.

It was during this period that Roy Bedichek became closely acquainted with Texas wildlife. A large part of his job involved going to schools all over the state, representing the UIL. While on these numerous trips he would often camp out because suitable lodging wasn't available.

His camping, born of necessity, soon stimulated his interest in wildlife, especially in birds. This interest soon became an obsession to learn and document everything he could about a Texas that he could see was slowly disappearing.

Urged by his close friends J. Frank Dobie and Walter Prescott Webb, he took a leave of absence for a year, beginning in February 1946, and went into seclusion at Friday Mountain Ranch, Webb's retreat southwest of Austin, to write *Adventures with a Texas Naturalist* (1947).

You cannot overestimate the significance of this book. Almost every list of The Best Books Ever Written About Texas has included *Adventures with a Texas Naturalist.*

Bedichek liked to rise several hours before daybreak and study or write in a separate building beside his home. Every day he worked in his garden, walked, or swam. He would often swim in the cool, clear, waters of Barton Springs, where a sculpture of Bedichek, Dobie, and Webb stands today (see photo).

Another of his books, *Karankaway Country* (1950), won the Carr P. Collins Award for the best Texas book of the year. A feat that he duplicated with his 1956 book, *Educational Competition: The Story of the University Interscholastic League of Texas.*

Without ever having been seriously ill, he died suddenly of heart failure on May 21, 1959. He was an excellent storyteller, a fine conversationalist, and a delightful communicator.

Like most authors, Roy Bedichek always had multiple writing projects going at any time. One of these projects resulted in a fourth book, *The Sense of Smell* (1960), which was published a year after his death.

Rusty Wier

Don't He Make You Wanna Dance?

The tall, slender man with a gray beard sits comfortably on the stool before the microphone, strumming his well-worn guitar. His trademark, custom made, riverboat-gambler, black hat provides little shade from the bright stage lights.

He's just finished plugging his newly released eighth album, *I Stood Up*. His many fans have waited impatiently for five long years for Rusty Wier's newest release.

As I watch him on stage, I realize that Rusty has changed little in the fifty years we've been friends. We both joke that we couldn't have grown up together, because neither of us ever grew up. It's true.

He opens his set with a broad smile, forgoing what used to be another of his trademarks, asking the audience, "Is there anyone here from Manchaca?" referring to the small town south of Austin where we miss-spent our youth.

Rusty and his family had moved into a ranch house down on the end of Frate-Barker Lane, not far from scenic downtown Manchaca. His folks, Dorsey Otto and Owana Wier, were always nice whenever I showed up at their place. I was fascinated by his mom's cool name; Owana. It fit this beautiful lady well and made her seem quite exotic.

She always greeted me with a big smile and something cool to drink. Like his mom, Rusty's dad also enjoyed a good laugh. He once asked me, "Jim, do you know why we named our boy Rusty?"

"No sir, can't say that I do."

"Well, we wanted a name for the boy that folks could associate with. And out here in farm country there's lots of fences. And what's hangin' on all those fence posts?"

"Barbed wire," I ventured, playing along.

"That's right. So, if you switch the last two letters of Rusty's name, you end up with Rusty Wire! Isn't that a hoot? We figured folks could remember that one."

Folks do remember Rusty. In Texas there are things and people that you only need one word to describe. Words like Alamo, Thump (Luling Watermelon Thump), Molly (Ivins), Kinky (Friedman), Liz (Carpenter), Willie (Nelson), and of course, Rusty.

His father owned the Tally Ho Restaurant at Seventh and Congress. That's where Rusty kicked off his entertainment career. Being an admitted "born ham," Rusty was only "knee-high to a duck" (about three) when he would ride his stick horse through the restaurant between the tables while the pianist played the "William Tell Overture." He must have enjoyed the attention, since he's been on stage regularly ever since.

Besides the Tally Ho, Dorsey Wier owned the Plantation restaurant near UT as well as some hotels down in Houston. The Plantation was a popular gathering spot for musicians, because back then it was just about the only place in town that stayed open all night. After we would finish playing at some club or fraternity house, we'd meet up at the Plantation to swap lies and guitar licks.

Rusty and I first met while riding the school bus to Porter Junior High. We were thrown together right off, since we normally sat in the back of the bus. Even then we were both a head taller than everyone else. (Now, with hats and boots we're both about six and a half feet tall.)

Being tall meant that our legs didn't fit into the knee area available on most school buses. So we migrated to the back of the bus to have a full seat to ourselves. This allowed us to turn sideways and stretch out.

Of course, sitting in the back of the bus also meant that we were a little more out of sight of our poor bus driver, Polly Jones. This wonderful lady, mother of my best friend Mark Jones, endured an endless string of pranks and mischief from the "back of the bus gang" for most of my school career.

Thank goodness folks would pick up hitchhikers back then, or we would have spent a lot of time walking to school. What did we do? Oh it was never anything bad, just some sort of mischief that would cause Polly to stop the bus, open the door, and roll her eyes and give us that, "you kids are going to be the death of me" look.

Meanwhile, we were all being perfectly quiet little angels in the back of the bus. Then Polly would run through the roll call of those she had chosen to walk to school that day. We would howl in protest and then get off. Often we would hitch a ride so quickly that we would be there to greet the bus at school, causing Polly to roll her eyes once again.

Rusty is still quite proud of achieving one of the high points of his young life at Porter Junior High. "I was the first boy in the girls' restroom in Porter Junior High. I didn't get caught, but everybody knew it was me. It was great."

Mischief.

Then there was the time that Rusty was riding the bus home from Travis High School. The back seats were filled, so he was sitting about halfway back. He was also sneaking a smoke. After years of practice, he had gotten so good at sneakin' smokes that he had puffed this one down to a butt. As the bus cruised down Manchaca Road, Rusty flicked out the burning butt. It then was caught by the wind and blew back into a window behind him. As if it had eyes, it headed straight down a girl's blouse. Now this wasn't a flat-chested young lady, and the smoldering cigarette butt found its way into her bra.

For those of us in the back of the bus, our first notification that there was a problem came when the most conservative young lady to ever set foot on that bus jumped up, ripped open her blouse, and yanked off her bra. We were amazed, pleased, and amused. She was none of these.

Long-suffering Polly pulled over immediately and started the interrogations. (This was in an age before Miranda warnings!) Having established that a cigarette butt was the culprit, Polly didn't even have to say anything. She turned and looked at Rusty; he shrugged and got off the bus, shaking his head. Mischief.

Rusty became musically hyperactive at about age seven. His parents didn't perform musically, but they enjoyed playing a variety of music, including lots of Dixieland. Rusty added lots of percussion to the recordings by playing pots and pans with spoons.

To preserve their kitchenware, the Wiers bought Rusty a set of drums when he was ten. Shortly thereafter, they set up a soundproof room to preserve their hearing and sanity.

Rusty considered playing in the school band. We all figured he was a shoe-in, because of all his experience. But, in typical Rusty fashion, the band didn't meet his standards. Riding home on the bus that day, he recounted, "They gave me these fat stupid sticks and had us playing on these stupid little pads, not drums, and then they wanted to play some really stupid music. I told 'em it was stupid. They didn't take it real well."

By age thirteen, Rusty was the drummer for a group called the Centennials. The only problem was that he wasn't old enough to drive and didn't have any way to get to the gigs. "They'd come pick me up, and Mom and Dad would say, 'OK, but he's gotta be back by eleven.'"

He laughs, adding, "It never happened. We never got home on time, but Mom and Dad always kept trying."

Rusty and the band put on another great show at the legendary Saxon Pub in Austin. Pictured with Rusty is John Fannin and Cole El Sateh.

The Centennials played some pretty good rock & roll, and for the next ten years, Rusty was in the middle of the early sixties rock scene. He performed with The Whig with Benny Rowe, and Lavender Hill Express with Layton DePenning and Gary P. Nunn.

The Whig was interesting for its name. Rusty was in the army reserve at the time. They required that your hair not touch your ears. Meanwhile, long hair was the rage in the music scene. Lots of guys in the reserve at the time solved this dilemma by buying a shorthaired wig. They would slap that shorthaired rascal on and could fit right in with the folks at the reserve meetings. The only thing that looked a little strange was that their sideburns were combed up, not down! So, in honor of this device, they called their group The Whig.

"During this time I was singing with a whole string of pick-up bands. One of my favorite Austin places was Charlie's Playhouse, located just east of I-35. They catered to lots of college kids, playing plenty of rock and folk music with lots of jazz overtones.

"The Playhouse was owned by Ernest Charles 'EC' Gilden. EC was a big, gregarious black man with a love for live music and running clubs. At the time he had two clubs named after himself, Charlie's Playhouse and Ernie's Chicken Shack, which was outside the city limits, on Webberville Road. Since Charlie's was in the Austin city limits, it had to close earlier than Ernie's. So each night when I closed the last set at Charlie's, my lines went something like, 'No sense in stopping the party, just head on out to Ernie's Chicken Shack.'"

Rusty learned a lot from the wise old musicians at Ernie's. Sometimes he would have a bottle to share, other times he would just eavesdrop. He learned not only technical skills about performing, he began to appreciate the beauty of the new sounds that were being created as different musical forms began to merge. And there were plenty of sounds merging as the Austin '60s scene mixed generous portions of rock, folk, blues, jazz, and country, to create the Austin Sound.

Rusty was a member of Lavender Hill Express, one of Austin's most popular local acts at that time. They played at most of the popular gathering places and anyplace else that had a microphone. Rusty wanted to call Lavender Hill Express "the Blue Mountain Train." "I guess I was trying to go country, even then."

When Gary P. Nunn put together a new band, Rusty was "not invited" to play with them. This allowed him time to look at where he was going musically. Rusty had decided that drums were fun, but nobody can name a live drummer. Guitars were where the action was; chick magnets, even if you just carried one around! So Rusty picked up a Mel Bay book of guitar chords and taught himself to play guitar.

To this day, Rusty and I still laugh that there are guitar pickers and guitar floggers. We're both floggers! My flogging days are past, but Rusty continues to carry the floggers' torch.

At that time the Chequered Flag was one of the best venues in town. I got the opportunity to play at the "Flag" a few times over the years. It was owned and managed by music legends Rod Kennedy, Segle Fry, and Allen Damron.

Rusty tells a humorous story about auditioning at the Flag. "I had decided to be a folk singer. I went down to the Chequered Flag and auditioned for Segle Fry and Allen Damron. At the end of the audition, they handed me a broom and said, 'Here, sweep the floor. You need to sit and watch people and learn.' Two days later I told them I figured that I had learned plenty and was ready to go on stage. They apparently weren't as convinced as I was. But, to me, sweeping seemed a whole lot like farm work, and I'd had all of that I wanted."

The music scene in Austin was really catching on. It attracted lots of talented, free-spirited musicians to the city. That lifestyle also attracted a good deal of attention from the media, which in turn attracted a lot of close scrutiny from the local law enforcement organizations. Many prominent Texas acts had grown tired of the "attention" and decided to head out to the left coast. Janis Joplin led the exodus, followed by Doug Sahm, Steve Miller, and the 13th Floor Elevators.

Rusty missed the first flight heading out west. He stayed in Austin and founded a folk trio with DePenning and John Inmon. They met with moderate success.

In August 1970 the Armadillo World Headquarters opened its doors. It soon became the focus of much of the city's musical life. With an eventual capacity of 1,500, the hall featured a varied fare of blues, rock, jazz, folk, and country music in an informal, open atmosphere.

The word soon spread that there was a great new venue down in the Lone Star State. Top touring acts like Frank Zappa, Willie Nelson, the Pointer Sisters, Bruce Springsteen, Steven Fromholz, and the Grateful Dead played the Armadillo. Local acts often opened these shows at the "Dillo," giving exposure to such future stars as Joe Ely, Marcia Ball, and Stevie Ray Vaughan.

When asked about the Dillo, Rusty laughs, "I wasn't part of the 'In Crowd' at the Armadillo, but I did play there a few times."

The Austin music scene continued to bubble and boil in the early seventies. Willie had returned from Nashville after his house there

Rusty relaxes between sets and chats with a fan.

burned. Waylon Jennings, Michael Murphey, and Steven Fromholz were all making big musical waves in Texas.

While Willie & Waylon and the boys were getting back to the basics of life in Luckenbach, Rusty finally decided to try California. L.A. wasn't quite ready for Rusty.

"I lived in L.A. for about six months on 38 cents. It could have been a whole lot more fun. Just wasn't a good fit."

But leaving L.A. did serve as a great source of inspiration for Rusty. "I left L.A., driving back home. It was a long drive. Lots of time to think. About the time I got outside of Dripping Springs, I got to thinking about how I'd been gone for so long, it just came to me... 'Don't it make you wanna dance, don't it make you wanna smile.'"

"Don't It Make You Wanna Dance" made Rusty a star. Bonnie Raitt's recording of the song was used in the John Travolta movie *Urban Cowboy*. The soundtrack album for the movie sold over two million and earned Rusty a Double Platinum Album.

The good times had officially begun. Rusty performed with Willie, Waylon, Ray Charles, Charlie Daniels, Lynyrd Skynyrd, the Atlanta Rhythm Section, Steven Fromholz, B.W. Stevenson, Asleep at the Wheel, Pure Prairie League, and the Allman Brothers. In those days, Rusty was often the headliner, with folks like George Strait as his opening act.

Every ten years or so, someone puts out a new release of "Don't It Make You Wanna Dance." Most recently it was Chris LeDoux. Jerry Jeff before that. Before that it was John Hiatt, Barbara Mandrell, Colleen Peterson, and of course Bonnie Raitt.

When asked about the song, Rusty flashes his still-boyish grin, "Jim, I truly do wish I could write about five more like it. Gosh, if I only sold one to half the people in the world, I would be doin' all right! I really appreciate simplicity in music. Grass roots feelings are essential to my music. My dad urged me to learn all of Hank Williams' songs. Simplicity."

Rusty has learned a lot of lessons in the music industry over the years. One lesson is that if he can get someone to sit down and listen to his music for a few minutes, he will play something of his that they will really like. Like I said in the chapter on storytelling in Texas, it's not bragging if it's a fact.

Wherever you are musically, Rusty will do something that will find you. It's a gift. In his normal set you will see a blend of his compositions with those of the Bee Gees, Righteous Brothers, and even a reggae version of a Bee Gees song.

Rusty has also learned a lot of lessons about life; some of these he wishes he had just skipped over. "It was the times. Nobody really saw where it was all headed." Let's just say that Rusty is a great resource for information on mistakes that are best avoided.

A friend of mine who is a pilot told me that a good airplane landing is "any landing you can walk away from." The same can be said about the destructive aspects of the music business. Surviving can be the ultimate challenge.

Rusty is a survivor. And he's had a hell of a lot of fun doing it.

It's 1990 and Joe Ables is preparing to open a new club in Austin. Construction workers are scurrying all over the site, completing what will become the legendary Saxon Pub. They are building on the stage, and the front door hasn't even been hung.

In the midst of this confusion, a tall guy with a hat and beard walks in like he owns the place. He walks over to the under-construction stage and announces that, "Yep, this'll do."

And so it has. Since its beginning Rusty has been a regular performer at the Saxon Pub.

As Rusty puts it, "I've been drinkin' on Joe's tab for twelve years now!"

Rusty is blessed with a great band. First, I'll correct a mistake by another writer. Almost every Thursday night a great musician, John Fannin, is on electric guitar. For the record, Larry "Snake Eye" Nye fills in occasionally when John Fannin is out.

The rest of the band consists of Andy Tarrant (bass), Cole El Sateh (piano), and Jeremy Bow (drums). All combine their towering musical talents with Rusty on acoustic guitar to produce magic. The times I've spent listening to these talented guys are treasures.

Part of the reason their music has worked so long is that Rusty has become a consummate professional entertainer. No matter what's going on in his life, and no matter how many people are at a show, Rusty leaves them all with a smile.

A heartbreaking example of this happened when his mother, Owana Wier, passed away, only twelve hours before his regular Thursday night show at the Saxon Pub. The audience never knew of his loss. He merely dedicated his first song, a cover of the song "To Love Somebody," to her.

"She didn't want me to miss a show." And he didn't. Rusty buried his mom the day after Mothers' Day. But the audiences never knew.

Rusty performs Wednesday nights at Gino's, a south Austin eatery and bar that features lots of live music. On Wednesdays Gino's has an open mike, where folks can come and try out their tunes on an audience. It's always a lot of fun.

On one of those Wednesday nights, Rusty and I were sitting at the bar between sets. I told him that his song "Quervo's Gold" is one of my favorites.

He laughed, "Jim, it's strange that you should mention that while we're sitting here. A few years back, my wife and I were sitting in just these chairs, and we wrote 'Quervo's Gold' together. We had decided to put together a song using all of the names on the liquor bottles behind the bar. It turned out OK." Actually, it's one of his most requested songs.

Whether it's at Gino's on Wednesdays, or the Saxon Pub on Thursdays, or any of a dozen other venues, the folks will be getting a good show.

"I've seen some bad shows, where the crowd got short-changed. That's not right. I always try to leave the folks smilin' and happy!"

He has left them happy, but one other thing has been important all of his life. To paraphrase Frank Sinatra, "Rusty did it his way."

Along the way he has often appeared on *Austin City Limits* and the Nashville Network Series *The Texas Connection*. He has also appeared in well-known television and radio campaigns for McDonald's, Lone Star Beer, the city of Austin, House of Jeans, and many, many others.

"It's been a wonderful ride. I'm making a living doing what I love to do. It doesn't get any better than that! But Jim, there's one other thing."

"What's that, Rusty?"

"I don't kiss nobody's ass!"

Mischief.

You can keep up with Rusty by checking www.RustyWier.com.

Don't It Make You Wanna Dance?

by Rusty Wier

I've been gone for so long, don't it feel good to get back home
To the friends and the people that you'd love to see
There's a twinkle that's in her eye both smiling as you go by
They know what you what you really wanna feel.

Chorus:
Don't it make you wanna dance, don't it make you wanna smile
When you're down, down, down in the country they can sing a while.
Don't it make you wanna dance, don't it make you wanna smile
When you're down, down, down out in the country they can sing a while.

Don't it feel just right tonight, gettin' loose 'neath the old moonlight
Gettin' down, gettin' funky, gettin' hot, gettin' real
Everyone has found a grin, so when the chorus comes around join in
Come on people won't you tell me how you really feel.

Chorus x3

Elizabeth Ellis

American and Texas Storyteller

I haven't known Elizabeth Ellis nearly long enough. She is my new-est old friend. We only met recently. I was talking with singer-songwriter Allen Damron about this book, and he said that it would not be complete without Elizabeth. I had heard of Elizabeth but had never had the opportunity to meet her. Allen took care of getting us together and the rest, well that's all just history.

We first got to sit down together in the little Czech town of West, Texas. This beautiful little town sits on IH-35, north of Waco We sat at the back table at Sulak's Restaurant, a great place to eat that has been a favorite of mine for over forty years. (Their kolaches are incredible! I keep telling folks this is a tough job!)

Elizabeth walked in with a smile that lit up the room. Immediately I realized that she is a very, very interesting lady. Not surprisingly, she has a vast collection of stories about almost anything you want to talk about. This is a common characteristic among storytellers. They tend to have certain topics that they favor. But everything they observe becomes raw material for stories.

Elizabeth Ellis tells traditional stories from cultures all over the world, with a special emphasis on the stories of Appalachia, where she grew up, and Texas, where she has lived for thirty years. She

Elizabeth Ellis and Jim talk about storytelling while eating at Sulak's, the great Czech restaurant in West, Texas (north of Waco on IH-35).

also tells stories of heroic American women. She can tailor each program to fit the needs of the audience and offers lecture-demonstrations, workshops, and mini-performances for students and people of all ages.

Elizabeth tells Texas stories, fairy tales, and folktales from cultures all over the world. She is recognized as a powerful teller of personal experience stories and tales of heroic American women. A native of Kentucky, Elizabeth grew up in a family of storytellers.

Since she became a full-time professional storyteller twenty-one years ago, she has traveled widely throughout North America, sharing her story magic with audiences from kindergarten students to adults. Elizabeth is a founding member of the Dallas Storytelling Guild and has been honored by the Tejas Storytelling Association with the John Henry Faulk Award and by the National Storytelling Association with the Circle of Excellence Award.

Elizabeth grew up in the Appalachian Mountains. From 1967 to 1969 she taught school in the Carter County School District for the National Teacher Corps. There she taught basic English and work skills to Job Corps participants.

In the fall of 1969 Elizabeth became a community services librarian for the Dallas Public Library. She worked there for ten years before becoming a professional storyteller.

Since 1979 Elizabeth has been the artist-in-residence at elementary, secondary schools, colleges, and universities, telling stories and conducting storytelling workshops for students, teachers, and parents.

In 1981, not long after she started telling stories professionally, she had become friends with Gayle Ross, then a gifted amateur storyteller. Elizabeth saw Gayle's potential and was encouraging her to become a professional storyteller.

Together they traveled to the National Storytelling Festival in Jonesborough, Tennessee. By the time they got back home they had decided to become the Twelve Moons Storytellers (one for each month). Together, they gave each other the confidence to step in front of an audience and tell their stories.

Fear of being in front of a crowd is one of the strongest fears in folks. It is hard to stand before a crowd and entertain them after they've had a bad day at the office. But the synergy between them worked, and Twelve Moons Storytellers became legendary.

Gayle Ross explained, "It was a silly way to handle things. Since I lived in Fredricksburg and Elizabeth lived in Dallas, wherever we performed, someone had to travel at least 250 miles! Economically, a very bad plan. But, there is no way I could have done it myself without Elizabeth's support."

Elizabeth is now a full-time free-lance storyteller in Dallas, Texas, and is one of the few tellers to have been featured more than five times at the National Storytelling Festival in Jonesborough. She had first appeared at the festival in 1981 as part of the Twelve Moons Storytellers. She returned in 1986 as a solo performer, making her mark as a riveting teller of the personal experience story.

In 1987 Elizabeth was the founding president of the Tejas Storytelling Association. She served on their board of directors from 1987-1992.

For several years Elizabeth had been a member of an Oklahoma storytelling group named Territory Tellers. From 1993 - 1994 she served on their board of directors and as their Texas representative

Noted for her ability to teach others how to tell, from 1994 -1996 Elizabeth served on the board of directors of the National Storytelling Association, serving as at-large representative from the national membership.

One of Elizabeth's many honors came in 1997, when she was chosen to receive the National Storytelling Association Circle of Excellence Award, which is being presented to individuals for their efforts in preserving the art and for setting standards of excellence in the field of storytelling.

Whether you are a storyteller or a listener, here are some great tips, from a master storyteller, that will help you appreciate the talent required.

Elizabeth states there are four kinds of stories, determined by the response given to each by the audience:

The first type is the Ha Ha — the funny story, all the way from slapstick to the literary story, humorous due to clever plotting.

The next is the Ah Ha — a story with an element of surprise, a story that explains, a ghost story, or a story that makes you say, "Oh, I get it!"

The third type is the Aaah! — a story, possibly an experience, a Bible story, a wide variety of stories that all take a deeper level of concentration than the first two types, but always get the reaction "Aaah!" upon their completion.

And the final type is the Amen — the story that literally means, "So be it."

This is the way life should be lived, and is often a good way to end the program. Elizabeth suggests starting with the lighter stories and moving into those that take more concentration, always going back to the lighter ones if you feel you are losing the audience.

Develop your own style of plan for making your program a success. Remember that there are as many different approaches to planning a program as there are storytellers. Some start with humor, some with a song, and others give a quick sampling of what is to come. The whole idea is to snag the audience early. When I am telling to a group of teenagers who have the attitude "Show me," I will often start with an urban legend, like the *Vanishing Hitchhiker*, which I locate as having happened to me in their area. I soon have their wide-eyed attention for the rest of the program.

Keep in touch with your audience. It is important to have a program planned, but if for some reason your plan isn't working, be prepared to change direction. And always make sure that when you finish, the audience still wants more. In other words, know when to get off that stage!

Over the years Elizabeth has performed at hundreds of national and international storytelling festivals, residencies, and conferences throughout North America, including the National Storytelling Festival, Kerrville Folk Festival, Winnipeg Folk Festival, and the Vancouver Folk Festival.

Elizabeth has a video available from H.W. Wilson Publishing Co. *The American Storytelling Series, Best Loved Stories told at the National Storytelling Festival.*

She also has a wonderful CD, *Mothers and Daughters, Daughters and Mothers* which was recorded live at the National Storytelling Festival. It is available from New Moon Productions.

You can find out more about Elizabeth at the web site http://www.geocities.com/SoHo/Study/1578/tellerpage.html#Ellis or at http://www.tejasstorytelling.com/Bio%20Elizabeth%20Ellis.htm or you can email her at leellis@verizon.net.

Here is one of Elizabeth's wonderful stories.

Jack and the Donkey

by Elizabeth Ellis

A whole lot of the folks who settled Texas came here from the Appalachian Mountains. They brought their stories with them, and a lot of them were about a guy named Jack—the guy who climbed the beanstalk. You remember him, right?

Jack got to looking around the homeplace one day. He realized he had a mule, and really wasn't using it for much of anything. So, he decided that he would take it to town and sell it, maybe make a little money off the deal.

He had a hired boy working for him at the time. The boy hardly ever got to go anywhere. So Jack asked the boy if he wanted to go with him. The two of them set off down the road to town, leading the mule.

Now Jack didn't live in a big place like Houston or Dallas. It was a little place. They didn't have enough people to have a "town drunk." They had to take turns at it.

It must have been Claude Hicks' turn to be the town drunk, 'cause he was coming home packing quite a load, if you know what I mean. He looked up and saw Jack and the boy leading that mule. He started to laugh, fit to kill. He said, "Jack, I always suspected about you that the light was on, but nobody was home! Why would anybody walk and lead a mule?"

Now Jack was one of those folks that has a firm grasp on the obvious. He couldn't always think things out on his own. But when somebody showed him something, he could see it plain as day. Jack got on the mule and started to ride it.

They hadn't gone any piece at all, when here came Mineola Haggard. She was the local schoolmarm. In fact, her motto should have been, "Your business is my business." You probably know some people like that. I do.

As soon as Mineola laid eyes on Jack, she said, "Aren't you a pretty looking thing, riding along up there like you think you're the foreman of the whole ranch. Look at that poor boy, dragging along in the dirt. Why don't you let that poor boy ride?"

So Jack got off the mule and hoisted the boy on its back. But the very next person they passed was old Brother Sizemore. He was the preacher at the First Church for the Perfection of the Spirit, kind of a professional "wet blanket." He would go to any kind of place where people were having a good time, and he would just ooze all over it until he put it out.

As soon as he saw the hired boy riding on the mule, he began to chastise and rebuke the child. He said, "Don't you know you're supposed to honor your elders? Get down off that animal and let that old man ride!" The hired boy was really crestfallen at being talked to like that. He slid off that mule.

He and Jack watched as old Brother Sizemore stomped off out of sight. Jack turned to the boy and said, "Maybe we ought to both ride it."

So the two of them got on the mule together. And they rode it right down in front of the First Church for the Perfection of the Spirit, old Brother Sizemore's church that I was telling you about. Now it just happened that it was Quilting Day. Those women had darned more husbands than they had socks. They came swarming out of that church like a tree of bees. They climbed all over Jack and that boy. They said, "Who does that mule belong to? We know it can't belong to you. If it did, you wouldn't treat it like that. Look at you, the two of you riding along on that poor little thing. You're gonna break it down. Why, you ought to be arrested for cruelty to dumb animals—if they could figure out which one of you was the dumb animal in the first place."

As the women flounced away, Jack turned to the hired boy and said, "Maybe we ought to both carry it!" He took out his jack knife, went over to the side of the road, and cut himself a good size sapling. He stripped all the branches off it. He came back and they tied that mule up like a prize Christmas turkey. They stuck that pole down between the mule's legs. Here they came into town, carrying that mule across their shoulders.

Right down in the middle of town in front of the county courthouse was the "whittling and spitting" bunch. You've seen those guys out in front of every courthouse in the entire state, haven't you? Well, there is always a ringleader among them, kind of the "head red," if you know what I mean. That fellow looked up and spotted Jack and the boy, carrying that mule. He commenced to laughing till you could have heard him all the way to the state capitol. He threw back his head and hollered, "Fellars, would you look at that!" And of course, they all turned and started hooting laughing.

Jack was so flabbergasted at being laughed at one more time, when he had tried every way in the world he could think of to please other people, that he lost his hold on his end of the pole. That poor hired boy couldn't hold that whole mule all by himself. That mule got away from them, and rolled right off the bridge into the East Fork of the Trinity River and drowned deader than a doornail.

And that just goes to prove that if you try to please everybody, you will end up pleasing nobody. And, like Jack, you'll be quite likely to lose your ass in the bargain.

Tim Henderson

Singer - Songwriter - Musician - Humorist - Storyteller

Photo courtesy of Marian Henderson.

It would have been easy for me to dislike Tim Henderson. Envy works that way. As a songwriter/lyricist, I stand in awe of Tim's talents. He shares my admiration with the likes of Lennon and

McCartney, Harry Chapin, Buddy Holly, Hank Williams, Paul Williams, and Jim Steinman. Each possesses that rare ability to transport the listener with his mastery of words and music, to wherever he decides to take you. And what wonderful places Tim will take you.

To be a good songwriter you must possess a diversity of skills. You need to be a storyteller, lyricist, arranger, and musician. You envision the journey then craft a vehicle to transport the listener. The ability to select phrases that "reach" the listener, giving them the picture in just a few words, is the basic requirement. Next you must be able to find the melody that matches the rhyme.

I'm not alone in my admiration of Tim's talent. Here are a few comments from other musicians:

Peter Yarrow (of Peter, Paul, and Mary): "Tim's music takes us on a journey of laughter and whimsy, from wistful poetry to playful exaggeration, all the gift of Tim's magical, masterful muse." And he added, "Tim's song 'Maria Consuelo' is a magnificent, moving, powerful, salt-of-the earth song."

Tom Paxton said, "I keep trying to think of a more purely representative American songwriter than Tim Henderson and, frankly, I'm stumped...There's a bit of Robert Service in Tim, a dash of Louis L'Amour, and a double shot of Mark Twain and Bret Harte."

The late, great songwriter-singer Townes Van Zandt — "His songs are soulful and solid, sprung from the soil of Texas. Sometimes witty, always wise. Never showy or shallow. His music has always impressed me as beautifully human."

I'm a fan of songwriters performing their own songs. I often hear additional meaning and inflection when they perform their works that would be lost by a singer with no emotional ties to the song. Many years ago Allen Damron was singing "Texas in His Ways," and there was no doubt in my mind he had written it. It was several years later when I found out that he hadn't. I was stunned.

Allen explained that Tim Henderson had written the song. I commented on the depth of emotion that came out when Allen sang it.

Then he explained, "That song means a tremendous amount to me. I love it because it's a beautiful song, but also because Tim Henderson wrote it about my father, Jack Damron."

Texas in His Ways

You can't tell him from the countryside,
he's dusty as the land,
And he's all crow's feet and wrinkles,
like the back of Granny's hand,
He ain't never had much learnin' but he still turned out OK.
He's got a lot of Texas in his ways.

His old blue jeans have faded to the color of his eyes,
And his hair is like the wispy clouds that mock a summer day,
Hell, he's never had much money but he'll make it through OK.
He's got more than a little Texas in his ways.

And on Friday night the Texan drives his pickup truck to town,
Drops his woman at the church and goes to drink a couple down,
He's a-listenin' to the jukebox while his woman kneels and prays,
"God, forgive him for the Texas in his ways."

He's the fabric of this land, and he's respected in his town,
He plays dominos on Sat'day while his woman shops around,
Shoots straight and tells the truth, and any debt he owes he pays,
There's more than a little Texas in his ways.

And on Sunday night the Texan drives his pickup truck to town,
Drops his woman at the church and goes to drink a couple down,
He's a-listenin' to the jukebox while his woman kneels and prays,
"God, forgive him for the Texas in his ways."

It was a few years later that Tim and I finally met; I've valued his friendship since, enjoyed his performances, and envied his writing ability. Tim wasn't born a Texan but he got here pretty quick and sure adapted well.

Tim was born in Charleston, West Virginia, on February 19, 1940. His parents were Carm and Bud Henderson. His father did shift work for DuPont for "entirely too many years...when you consider he always had either a second job or was working the farm for another forty hours a week."

Tim Henderson at age 3.
Photo courtesy of Marian Henderson.

But he always found time for his family. They had five kids and adopted two. Yet, they put all the kids through parochial school. The school was the one big luxury of their lives. They were poor in the unknowing way that Appalachian Mountain people always are.

The family was always working the garden and livestock, so there was always plenty to eat. Hand-me-down clothes were the rule. As Tim says, "The only dignified thing about them is their perseverance, wisdom, and love."

Tim's mother was teaching school, which left much of the rearing of the children to his maternal grandparents, Jim and Macel Hagerty. As Tim described them, "They did most of the scolding and molding that made us all the good folks we kids turned into. My grandmother was a sharp-looking little thing who sang and played the dulcimer. My grandfather was a cavalryman who turned down the Buffalo Bill Wild West Show to marry her."

He went on to add, "The line they drew was straight and narrow. Deviation was corrected with a broom. Granny knew the wild medicinal herbs. Grandaddy lied a lot, but he told the best tales!"

So Tim came by his storytelling interest like most of us, by growing up listening to the tales of the spinners.

His paternal grandparents, Karl and Noll Henderson, were more distant, despite living in the same town. They only saw them Sundays and special occasions.

Tim describes Karl as "an erratic but gifted renaissance type who drifted in and out of fortunes. Stole his first one by plundering a silver mine in Mexico when most of the other miners had been massacred by one side or the other of the Villa/Carranza mess. He was a former local dragon of the KKK, who couldn't adjust to a Catholic son and daughter. But Lordy, he sure was a talented and inventive cusser."

Tim graduated from Charleston Catholic High School in 1957. He majored mostly in "hunting and fishing, which I did better than most." He played football "in a truly unexceptional manner. I was a singularly unprepossessing varsity swimmer for Virginia Polytechnic Institute in 1959."

Almost everybody attending VPI at that time was a member of their military training corps. By 1959, after two years at VPI, Tim was convinced there were two fields he no longer wanted any part of, nuclear engineering and the military.

He returned to Charleston and went to work for Union Carbide. He worked his way up from janitor to lab technician, while studying chemistry at night at West Virginia State College.

In a growing-up-in-the-'60s moment, Tim switched his major from chemistry to the humanities. Not unpredictably, Union Carbide also switched him, from a defense employed deferment to "Draft Grade 1-A Prime Cut."

Following one smooth move with another, in 1962 Tim "outsmarted himself by beating Uncle Sam to the punch and enlisting in the air force." Uncle figured that since Tim preferred the humanities, he would love to learn Russian; let's make Tim an electronic spy. For four years and a month, Tim was a Russian translator (etc.). Most of his time was spent in Germany, but he also saw Cyprus, Turkey, Italy, and the Aleutians.

Throughout his four years in the air force, Tim was learning. He had learned enough by this point that when he found out his next duty station was to be Monterey... studying Vietnamese, he excused himself and promptly exited the military experience.

Returning home, with the GI Bill in his pocket, he started taking courses in computers. An old friend, a highway engineer with the state of West Virginia Department of Highways, hired Tim as a tech writer. Since he lacked a college degree, they couldn't pay him but half what they had paid the person he replaced. To correct this, Tim went back to State. He completed his B.A. degree in English and German in 1971.

Tim Henderson, Janey Lake, and Pete Seeger.
Photo courtesy of Marian Henderson.

On the family front, in 1970 Tim had married the love of his life, Marian. To "keep body and bride together" he worked at a variety of jobs including running a newspaper, directing a public TV series, and doing some technical translating in German and Russian.

He also had one of the legendary jobs in America; Tim was a Fuller Brush salesman! (Willie Nelson sold some encyclopedias door-to-door.)

There was one other job that would have a profound influence on Tim, and his music, for the rest of his life. For one summer he worked in the coal mines. Here are the lyrics to one of my favorite songs of Tim's:

Black Hearted Mountain

Well, my Grandpa knew this mountain
her hardwoods tall and clean
stamped against the turquoise sky
like an emerald serene.

She stored jade in each and every hollow
where the silver springs ran cold.
But, the downfall of the mountain
was a heart of blackest coal.

The panther prowled this mountain.
And the eagle nested here.
Grouse and bear and turkey,
the mountain elk and deer.

They grazed the upland meadows,
at least that's what I've been told.
a living, breathing, mountain
with a heart of blackest coal.

You big black hearted mountain,
I just stood and watched you die.
While the dusty smoke of coal fires
streaked across the turquoise sky.

They made a mesa of my mountain
Hell they hollowed out her hills
Ripped and tore her entrails out
with bulldozers and with drills.

Pulled down her hardwood forests,
to line the tunnel holes.
that pierced the virgin mountain
to her heart of blackest coal.

Now my big black hearted mountain,
hunts the winter sky alone.
Deep within her hollow heart,
the rotten timbers groan.

And the night wind wails around her,
like a lost tormented soul.
A mountain that was murdered,
for her heart of blackest coal.

In 1972 Tim moved to Texas and entered the UT Austin graduate school, studying German. He also taught undergraduate technical German. As he puts it, "I taught for three years and was damn good at it. But when my GI Bill ran out, so did my enthusiasm for teaching at $325 a month."

The fact that he and Marian now had twins, Scott and Katie, may have had a lot to do with some of that financial dissatisfaction. Tim is a very funny man. He thinks funny. An example of this was a discussion about the expense of raising kids. Tim stopped to speculate on how much it costs, per pound, to raise a child. What would the market price be? Then he added, "Of course you would have to offer a discount on teenagers!"

Throughout his early years in Texas, Tim was writing and selling music. For those of you unfamiliar with the writing business, it is a very tough way to make a living. Tim got a big laugh out of the story about the writer who won the lottery. When asked what he would do with the money, he said, "Oh I'll just keep writing until the money runs out!"

Tim's "day jobs" have included faceting and selling precious stones, running sewer plants, working as a short-order cook, selling real estate, digging ditches, driving a dump truck, giving guitar lessons, and "writing sound tracks for El Cheapo and government-grant movies and far off-off Broadway shows." He also told jokes, wrote for newspapers, did some dynamiting, built houses, cleaned out manholes, and prospected for opals, turquoise, topaz, and gold. Summarizing that period, he commented, "I never found any good opals, or gold, and one of the houses fell down."

Allen Damron and Tim Henderson perform at the Kerrville Folk Festival in 1979. Photo courtesy of Marian Henderson.

Back on the singing-songwriting front, having received numerous glowing reviews of his ability, Tim went on tour. Later he summarized the experience with, "songwriting has never paid and is often overlooked or even scorned. It made it possible for me to tour nationally three years running and only go 15K in the hole!"

Like I said earlier, the true test of a storyteller is whether he or she can take you into another time and place. Here is another example of Tim's skill:

Lucky as You

All the cracks in the ceiling
are a roadmap that's leadin' him nowhere.
His life's a raw deal, and it's lost its appeal,
till he just don't care.

All the years plowed his face,
but the wisdom they sowed never grew.
And he's never found love.
He's just not as lucky as you.

In the big chain motel,
with the dry plastic smell of tomorrow.
Oh, he's doin' real well,
at least he handles the trouble he borrows.

His whole life's a gamble,
and one that he's liable to lose.
'Cause he never found love.
He's just not as lucky as you.

Love is so precious.
Fools keep it all to themselves.
But it ain't worth a thing,
unless you spend it on somebody else.

Oh, he's pickin' his best,
so he'll find the success he's been chasing.
In his used memories,
is the future he sees he'll be facing.

And the road that he's on
is the one only fools and pickers would choose
'cause he'll never find love.
He's just not as lucky as you.

No he'll never find love,
he's just not as lucky as you.

For the last twenty years, Tim's day job has been as a technical writer-translator for many of the leading technology firms in Austin. He is one of the most respected writers in the very competitive Austin writing community.

Peter Yarrow (of Peter, Paul, and Mary) and Tim perform together.
Photo courtesy of Marian Henderson.

Looking at his life, Tim says, "Right now I write books on computers about computers. The pockets are fairly full. I don't hate anybody, and I can't think of anything I'm particularly sorry for having done. I love my family and living in Austin. I like watching my kids grow and sleeping in my own hard bed at night. I like my wife a lot, too. Even after all these years, she is still full of surprises."

Throughout his life, Tim has never stopped writing. He has published over 200 songs, which have been performed by a wide variety of entertainers. His most performed song is "Maria Consuela."

Songwriters often have little control over when and where a song appears. "Maria Consuela" was like that. Here's how Tim described it, "I wrote 'Maria Consuela' on a hot Texas summer afternoon while backwashing filters in a water plant in Lakeway, Texas. I had been planning to write something like Maria for about a year. She came gushing out while the front part of my mind was OCCUPADO. I'm blessed with a memory that permits me to compose in my mind just as though I had a paper and pen available. My favorite time to compose is at night, driving on a long trip."

Tim then sat down with old friend Allen Damron, and they added a few final touches to this wonderful song. Please note the true-to-life details that help bring the story to life (more about that later).

Maria Consuelo Arroyo

Tim Henderson & Allen Wayne Damron

Maria Consuelo Arroyo was born
and raised on the south side of town,
With eyes holding midnight, the face of an angel come down,
In softness and beauty she grew like a rose without thorns,
At fifteen she married, at sixteen her first child was born.

And time is a lover,
the planter in ripeness who harvests your dreams;
And time is the river that sweeps us along in its stream,
It brings us together, then forces us cruelly apart.

And there's no wrinkled crone, in her dry skin and bones,
Who's not a young girl in her heart.

Maria Consuelo Arroyo, she bore seven
more on the south side of town,
And her love for her family like soft rain came whispering down,
Like flowers in a garden, they flourished in beauty and grace,
With their eyes, like dark mirrors, reflecting the love in her face.

And time is the traitor, yes, time is the villain
who stalks on our stage,
The bringer of heartache, the bringer of wrinkles and age,
He brings us together, then forces us cruelly apart,
And there's no wrinkled crone, in her dry skin and bones,
Who is not a young girl in her heart.

Maria Consuelo Arroyo, her man fell in
battle across wine dark seas,
And her children were scattered like
feathers that ride down the breeze.
She kneels in the darkness, nine candles she lights every day.
And Padre Alphonso remembers their names, when he prays,
And time's the black angel, a dark curandero
who brings the long sleep.

And time is a shepherd who's keeping good watch on his sheep,
So he brings back together the souls that he once tore apart,
And he comforts old crones in their dry skin and bones,
For he still loves the girl in their heart.

And time is a lover, the planter in ripeness
who harvests your dreams...

As a testament to the clarity and beauty of the song, Tim has been approached by numerous folks who have explained to him, in detail, that the song is about one of their relatives. And they want to know how he got their relative's story. They are incredulous when he explains that he made up the entire story and "used it for its internal cadence." One Latin American studies teacher in Arizona went so far as to write to find out more about Maria, where and when she lived, etc.

Maria Consuela was the result of two cultures meeting within Tim. "I love the music of the Latin cultures of Texas and Mexico. There are strong superstitious and religious similarities between the Indios and the mountain people of my West Virginia childhood. I was raised Catholic, and my maternal grandmother was a witch woman, or herb doctor. I observed the role life assigned to both my grandmothers. They were forced by their societies into a reactive rather than an active role in life, relying on a husband/father/provider, and all temporal and spiritual communication occurring through the good offices of males.

"If there is a single thing I am trying to emphasize in 'Maria Consuela' it is the fact that all Maria could do was to love and endure."

It continued to quickly spread in the music community. Tim performed it at a campfire sing-around at the Kerrville Folk Festival. Peter Yarrow rushed across the fire to ask for a demo. Allen Damron had used the song from within a month of when it was written. He circulated it to Chicago. Bob Gibson caught Allen performing it there and played it at Carnegie Hall with Tom Paxton, Odetta, and Josh White Jr. It received a standing ovation.

If "Maria" was a plague, then Allen Damron was the vector by which it was spread nationwide. Allen sang it to Katie Lee at a folksingers thing in Mountain Home, Arkansas. She called Tim at 2 A.M. that very night, seeking permission to use it. A third-hand demo tape of "Maria" fell into the hands of Chuck Glaser, in Nashville. He and his brothers had broken up as a singing group and had been fighting for years. Their father died, and after the funeral Chuck played "Maria" for brothers Jim and Tompal, saying he hoped this would be the song that would bring them back together. It did. Shocking Tim, they recorded "Maria" in a Nashville Elektra/Asylum studio and got *her* on the country charts. He says, "I still have a hard time wrapping my mind around the concept of 'Maria' as a honky-tonk ballad."

But shock is the name of the game where "Maria" is concerned. Imagine getting a phone call telling you that Katie Lee had just sung "Maria" on the MacNeil-Lehrer Report the evening before. National news! "Maria" sure gets around.

I've mentioned Tim's wonderful sense of humor, and here is an example:

The Privy House

Now my family gets together and we talk of bygone days,
And how things was down on the farm, compared to city ways,
There's some things we remember well can make a fellow blush,
And you can say I'm gettin' soft, but I like commodes that flush.

For the wind would howl and the wind would roar,
Up through the cracks in the privy house floor,
Guess the coldest times I ever saw,
Was settin' in the privy when the seat won't thaw.

Now the thing that I remember 'bout my shiftless brother, Pete,
Was the way you'd hear him holler when he'd plunk down on that seat,
And his teeth would still be chatterin'
when he'd come back through the door,
And he'd cuss and swear he'd never use that privy house no more.

Said, "Bundle up and wear warm clothes,
It don't help a bit when a chilly wind blows,
Cold inside and you set and freeze,
And the ice will form on both your knees."

But them icy winds that froze you there a-settin' wasn't all,
For that privy had its hazards from the spring right through the fall,
Ain't nothin' quite as scary as a swarm of angry bees,

When you're stuck there in the outhouse with
your pants around your knees,

And a copperhead or a rattlesnake,
Sittin' in the privy with you makes you shake,
Your eyes are searchin' to and fro,
But you know you've got no place to go.

When you're out there in the outhouse, settin' broilin' in the sun,
And your pants are 'round your ankles, so you can't just cut and run,
And you know, deep down inside you, you're just so much eatin'-meat,
To the sassy fat black widow that's a-creepin' 'crosst the seat.

Watch your tail, watch your feet,
When you set on a privy house seat,
Down inside is black as coal,
But you'd better look first down the privy seat hole.

But the thing that brought my urge to use an outhouse to an end,
Was the time the black bear came inside to get out of the wind,
Grandmaw told me, up in heaven, how the good souls learn to fly,
Well, I went flyin' down the mountain
with a big old bear (bare?) behind.

Rainy day and a leaky roof,
In an outhouse small as a telephone booth,
Nothin' else can give you piles,
Like settin' in a privy with a bear that's wild.

And the wind would howl and the wind would roar,
Up through the cracks in the privy house floor
And the coldest times I ever saw,
Was a-settin' in the privy when the seat won't thaw...

Tim does a few appearances each year. I'm proud to say that several have been with me. Please keep your eyes open for him to be appearing in your area. Don't miss the chance to see this very talented entertainer. If your local music store doesn't have his CDs and tapes, send me an email and I'll help you out. Send it to Jim@JimGramon.com.

This shot captures the humor that runs through Tim's performances. Don't miss the chance to see Tim perform, or at the very least pick up copies of his wonderful CDs and tapes.

Old Wil

A recurring theme in my books is that there are storytellers all around us. And, that they tell the stories in a wide variety of ways. I do the same thing. Often when I start working on a story, I'm not sure what form it will finally take. Perhaps it will end up as a short story, anecdote, joke, song, or even as a poem.

I know, poem is a four-letter word in many circles. But poetry is no different from songs, there are good 'uns and bad 'uns, and even some really, really, bad 'uns.

Nobody knew that I still write poetry. Nobody knew that I had been selected as a member of the Cowboy Poets Society. So you can imagine everyone's shock and embarrassment upon learning that one of my poems had been selected to be featured at the Austin International Poetry Festival! (I was their token cowboy!)

The poem, "Old Wil," came from the same background that most of my stories come from: growing up farmin', ranchin', and storytellin'. "Old Wil" is based on an actual event, and it represents a lifestyle that is, unfortunately, vanishing. But in rural Texas there is still a strong sense of community, caring, and sharing that we don't see enough of today.

Old Wil

Old Wil was a Texas rancher,
been one all his life.
Spent his days a herdin' strays.
He never took a wife.

A better friend could not be found.
A truer soul could not be had.

Always there beside you,
when the times were really bad.

But doctors weren't no friends of his
"They just help you go.
God's my doctor, and He taught me
everything I need to know."

So when word came down to the domino hall,
that the hospital had checked Wil in,
they knew it was heaven's call
and soon Wil would be with Him.

His friends gathered to offer help
Wil said, "Thanks, but there's nothin' you can do.
I sure do miss my old bull's beller
and hearin' my longhorns moo."

Ya know there ain't nothin' like it
under a star-filled Texas sky.
The lowin' and the bawlin'
just make you wanta sigh.

Late that day Ol' Wil was pretty weak.
Folks knew he was a nearin' the end.
When, from below his window,
a beautiful sound came a driftin' in.

The nurse said, "Wil you better sit up.
There's somethin' for you to see.
In all my years in Texas,
this is somethin' new to me."

Wil sat up and took a look,
rubbed his eyes, and looked again,
The parkin' lot was full of his herd
bein' wrangled by his friends.

Wil went to sleep, that one last night
to the music of his millin' herd.
He wanted to thank them all,
but he just couldn't find the words.

But, they all knew just how he felt
'Cause he felt just like them.
That's what true friends are all about,
they're with you to the end.

That was the end of the original poem. But it just wouldn't leave me alone. It somehow seemed incomplete. I finally realized that I hadn't really addressed how Wil would fit into the afterlife. So, two weeks later, I penned these additional lines.

But, the story doesn't end there,
when Ol' Wil died that night.
When he went to meet St. Peter,
they got into a fight.

See, St. Peter was goin' to send Wil to heaven
but Ol' Wil said no, he wanted a change.
So now, while other angels are a strummin' their harps,
Ol' Wil's out ridin' the Texas range.

Mike Blakely

Author - Songwriter - Musician

He sat quietly at a huge round table in the large ballroom. Anywhere else in the world he would have looked out of place in a somewhat formal ballroom. But not in Austin. The man's cowboy hat was tipped back (he was wearing a summer one). His moustache drooped a little at the edges of his mouth. Of course to me, that big round table sure looked like a Liars' Table, so I moseyed on over to sit in.

Although he was sitting quietly, I knew this guy had a lot to share because his eyes never stopped. He was taking in everything in the room from beneath the broad brim of his hat. So I wasn't really surprised that he was one of the featured authors at this writers' conference.

That was my first meeting with Mike Blakely, talented author, songwriter, musician, young, good-looking. Yep, Mike could be pretty easy to hate if he weren't so darn nice.

The May 2001 issue of *Texas Monthly* lists Mike Blakely as one of Texas's leading writers. This was based on the author's ability to produce either imaginative or significant works about Texas. High praise that he has earned.

Born in 1958, Mike Blakely grew up in a Texas ranching family near Halletsville. His parents, Patricia Dawn Blakely and Dr. James E. "Doc" Blakely, also had another son, James Perry Blakely, two years older than Mike. The boys had a great childhood on the farm. Mike loved it from the beginning and started herding cattle on horseback by the age of six, and it has been that way ever since.

"I remember that first roundup fondly," Mike recalls. "It was on a ranch we were taking care of for a friend near Halletsville. I was just a kid, but I had herded cattle around the pens afoot. That first time I loped my horse around the herd to turn it, and the herd actually went the way I wanted it to go—that's the moment I got hooked on cowboying. That was pretty powerful stuff for a six-year-old kid."

Mike's mom was a grade-school teacher for some time, then she bought and ran a successful retail store in Wharton. Later she began investing in real estate. At one time Mike worked for her, maintaining a dozen houses and apartments. Now she stays busy running the ranch with Mike's dad.

"Doc" Blakely has a Ph.D. in Animal Sciences and taught at Wharton County Junior College (WCJC) for ten years. Now Doc has always had a sense of humor and is a talented musician, playing the fiddle, mandolin, and guitar. But during this time he also discovered that he is a very funny man.

He began moonlighting as an after-dinner speaker and eventually quit teaching to go full-time, nationwide, as a speaker. Today he does occasional engagements when the demands of ranching allow.

The Blakely family also introduced Mike to music and travel. He began playing guitar at eight years of age, and by the time he turned fourteen, Mike had visited a dozen foreign countries in Central America and Europe.

Mike Blakely and Johnny Gringo perform at the
Too Damn Friendly Bar in scenic downtown Johnson City.

While in high school, Mike began performing with a popular dance band called Redwood, playing in dance halls all over the Coastal Bend region of Texas.

"I was the only high school kid in the band," he says. "The rest of the guys were in their twenties and thirties and were really talented veteran musicians. They gave me a pretty hard time because I was so green, but I learned a lot from them. I was writing my own songs by that time, but I never had the nerve to play any of them for the band."

James Perry Blakely, two years older than Mike, rodeoed and was a volunteer fireman. He got married and joined the Marines. He had a daughter, Torie. James was killed in an off-duty cliff-climbing accident in Washington State, where he was stationed with the Marines. He was only twenty-two.

A few years after James died, Mike found one of James's old cowboy hats in a storage room. He took it to Manny Gammage at Texas Hatters to have it restored so he could wear it. That's how Mike and Manny became friends. It took Mike fifteen years to write the song about his brother's hat, and how Manny fixed it. By that time Manny himself had passed over to what Mike calls the "Great Mystery."

So the song became a tribute to both Mike's brother and to Manny. It's called "The Hatter's Hymn" and is on the *Ghost Town Council* CD released in July 2002. Since Steven Fromholz and Rusty Wier both had hats made by Manny, they agreed to sing backup on the song, too.

After graduating from high school in Wharton, Texas, in 1977, Mike spent four years as a helicopter mechanic in the U.S. Air Force, serving at Kirtland Air Force Base, Albuquerque, New Mexico, and Osan Air Base, South Korea. Like lots of folks, the GI Bill would help him pursue his education.

Mike admits he didn't take high school very seriously. So he was a bit surprised when he found himself missing the writing assignments after he got out. About the same time, his high school English teacher happened to see his mom in the grocery store back home and mentioned to her that Mike had shown some promise as a writer. When Mike heard that, he made the decision to go to college and earn a journalism degree.

Graduating from The University of Texas at Austin with a Bachelor of Journalism degree in 1984, Mike began free-lancing with newspapers and magazines. He launched his self-syndicated column on Texas history and folklore, "Lone Star Legacy," in 1985, the year before the Texas Sesquicentennial celebration. The column ran for three years in some fifty newspapers across the state, including *The*

Dallas Morning News, the *Houston Chronicle*, and the *Austin American-Statesman*.

"I had always been interested in frontier history, especially in Texas. J. Frank Dobie was one of my favorite writers. So, it was a natural thing for me to write about old-time Texas, and the public interest stirred up by the Sesquicentennial gave me the chance to do it."

Mike's reputation as a magazine writer continued to grow, along with his list of credits, which included *Texas Highways, The Cattleman, American West, Western Horseman, Ultra*, and many others.

Writers are told, "write what you know," so it was a natural fit for Mike to also start writing hunting and fishing articles for *Texas Sportsman, Sports Afield*, and *Sporting Classics*. He even wrote a regular column on hunting and fishing folklore and history for *Texas Fish & Game*.

The intense historical research required to turn out his weekly and monthly columns provided Mike with the background material he needed to write his first few novels. After publishing hundreds of newspaper and magazine pieces, he sold his first novel, *The Glory Trail*, which was released in 1990.

"The great western writer Elmer Kelton was a friend of my father's," Mike says, "and he recommended that I join Western Writers of America. I joined in 1992 and went to the convention. There, I met Bob Gleason, editor-in-chief of Tor/Forge Books. I also met Tom Doherty, the founder of the company. We hit it off, and Forge Books ended up offering me a contract for several novels. So, my career began to take shape, and I got more involved with the inner workings of Western Writers of America.

In 1994 Mike's novel *Shortgrass Song* became a finalist for the prestigious Spur Award for Best Novel of the West, given annually by Western Writers of America. The story of a drifting cowboy musician, set from 1860-1884, *Shortgrass Song* led Mike's career as an author in a new direction. He began writing bigger, more historically involved novels. The sequel to *Shortgrass Song*, called *Too Long at the Dance*, followed the same recipe and garnered stellar reviews. Mike's next novel, *Comanche Dawn*, received rave reviews and again earned Mike the distinction as a finalist for the Spur Award in 1998.

From his home in Marble Falls, Mike had become one of America's leading western writers. He became more involved in Western Writers of America and served as membership chairman and was elected to their board. He became vice president, then served as president of the association from 1998 to 2000.

During this period, Mike's music had taken a bit of a backseat to his books. But all the while he was writing songs and poetry, to provide breaks from the books. Soon he had accumulated quite a stack of original tunes that begged to be performed.

Having learned many authentic cowboy ballads as research for *Shortgrass Song*, he began writing in the same vein, and soon he was performing original and traditional western songs all over the country. Teaming up with his father, rancher/humorist/musician Doc Blakely, Mike created an act called "The Swing Riders," focusing on the convention market. The Swing Riders have since played to standing ovations for audiences coast to coast and border to border. Their tightly rehearsed two-man show features fiddle tunes, cowboy humor, and trail drive songs.

At the same time, Mike was becoming known as a songwriter. Teaming up with John Arthur Martinez and Alex Harvey, Mike co-wrote a rollicking Tex-Mex song called "Seguro Que Hell Yes!" The song was the lead single on a Grammy-winning album recorded by Flaco Jimenez and featured the lead vocals of Raul Malo of the Mavericks and the back-up vocals of Radney Foster and LeRoy Parnell.

In 1994 Mike recorded his first CD, *Ride the River*. The disc included his song, "Charlie Siringo," which has since become a favorite on the cowboy music and poetry circuit. Also from *Ride the River*, an English-Spanish ballad called "Mira Las Palomas" would be recorded as a duo by noted Texas performers Geronimo Trevino III and Johnny Rodriguez. The CD *Ride the River* won Album of the Year honors at the Hill Country Music Awards.

Soon, the Mike Blakely Band, later to be known as Mike Blakely Y Los Yahoos, began performing across the Southwest. The new trio included Larry "Snake-Eye" Nye and Donnie "Walkin' Dawg" Price. A brilliant guitar player, Larry Nye is also the owner of Lazy L Recording Studios where Mike records. Donnie Price serves not only as bass player for the band but also covers bookings and publicity.

Los Yahoos play everywhere from beer joints and honky-tonks to five-star hotels. The group proved versatile and enormously popular. In addition to western tunes, Los Yahoos also play Mike's country, blues, rock, and rockabilly tunes. Los Yahoos have even toured Italy and Switzerland and found enthusiastic acceptance on the international market.

With the release of Mike's second CD, *West of You*, Los Yahoos assumed a more aggressive approach to marketing their unique brand of music. The band formed its own independent record label, called Swing Rider Records. After a year of market research and preparation, the fledging label decided to release *West of You* in January 2001.

Much to Mike's surprise, one tune, the epic western story song "The Last Comanche Moon," became the most requested song on KFAN for three solid months. "The song is almost seven minutes long," Mike says, "so I didn't even recommend it to the DJs as one they might want to play. I thought it was too long for radio. But the program director at KFAN, J.D. Rose, liked it and began playing it on his show, and pretty soon the requests started coming in."

Because KFAN (www.texasrebelradio.com) had won the distinction of being the most-listened-to radio station in the world on the Internet at the time, some of those requests for "The Last Comanche Moon" were coming from places like Denmark, England, and Australia. Two other songs from the CD—"It's About to Get

Western" and "Here's to Horses"—were recorded by Texas legend Gary P. Nunn on his CD, *It's a Texas Thang*, released in October of 2000.

Swing Rider Records even has a cooperative agreement with Forge Books to promote the sales of Mike's books and CDs in retail stores that handle both mediums, such as Borders, Barnes & Noble, Hastings, and Wal-Mart.

But now Mike encountered a unique phenomena of the publishing industry. The oldest lie in the book business is, "We are looking for something different." Publishers seldom will do anything that is different. They want a successful track record before they invest. Makes sense, except that if it is something new, it has no track record.

So, when Mike (a western writer) tried to sell *Summer of Pearls*, which is more of a southern novel than a western novel, the publishers were reluctant. But the novel was good enough to overcome their objections, and it came out in September of 2000. Forge Books took the initiative to publish the title, and since its release, *Summer of Pearls* has enjoyed excellent reviews and high praise from readers all over the country.

I went to interview Mike in Marble Falls. We were going to have a couple of hours to talk. We met at a local restaurant, and he entered with a guy that reminded me of the actor Gene Hackman.

Mike introduced me to author/singer/songwriter W.C. Jameson. (He also writes for Republic of Texas Press.) Mike went on to explain that he had gotten some studio time and that they were headed over to work on the new CD *Ghost Town Council*. So I tagged along and we spent the day in the studio.

Larry Nye was already there when we arrived at the studio. From the moment we arrived it was obvious that Mike, W.C., and Larry are all very talented professionals. They went about their work with a quiet focus on creating a "perfect" CD.

As an independent record label owner, Mike was preparing to release an album of original songs by W.C. Jameson. At the same

W.C. Jameson, Larry Nye, Mike Blakely, and Johnny Gringo
enjoy some great BBQ at Coopers, during a break in recording.

time, Mike was busy recording an album by the new band, called *Ghost Town Council*. Mike is a member of the band, along with W.C. Jameson, Larry Nye, Donnie Price, and new singing sensation Julie Anne Sckittone.

"After we release *Ghost Town Council*, I'll be ready to record my third solo album as a singer-songwriter," Mike says. "I've got songs that I've been playing live for years now but haven't had a chance to record. The third album will be a little more country. More Americana. But I think I'll always include a cowboy song or two on each CD I record."

Mike lives close to the land and nature. It's where he came from and who he is. He lives in a one-room cabin on his ranch (Rancho Quien Sabe [Who Knows?]) outside of Marble Falls, Texas. There he enjoys hunting and fishing and raising and training horses.

It only makes sense that when a creative person like Mike gets an idea, that it "comes out" in more than one form. One of his characters, the villainous Bill "Snakehead" Jackson, is the narrator of Mike's tune, "The Whiskey Trader's Song," and he also appears as the major antagonist in the novel *Moon Medicine*. The story told in the Blakely ballad "Mira Las Palomas" matches a remarkably similar episode in Mike's novel *Vendetta Gold*. And the lyrics to Mike's song "Too Long at the Dance" can be found in the narrative of his novel by the same name.

What a deal! How often is it that you can you buy the novel, the CD, and go hear the artist play? I think you are probably beginning to see why I respect Mike Blakely's many talents (despite his disgusting lack of aging).

Folks often ask how he can successfully write both books and music. He answers, "They actually work very well together. From a

Steven Fromholz, Jim, and Mike Blakely on stage at the Friendly Bar.

207

marketing standpoint, they help promote each other. From a creative perspective, one takes up where the other lets off. I can't write a novel while I'm driving down the road, but I can write a song behind the wheel and have written many of them that way."

Mike continues, "When I write a novel, I have to hide away in my cabin alone and shun the rest of the world for a few hours a day. It can be a lonely existence. Playing live music is the antidote to that. When I play a song, I get immediate feedback from the audience. When I finish writing a book, I may not get any response from the public for months. I don't see how I could do one without the other."

I asked Mike about the folks who have influenced him, besides his parents and Elmer Kelton. The question seemed to hit a special chord. You can tell from his responses how much his writing means to Mike. "One influence is Alex Harvey. I wrote a few tunes with Alex, including 'Seguro Que Hell Yes!' which also included my amigo John Arthur Martinez, the originator and co-writer of the tune." (The song was recorded by Flaco Jimenez on his self-titled Arista-Texas album. In 1995 it won a Grammy for best Mexican-American performance.) "I picked up a lot about singing from the soul by hanging around with Alex Harvey in Texas and Nashville.

"Another influence is the great singer/songwriter and Country Music Hall-of-Famer Floyd Tillman. I met Floyd about 1985 when I interviewed him several times for an article on him that I wrote for *Texas Highways Magazine*. Floyd still lives here in Marble Falls, and I see him occasionally at the post office. Floyd is also quite a showman and a monster songwriter."

Now just sit back and enjoy a couple of brief examples of Mike's wonderful prose.

Excerpt from Mike's newest book, Moon Medicine

Try to imagine that country in those days. I will do my best to help you. Let my recollections fire your imagination until my descriptions play out before your mind's eye like a living work of art, accompanied by all the sounds and smells and sensations of the wild country.

Imagine your buckskins sticking hot to your skin where the sun beats down. A gust peppers your eyeball with grit and parches your mouth with the dry bitter taste of alkali dust.

You ride, your saddle pressed hard against your thighs, the rhythm of your pony's gait a part of your very existence now. Through your squint, you sweep the horizon in a never-ending search for something exhilarating or fatal. You ride all day, day after day, without finding a house, or a road, or a fence, or even a wisp of cook fire smoke. All that you find is wild, from the prairie dogs that perch above their holes and bark, to the antelopes that stalk you out of curiosity, only to turn and flee at your scent.

You watch a cloud the size of a feudal fiefdom walk past you on stilts of lightning, an impossible daddy-longlegs spider out for a stroll. You only smell the rain, sweet and musky, but you appreciate the spider's shadow, for you will not see a tree large enough to throw shade until you find running water two days ahead.

Your saddle leather makes a creaking sound you will hear tonight in your fitful dreams. Your mouth reminds your hand to touch the canteen, but you know you must not drink yet. Your pony looks sidewise at a rattling snake that, uncoiled, would rival a shepherd's staff. You waste no time with reptiles. You soak in the beauty of the open country until you cannot hold any more of it. Your senses saturated, you feel you must scream, or weep, or gallop needlessly, or go mad. But you just ride on and on and on, and hope for water, and watch for enemies, and wish for wings. You eat in the saddle, and laugh a little with friends, and sing songs under your breath. You ride until you wish you could do anything but ride, be it float, sail, sleep, sit, dance, crawl, slide, roll, stumble, or swim. But all you can do is get down and walk for a while.

You wonder what brought you here.

You began this morning, with the wolves singing and the stars fading. You will ride until you can no longer see the ground under your pony's hooves. Then you will listen to shrieks and howls and hoots of wild things. You will ride again by the rising moon, then by the sun that soars higher to humble you with its fierce glare. You ride and ride and ride. Grass gives way to cactus. The coyote skulks in the distance, an amber-eyed trickster. The hawk dives at twilight and the young cottontail screams his death song. You camp at a pond where a flock of redwing blackbirds flies as if possessed of a single mind, rattling as it plunges at once into a tangle of reeds and tules. You listen to the low moan of bullfrogs and contemplate how a frog ever arrived here, at this isolated pool — perhaps as an egg stuck to the leg of a heron.

You wake early and ride. Finally, in the distance, like a great hazy vision, you see the massive purple shoulders of the Guadalupe Range begin to materialize, and your heart leaps.

You give thanks for your delivery, in spite of the very real prospects of battle, torture, and death. You have ridden well and arrived sound. Now you must accomplish a task that you have come to think of as well-nigh impossible. You will do it, or die.

You can keep up with Mike and his band on www.MikeBlakely.com.

Walter Prescott Webb

(1888-1963)

I never had the pleasure of meeting Walter Prescott Webb, but I have heard much about him from friends who knew him. Friends like John Henry Faulk and Cactus Pryor.

Mr. Webb and I do have one other tie. When I got my B.S. (lots of it) from UT, I was also certified as a secondary sciences teacher. I taught ninth grade physics at Walter Prescott Webb Junior High in Austin.

Walter Prescott Webb was the philosopher portion of the Texas Triumvirate. Along with J. Frank Dobie and Roy Bedichek, they formed a small think tank. They would meet regularly at the beautiful Barton Springs pool, in Austin's Zilker Park. A statue of the three now stands at their old meeting place by the pool, beneath the magnificent shade trees.

Webb was a philosopher-historian. Dobie was the folklorist storyteller. Roy Bedichek was a gifted naturalist and environmentalist. When you study the works of these three intellectuals, you will see the growing influence of the others on each of them.

They would vehemently argue issues based on conviction and respect. New concepts were hatched and old ones refined in numerous intellectual disciplines. Beneath the shade trees they discussed the various aspects of life on this planet and where people fit into nature—in particular, how we fit into Texas nature.

Webb was born on a farm in Panola County, Texas, on April 3, 1888, the son of Casner P. and Mary Elizabeth (Kyle) Webb. Webb's father was a schoolteacher and farmer.

The family had originally moved to Texas from Aberdeen, Mississippi. They first moved to Caledonia, located in Rusk County. Later they moved into the Panola area of far East Texas.

That region of the state made a strong negative impression on Webb. Life there was rough and boring and didn't sit well with him. Looking for some way out, he sent a letter to the editor of a literary magazine, the *Sunny South*, asking how he could become a writer. Amazingly, William Hinds, a toy manufacturer in New York, got his letter and responded. Hinds encouraged young Webb to keep his sights on "lofty goals."

Keeping this advice in mind, Webb finished high school in Ranger. He also earned a teaching certificate and taught at several small Texas schools. Webb and Mr. Hinds had remained in touch all these years. So when Webb decided to go to the University of Texas, Mr. Hinds assisted him.

At UT, at the age of twenty-seven, Walter Prescott Webb received his Bachelor of Arts degree in 1915. On September 16, 1916, Webb married Jane Elizabeth Oliphant. They had one daughter.

Teaching in high school did not offer Webb all the challenges, or compensation, that he needed. So he also worked at a variety of other jobs, including that of bookkeeper for Southwest Texas State Teachers College in San Marcos, and as an optometrist's assistant in San Antonio.

In 1918, while teaching at Main High School, Webb was invited to join the history faculty of the University of Texas. He enthusiastically jumped at the opportunity and began working on his master's degree as soon as he arrived.

In 1920, after receiving his master's, he was encouraged to seek a doctorate. In an effort to expand his educational base, he enrolled at the University of Chicago. This was the period Webb would later refer to as his year of "educational outbreeding."

He was very disappointed in what he found in Chicago, and he was also homesick for Texas. But his interest in history had been stimulated, and since he didn't like what others had done, he decided to write his own history books.

In 1931 his years of research and writing produced *The Great Plains*. It was acclaimed at the time as "a new interpretation of the American West." In 1939 the Social Science Research Council cited it as the most outstanding contribution to American history since World War I. The book was also the winner of Columbia University's Loubat prize.

Since he had not only done the research but had literally written the book on the subject, the University of Texas granted Webb a Ph.D. in 1932.

In 1939 Webb became director of the Texas State Historical Association. During his seven-year tenure, he expanded and improved their publication, *Southwestern Historical Quarterly*. Webb also decided to create an encyclopedia about Texas. Several years later, in 1952, the resulting document was published as the *Handbook of Texas*.

Over the years Webb took brief teaching positions away from the University of Texas. In 1942 he was the Harmsworth Professor of American History at Oxford University.

Great educators often develop new ways to look at the available information. In this way Webb became famous for his books and seminars on the Great Plains and the Great Frontier. In them he developed two major new historical concepts.

In the Great Plains thesis he stated that the westward settlement of the United States had been briefly stalled at the ninety-eighth meridian, a point of demarcation separating the wooded environment to the east from the arid environment of the west. Technology soon provided them with the answers they needed, in the form of the six-shooter, barbed wire, and the windmill. With these advances in hand, they could proceed with much improved chances of success in this rough territory.

His second insight, the Great Frontier thesis, was published in his book of the same title, in 1952. Many consider this to be Webb's most insightful and intellectually stimulating theory.

In *The Great Frontier* Webb proposed a "boom hypothesis." It goes this way: The new lands discovered by Columbus and other explorers in the late fifteenth century precipitated the rise of great wealth and new institutions such as democracy and capitalism. But by 1900 the new lands had disappeared, the frontier had closed, and institutions were under stress, resulting in the ecological and economic problems that have plagued the twentieth century.

Historians are not in agreement about this theory. They split over the concept, and for many years serious debates have raged. In 1972, eleven years after his death, an international symposium was held to further discuss this theory.

In all, Webb wrote or edited more than twenty books. Here is a brief look at some of the most prominent ones.

In 1935 he published *The Texas Rangers: A Century of Frontier Defense*, a study of frontier law enforcement by the rangers. Though well received by others, Webb was his own harshest critic. He said the book was filled with "a large collection of deadening facts."

Divided We Stand: The Crisis of a Frontierless Democracy (1937) analyzed the practices of corporations, which Webb contended promoted economic sectionalism to the disadvantage of the southern states.

More Water for Texas: The Problem and the Plan (1954) was a labor of love for Webb. He was a founding father of the conservation movement in Texas. Even then he realized that water would be the critical resource in the future. So it is no coincidence that he and J. Frank Dobie and Roy Bedichek met at Barton Springs whenever possible.

He also published a collection of his essays, *An Honest Preface, and Other Essays*, in 1959.

When he wasn't fostering the development of historical or conservation programs in Texas, he was often dealing with philosophical issues. In that capacity he was one of the charter members and later a fellow of the Texas Institute of Letters. He was also a member of the Philosophical Society of Texas.

At times Webb served as president of both the Mississippi Valley Historical Association (1954-55) and the American Historical Association (1958).

Webb received honorary degrees from the University of Chicago, Southern Methodist University, and Oxford University in England.

He held two Guggenheim fellowships and acted as special advisor to Senator Lyndon Baines Johnson on water needs of the South and West. He received a $10,000 award from the American Council of Learned Societies for distinguished service to scholarship. The United States Bureau of Reclamation also gave him an award for distinguished service to conservation.

On June 28, 1960, Webb's wife, Jane, died. They had been married for forty-four years. They had one daughter. On December 14, 1961, Webb married Terrell (Dobbs) Maverick. She was the widow of F. Maury Maverick, of San Antonio.

Walter Prescott Webb was killed in an automobile accident near Austin on March 8, 1963. He was buried in the Texas State Cemetery by proclamation of Governor John B. Connally. At the time of his death, Webb was working on a television series on American civilization, with a grant from the Ford Foundation.

Observations by Walter Prescott Webb

Here are a few quotes, attributed to Webb, that were shared with me over the years.

"So far as I have been able to find, there is scarcely a hint of humor, hardly a particle of wit in whole libraries of history books." (To that I say, AMEN. I was halfway through college before I ever had an interesting history class!)

He told John Henry Faulk, "Young historians should study my career. It will give them a lot of pointers on what they shouldn't do!"

About being elected president of the Historical Society, "This is one of the most improbable accidents in the history of the profession."

Additional Info: Walter Prescott Webb Historical Society academic.dt.uh.edu/~smith042/.

Abbott, Texas

On Interstate Highway 35, ten miles south of Hillsboro, is the exit for the beautiful little farm community of Abbott. The town of Abbott, named for Jo Abbott, was founded as a railroad town on the Missouri, Kansas and Texas line in 1881. In 1882 the first Abbott post office was established. It served the town until 1928.

In the late 1800s the town grew as cotton became the prominent crop of the South. Half a century later those very same cotton fields would become the learning grounds for a legendary Texan.

During that period the city prospered with two cotton gins, a gristmill, and a wide variety of other professional and commercial businesses. Three churches were also established at this time.

The Abbott school system was founded in the mid-1880s. By 1929 the school district had been fully accredited through the eleventh grade.

Most construction of that period was all wooden. Towns had not developed construction codes requiring fire breaks between town buildings. As a result Abbott had three major fires in 1897, 1903, and 1904. After each catastrophe, the town was rebuilt, a little more carefully each time.

In 1913 life in Abbott changed completely with the arrival of electricity. Electric power for the city was a by-product of the arrival of the Electric InterUrban Railway. In combination with the Katy, the InterUrban transported people and products over two hundred miles of tracks, connecting several towns throughout north central Texas.

Downtown Abbott, Texas.

Abbott finally incorporated in 1916 and a couple of years later started construction of a highway through town, parallel to the railroad line. The highway was completed in 1920.

Like most of America, the Great Depression hit Abbott hard. The steady decline in business resulted in Abbott being dropped as a regular train stop. However, they could flag it down if needed.

This area of Texas was settled predominantly by Czech farmers. One of my favorite towns in the area is West. I always stop there on my way to and from Dallas because they have a great selection of kolaches (the wonderful Czech pastry). Until a few years ago the town newspaper was still in Czech. (I know because I bought one before realizing we had translation issues.)

In the 1990 census the population of Abbott was 314. This typically quiet small Texas town was a good place to grow and learn a lot about life. Our next legend used his incredible talent to translate all these experiences into his art.

Abbott City Hall.

Willie

WANTED
Photo courtesy of Aaron Allan.

It's after midnight, and this book manuscript is due to my publisher in just a few days. I have decided that Willie Nelson is a writer's nightmare. Despite the looming deadline, I can't find the right title for this chapter. How do you capture a phenomena like Willie in a couple of words? (No wonder so many writers are drinkers!)

The Reverend Horton Heat had his own title for Willie, when he said, "No matter who holds the deed, Willie owns the land. He's the King of Texas!"

It is understandable that folks feel that way. But "King Willie" doesn't seem to fit this truly humble, helpful, self-deprecating man.

Poodie Locke, Willie's longtime stage manager, puts a different spin on it: "Willie Nelson is the King of the common man."

In Texas there are times when you only need to use one word to convey your meaning. The Thump (Luling Watermelon Thump), Molly (Ivins), Waylon (Jennings), and Willie. And now it is obvious, the only title needed is "Willie."

Texans have followed the life and career of our native son with pride and confusion for many decades. Pride, because of his towering talent in so many areas. Confusion, because he is so talented in so many areas that we aren't sure how to describe him or what he will be doing next. So we just say "Willie," and everyone nods and smiles.

There is another indicator of the diversity of Willie's talent and diverse abilities. No matter where I've been, I've never heard anyone ask, "Do you like Willie's music?"

It's a silly question, because Willie has done so many wonderful types of music that everybody likes something of his. The question that is asked is, "What is your favorite Willie song?" Whatever you like, Willie has probably done a whole album of it. He has done country, jazz, soul, gospel, cow jazz, pop, big band, reggae, and lots of music that falls in between these groups.

Another problem with writing Willie's biography is that he has reached such a mythical stature that it has become more and more difficult to separate fact from myth. There is never a question of having enough material to write an interesting chapter on Willie. (He has been very good about providing plenty of humorous items for fans and writers throughout his career.) The only questions are which material to use and which of it is true. (I'm reminded of the

Cherokee observation that "All stories are true, even the ones that haven't happened.")

I first met Willie in Austin, back in his "Willie who?" days, in the mid-sixties. He was living in Nashville, beginning to make some waves as a songwriter. But he never lost touch with his Texas roots or his hundreds of Texas musician friends. Everyone in Austin music was hustling to find a gig (some things never change!). We crossed paths a couple of times at places like the Chequered Flag and the Split Rail. We were finally introduced at the old Plantation restaurant (about the only place in Austin that stayed open all night).

I was a tall skinny kid, six foot four and one forty five. I felt fat when I first saw Willie. He was rail thin, but not that emaciated, ninety-eight-pound-weakling type of thin. No, Willie was a work-ing-on-the-farm-wiry kind of thin. His skin color was pale with red highlights, the blue eyes took everything in, and the fingers were heavily callused. One look told me that this was a full-time musician.

Let me explain that. Most musicians have day jobs, to pay the bills, to take care of their habits, like eating. These jobs always take place in the daylight (to keep their nights free to perform). The result is that they get a little bit of a tan. However, most full-time musicians don't come out in the daytime, unless it's absolutely nec-essary (like to buy new guitar strings). They come out in the evening, play sets off and on till after midnight, then go meet other musicians somewhere and jam, showing off their new licks and shar-ing what they've learned. "The life" can be lots of fun, but not a lot of sunlight!

Like everyone else, I was drawn to Willie. His easy, approachable manner made him easy to talk to. If you had asked us then, we could have told you that Willie was something special. Although none of us could agree on why, it was obvious to everyone that this talented man was going to make a big mark on the music industry.

And then there was his "sound"—the soothing, comfortable quality of Willie's voice and guitar. Some musicians assault you with a barrage of sound, confusing loud music with good music. Willie learned early that less can be more. Skillfully he brings the listener into the musical story he's telling.

And what wonderful stories he has told us! He has had well over a hundred successful albums. It's a running joke among his fans that if they have all of his albums, they don't have room left for much else.

That night at the Plantation, I don't recall specifics of what was said. There was just an overriding feeling that I had met a neat guy, and that someday I would look back on that night fondly. And I do.

Willie backstage at his 1999 4th of July Picnic. Photo courtesy of Aaron Allan.

I wish I could say I'm a close friend of Willie's. Although I've been told that he enjoyed my books, in fact I'm just an acquaintance and fan, one of millions. We crossed paths for a few years back then. But most of the time I just observed him, in awe of this talented musician and songwriter. I was really a songwriter at heart, and much of that awe was for Willie's ability to tell a story that people can easily relate to, in a very few words. Try it sometime.

Only a few songwriters have written songs that have consistently touched me in the way that Willie has. Kris Kristofferson, Harry Chapin, Steven Fromholz, Tim Henderson, Allen Damron, Aaron Allan, and Bobby Bridger immediately come to mind.

So, where did all of Willie's ability come from?

You've read the story of Abbott, Texas. It is no more remarkable than a hundred other small Texas towns. Yet, from this quiet community came a songwriter, singer, musician, actor, and storyteller, all rolled into one, Willie Nelson. And his very talented band member, sister, singer, songwriter, and great musician, Bobbie Lee Nelson.

What was it about that small community that allowed Willie to explore his talents? With self-deprecating humor, Willie says, "I was dumb enough to think I could do anything. And I was lucky enough to do lots of 'em." (More about "Luck" later.)

Let's just start with the basic facts about Willie's background:

Willie Hugh Nelson was born in Fort Worth, Texas, on April 30, 1933, to Ira and Myrle Nelson. But he did all of his growing up in the little farm community of Abbott. Family circumstances resulted in Willie being raised by Ira's parents. He only had one sibling, a sister, Bobbie Lee.

Music was always a part of the Nelson household. The family was deeply into church activities and the associated gospel music. But the family also listened to the radio whenever possible and kept the phonograph spinning. The music available was mostly country, with some jazz, big band, western swing, and even the blues. Even at this young age, Willie was particularly fascinated by the DJs on the radio shows (more about that later). Willie had a good eye for quality even then, because his favorite was Bob Wills.

First signs of his ability as an entertainer came in the form of a public performance at the age of four, when Willie recited a poem he had written, at a church picnic. Encouraged by what he saw, Daddy Nelson bought Willie his first guitar, a Sears and Roebuck Stella, at the age of six. As Willie would later put it, "Then I started putting melodies to all those poems I had written."

Willie and Bobbie learned music through mail-order courses taught to them by their grandparents. By the age of ten, Willie had started performing as part of a polka band.

Willie's school years had a profound influence on his artistry today. He soaked up whatever music he heard. He learned Latin rhythms and about Corridas from his fellow workers in the fields. Willie learned to appreciate the Big Band era performers like the Mills Brothers, Andrews Sisters, Frank Sinatra, and Hoagy Carmichael.

During these years, Willie later explained, "I loved listening to the radio. I knew early on that I wanted to be involved with the music business. Being a DJ seemed like the greatest job in the world. During that time, one of the folks I aspired to be like was Aaron Allan. I really liked what he was doing, with the deejaying, songwriting, and singing. I also listened to the Grand Ole Opry out of Nashville, on WSM, and I listened to WLS out of Chicago." During his teen years Willie played a lot of honky-tonk music with folks like Bud Fletcher.

After a brief tour in the U.S. Air Force, Willie set his sights on getting a job as a DJ. He submitted applications to several stations, particularly KBOP in Pleasanton. He was particularly interested in working there, because it would give him a chance to work with someone he had admired for years, Aaron Allen.

As fate would have it, Aaron got a job offer and left KBOP to go work at WOAI in San Antonio. So they never worked together. But Aaron leaving KBOP was good news for Willie, because he was hired to replace Aaron.

Willie really hit the road when he left KBOP and went to Vancouver, Washington, where he deejayed for KVAN. During that time his mom was living in nearby Eugene. While at KVAN, Willie built up a following of listeners.

Convinced by his fans that there was a market for his music, in 1956 Willie self-financed his first recording. It was done in the basement of an acquaintance's home. The A-side was "No Place For Me," and on the back was "Lumberjack." The record caught on with his radio listeners well enough to convince Willie that he "might have a future in music."

In 1960 Willie visited Nashville. He was hanging out at Tootsie's Orchid Lounge with other songwriters including Hank Cochran, Mel

Tillis, Roger Miller, and Kris Kristofferson (how's that for a cast of characters?). After talking about the business with these talented folks, Willie decided that Nashville was where he needed to be. So in 1960 he moved there.

By 1962 Willie was married to his second wife, singer Shirley Collie. Together they did two Top 10 duets, "Willingly" and "Touch Me." Shortly after that came his first number one hit, Faron Young's version of "Hello Walls." Other hits soon followed, including "Crazy" (Patsy Cline) and "Nightlife" (Ray Price).

Hits came and went for Willie. The life of a successful songwriter in Nashville isn't the good life. As he would later put it, *"Picking up hookers instead of my pen, I let the words of my youth fade away."*

By December 1970 Willie was so depressed that he just lay down on a Nashville street one night, hoping that a car would run over him! In his despair he had just completed a song called "What Can They Do To Me Now?"

The following night, December 23, 1970, the path of American music was forever altered when Willie's house in Ridgetop, Tennessee, burned down. The fire was a shock, and it forced Willie to take stock of his life. It was then that a homesick Willie packed up his family and band and returned to Texas.

Earlier in the book we discussed how the late sixties in Austin had been a melting pot of talent and diverse musical styles. Willie wanted to be doing more than "pure country" music, and he felt that Austin was more open to his new ideas than the Nashville establishment. And he was very right.

Music was evolving and growing. Elvis, the Beatles, folk music, and other genre were all being felt by the listeners, but not by the country music establishment in Nashville. They actually began to entrench themselves, "guarding" country music against these "outside influences."

Willie's move quickly paid dividends when *Shotgun Willie* came out in 1973, for Atlantic Records. Next came *Red Headed Stranger*, the 1975 album with the blockbuster hit "Blue Eyes Crying in the

Rain." Suddenly, from outside the establishment, one of country music's top stars was producing smash albums that didn't conform to Nashville's thinking.

Simplicity was one of the key ingredients to this new sound. Willie preferred simple instrumentation. Often he recorded in small, simple studios that didn't have that "polished professional sound" but did have "a warm homey sound" that the people loved. This is something Willie continues to do. He laughs about driving the sound engineers at the recording studios crazy. Instead of hooking up mics on both his guitar and his voice, "I'll just have one mic, play the gui-tar acoustically, and let the guitar run through the voice mic." Simplicity.

Though Willie was always looking at, and liking, different types of music, it was the country music folks who "kept the light on" for him. His albums were "different" from typical country tunes. But once they got over the initial surprise, they found they loved the stories, melodies, Willie's down-home song lyrics, and of course, Trigger.

No, not Roy Rogers' horse. Trigger the guitar.

Willie and Trigger perform at a Farm Aid concert.

Trigger and Snubnose

Willie only uses two guitars. His favorite is Trigger, a thirty-three-year-old Martin N-20. Willie bought it sight unseen in 1969 because he was in a bind. The Baldwin Company had given him an amp and a classical guitar with a three-cord stereo pickup. He liked the three-cord stereo pickup, but somehow he had "managed to beat that guitar up pretty bad."

Willie sent the busted guitar to his friend in Nashville, Shot Jackson. He hoped Jackson could repair it. No such luck. Too far gone.

"Shot, what else do you have around?" Willie asked.

"Well, Willie, I've got a Martin here on the shelf for only $750."

"Can you put the three-cord stereo pickup on it?"

"Yep."

"I'll take it."

It was a good deal, even if Willie was a thousand miles away, buying it sight unseen. As Willie puts it, "When I got it I knew that I had picked up something special. I like to just sit around in a room and play it. I just like the sound of it."

Why did Willie name his guitar Trigger? "Well, Roy Rogers had a horse named Trigger, and I figured "This is my horse!" Then he adds, "It has such a great tone!"

Today Trigger looks like it's been rode hard. It even has a big hole in it. But it still puts out a wonderful sound that meshes perfectly with its owner. Trigger is covered with over a hundred autographs of Willie's friends.

Trigger is now one of the most recognizable musical instruments in the world. Ranking up there with the likes of the legendary Stradivarius violins and B.B. King's life-saving guitar, Lucille.

The trials and travails of Trigger have paralleled those of Willie. Upon arriving at his burning home in Nashville, the one thing Willie made sure was rescued was Trigger.

Many years later, when Willie had a "little disagreement" with the IRS, his first concern was whether they would try to seize

Trigger. To prevent that from happening, Trigger took it on the lam and hid out at his manager's house until the heat died down.

The duo of Willie and Trigger continue to provide wonderful music today. Several songs on his most recent albums consist of just Willie and Trigger, no other accompaniment.

Trigger is so highly thought of in the industry, that the Martin company has produced the Willie Nelson Limited Edition N-20WN guitar.

Here's an interesting tidbit: When he was asked what type of strings he uses, Willie didn't know. One of his roadies, Tunin' Tom, takes care of keeping Trigger strung and tuned.

Snubnose is what Willie calls his other guitar. It is a semi-hollow electric model. He plays mostly blues numbers on it.

With Trigger's help, Willie put out four smash albums in the seventies. *Shotgun Willie*, *Phases and Stages*, *Red Headed Stranger*, and *Stardust* took over the country music charts and were soon showing up on the pop charts also.

Folks have fun at Willie's 4th of July Picnic.
Photo courtesy of Aaron Allan.

One of the most endearing things about Willie is that he never forgot about his roots. Farm life in Abbott wasn't left behind. It was out of his concern for the well-being of the farmers that he co-founded Farm Aid, a series of charity concerts for farmers in need of a hand. Willie donates a great deal of his time to a vast number of other worthwhile organizations.

No other musical artist has been successful in so many diverse forms of music. He is always looking for something new to learn about music. This new knowledge is soon incorporated into the process of reinventing himself. Which explains the huge diversity of musical genre that he has performed well in.

Luck, Texas

Earlier I mentioned that there would be some additional comments about Luck. In this case we are talking about the ghost town movie set that Willie owns in the Texas Hill Country just west of Austin. There are two streets in Luck on which there is a livery stable, a grocery store, a hotel, and a sheriff's office. Like most towns of that bygone era, the church and the saloon are on the opposite ends of town.

His movie *Red Headed Stranger* was filmed in Luck. Some installments of *Lonesome Dove* and *Dr. Quinn, Medicine Woman* were also filmed in Luck.

Willie does a lot of relaxing and even some recording in Luck. As he always puts it, "Either you are in Luck, or you're out of Luck!"

When he's "in Luck" Willie is normally in the saloon. It's not as bad as it sounds. The saloon is the only real building in the town; the rest are just movie prop facades. The bar isn't lined with bottles, but with CDs, a coffee maker, and memorabilia from years of music.

It's in the saloon that the family band gathers, including Jackie King (guitar), Paul English (drums), Bee Spears (bass), Bill English (percussion), Jody Payne (guitar and vocals), Mickey Raphael (harmonica), and of course Bobbie Lee Nelson, Willie's sister on piano.

It's in the back office of the saloon that Willie has his office and sometime recording studio. It was here, in the fairly tiny office, that his wonderful album *Rainbow Connection* was recorded.

One of the regulars at the saloon is a new friend of mine, Ben Dorcy. James White, owner of the Broken Spoke introduced Ben to me as "the oldest roadie in the world." I don't know about that, but Ben has been at it for a while. Over the years he has worked for John Wayne, Buck Owens, and many others. Ben just flashes a small smile and moves on.

Ben Dorcy "the world's oldest roadie" and James White, owner of the Broken Spoke. Ben stops by when he's not on tour with Willie.

It's only appropriate that this quiet western movie set would serve as the worldwide headquarters for the vast industry that is Willie Nelson. He has more professions than most people have pencils. There's the singing, songwriting, recording studio executive; Farm Aid executive; movie star; author; and he has just come out with his own liquor label. What's that you ask? Why it's Whiskey River whiskey, of course!

So what is Willie's average day like? Well he's sixty-nine, jogs five miles a day, plays 18 holes of golf, does shows that last two and a half hours, and then signs autographs until everyone who wants one, gets one, which normally takes about two hours!

Poodie Locke, always a wizard with the words, says, "Willie's an animal!"

Lisa Fletcher, who works at Willie's recording studio, told me she had been with him ten years and had never seen him as busy as he is today. He is currently on the road about 275 days a year, doing anywhere from 200-250 shows!

To get a great glimpse of Willie's daily life, check out his new book, *The Facts of Life and Other Dirty Jokes*, from Random House.

When asked about when he will retire, Willie laughs, "All I do now is play music and golf. Which one should I give up?"

Actually Willie has announced that he intends to retire...in about a dozen years!

Stories

Here are a couple of classic Willie stories. It was late one afternoon in the New Mexico desert, when two lovely young ladies (friends of mine) were flagged down by a harried and quite inebriated bus driver waving a map. He asked the girls if they knew where a particular town was. Taking the drunk driver's hand, they pointed it toward the other side of the map from where they were.

"Oh crap, that's five hundred miles! We're supposed to be on stage there in an hour! Are you sure we aren't near there?"

The girls assured the driver he wasn't anywhere near his destination.

"Oh well, we might as well just stay right here and have a party. Y'all are sure welcome to join us."

And so they did. It was a more trusting time, and they climbed on the bus, and much to their surprise, there sat Willie, Johnny Cash, and the band. The party was well under way, and let's just say that a good time was had by all.

Poodie Locke tells about the time in the seventies that they were all down in Peru, with Dennis Hopper. "Dennis ate about five pounds of mushrooms. He was as high as a hoot owl! So there's me and Willie trying to get Dennis down off the top of a telephone pole, and he's naked! Those were some wild times!"

Of course, there were some stories that I couldn't tell, like:

Oh Willwee, oh Willwee, oh Willwee!

You'll have to ask me about that one next time we get together.

So, here's to you, Willie.

Hang in there, partner, and thanks for taking us along with you on a wonderful ride!

Pictures Too Good to Leave Out

James Gramon (my son) sits with music legend Steven Fromholz
and Tom "The Rev" Heger. They are having breakfast at the fabled
Manchaca Fire Hall. May it stay open forever!

Rod Kennedy and Jim backstage at the Kerrville Folk Festival.

O'Henry Awards authors. Talk about a wild bunch of authors and friends!!!
(l-r) Joan Upton Hall, David Marion Wilkinson teasing
Lori Aurelia Williams, Lila Guzman, Bill Crawford, H.W. Bill Brands,
Jim, Spike Gillespie (poor Spike stayed cracked up, worried that I
was behind her!), Katherine Tanney, and Mike Blakely.

Larry Nye and Steven Fromholz perform while Linda Wiles, owner of the Too Damn Friendly Bar, emcees in scenic downtown Johnson City.

Jim and Liz Carpenter share reading materials at a book signing.

Les and Jo Virgil at the annual Austin Liars' Contest, held each February. It was Jo's great idea; she's the Barnes & Noble manager in West Lake.

The G-BATS (Getting Better All the Time), a wonderful singing group.
They sang at Liz Carpenter's roast. Liz is a founding member.

John Kelso, author and columnist at Jim's annual Austin Liars' Contest.

Doc Moore tells a biggun at the Austin Liars' Contest.
He was the winner of the fun February 2002 event.

Storytelling and Folklore Festival Calendar

Author's Note: The number of storytelling organizations and events is increasing every day. There are hundreds around Texas. Most of these are affiliated with some larger group, like the Tejas Storytelling Association. The following list is designed to put you in touch with the leading organizations that will provide you with the info you need to find the group nearest you.

My book *FUN Texas Festivals and Events* has over 1,600 events. If you know of an event that should be on this list, please email me at Jim@JimGramon.com and I will spread the word. Please note that this info has been collected from a wide variety of sources. I've done my best to verify the info, but occasionally things do change. So I urge you to always contact these organizations, and CALL BEFORE YOU GO.

See you there, Jim

January

EL PASO: Southwestern International Livestock Show & Rodeo This annual event is fun for the whole family. Events include horse shows, western gala, cattle drive, team roping championship, chili cookoff; also, Junior Livestock Show and Auction, a media rodeo, and a piglet roundup. Saddle up, partner! Location: El Paso County Coliseum. For information call: (915) 532-1401.

February

HOUSTON: Annual World Championship Bar-B-Que Cookoff Corporate and Go-Texas cookoff teams will feature the most creative in barbecue decor, with pits disguised as fire engines, covered wagons, airplanes, and waste disposal trucks, just to name a few. Live bands and other entertainment will be performing throughout the contest. This event is held in conjunction with the Houston Livestock Show & Rodeo. For information call (713) 791-9000, or go to www.hlsr.com.

HOUSTON: Houston Livestock Show and Rodeo Big city, big rodeo. World's largest stock show; live country music performances by the genre's biggest stars, and top-notch PRCA rodeo action in the comfort of the famous Astrodome. Parade, carnival, and barbecue cookoff, too. For more information call (713) 791-9000, or go to www.hlsr.com.

BROWNSVILLE: Charro Days Celebrated with a four-day Latin Festival each year since 1938, complete with elaborate costuming, carnivals, parades, dances. A program of events is held in both Brownsville, and its sister city, Matamoros, Mexico. This is a spectacular and colorful event with spectators and participants dressing up in traditional Mexican costume. Admission is free. For information call (956) 542-4245. This festival begins on the last Thursday in February.

TYLER: Squatty Pines Storytelling Festival Retreat with us to the East Texas piney woods on the shores of beautiful Lake Tyler for three days of stories, music, workshops, hayrides, fishing, hiking and more, all sponsored by the East Texas Storytellers, www.homestead.com/EastTexasTellers.

MERCEDES: South Texas Music Festival A three-day festival of country, bluegrass, folk, western, religious, mariachi, tejano, Mexican hat dance, folkloric dancers, and clogging held at the 130-acre Rio Grande Valley Show Grounds, http://www.music-fst99.com/.

ALPINE: The Annual Texas Cowboy Poetry Gathering This event is held on the campus of Sul Ross State University in the mountains of Texas, in the Big Bend Country. Poetry, music, storytelling, dancing, great food, and the Trappings of Texas are all a part of the second oldest cowboy gathering in the United States. As part of the gathering, Trappings of Texas will open in the Museum of the Big Bend. This fine western art and custom cowboy gear exhibit is the oldest in the United States and features the best of the best saddlemakers, braiders, silver engravers, artists, and more. Educational seminars on making gear and ranch history are all part of this exciting weekend. For more information call (915) 837-2326 or go to http://www.tourtexas.com/alpine/alpine.html.

March

EL PASO: Siglo De Oro Drama Festival Location: Chamizal National Memorial, 800 S. San Marcial, El Paso. In its 27th year, this festival celebrates the literature and linguistic ties still shared by Spain and the border region of Mexico and the United States. The festival brings the best amateur and professional groups to the Chamizal stage, presenting works of the Spanish masters, both in English and Spanish. Participants come from as far away as Puerto Rico, Spain, and Jerusalem. Call: (915) 532-7273, ext. 102 or go to http://www.tourtexas.com/elpaso/el-paso.html.

DENTON: Tejas (Texas) Storytelling Festival The last weekend in March, the festival is held in Denton's Civic Center Park. See www.tejasstorytelling.com for more information.

DALLAS: Annual North Texas Irish Festival Location: Fair Park, Dallas, Texas. In early March this two-day festival provides top entertainers, nonstop music, and dance on multiple stages; North Texas Step Dancing Fiesta; storytellers; street performers; cultural events & exhibits; Irish food and beverages; vendors; Urchin Street Faire for the kids; parade of Celtic dogs; workshops and much more. Info: (214) 821-4174 or go to http://www.tourtexas.com/dallas/dallas.html.

AUSTIN: Star of Texas Fair and Rodeo Cost: $5 to park, $3 to enter gate. Rodeo tickets serve as a gate pass. Location: Travis County Exposition and Heritage Center, Austin, Texas. For info call (512) 467-9811. Held annually every March.

GLEN ROSE: North Texas Longhorn Show Come and see Texas longhorns up close when top breeders of North Texas meet to display one of the oldest breeds of Texas cows. Cost: Free. Location: Expo Center, Hwy 67, Glen Rose, Texas. For more info call the Expo Center at (254) 897-4509.

GLEN ROSE: Snaketales Learn about the myth and magic of these resplendent reptiles at a day of snake presentations by the Herp Society and other friends of snakes. Enjoy storytelling, demonstrations, fun and facts...all for the snake's sake. Snaketales activities are included in your admission to Fossil Rim Wildlife Center. Cost: $ call for admission. Location: Hwy. 67, Glen Rose, Texas. For more info call (254) 897-2960.

WINEDALE: Annual Winedale Spring Festival and Texas Crafts Exhibition Features Texas contemporary craftspeople, as well as demonstrations of traditional crafts, music, dancing, and a barbecue. Winedale is near Round Top, Texas. Telephone (409) 278-3530.

DALLAS: Texaspride Celebration Features recording artists, Mexican dancers, Comanche storyteller, Buffalo Soldiers, Texas Rangers, historical exhibits, and much more. Hall of State, Fair Park. Call (214) 426-1959.

FORT MCKAVETT: Annual Living History Day Features infantry and cavalry drills by reenactors. Fort McKavett State Historic Park. Call (915) 396-2358 for more information.

CORPUS CHRISTI: Spring Round-Up Celebration of Ranching Heritage in Aransas County Includes cowboy poetry and song, reenactments, food, and demonstrations. Also features a special ranching heritage exhibit at the Fulton Mansion. Call (361) 729-0386 for information.

SAN FELIPE: Annual Colonial Texas Heritage Festival Features reenactments, Buffalo Soldiers, crafts, food, and historic tours. Stephen F. Austin State Historic Park. (409) 885-3613.

GOLIAD: Annual Goliad Massacre Reenactment Recreation of the occupation of Fort Defiance by Col. Fannin and the massacre, followed by a memorial service and pilgrimage to the Fannin Memorial. Presidio La Bahia. (361) 645-3563.

DENTON: Texas Storytelling Festival Features storytellers from across the country, includes ghost stories, bilingual, and children's concerts. Civic Center Park. Call (940) 387-8336 or (972) 991-8871.

GLEN ROSE: Bluegrass Jamboree at Oakdale Park Our Bluegrass Jamboree four-day program runs rain or shine. Stage show starts at 6:15 p.m. on Thursday, with a planned program of bands, and runs until 12:15 p.m. Sunday. Informal jam sessions are scattered throughout the park. For the early birds, the pickin' and grinnin' starts the weekend before the show. Come early and stay late. Cost: $11. Location: Oakdale Park, Glen Rose, Texas. For more information call Oakdale Park (254) 897-2321.

April

GLEN ROSE: Larry Joe Taylor's Texas Music Festival This year it is in Meridian; last year it was a three-day gathering of 3,000 fans in Glen Rose, along the banks of the Brazos. This collection of cookers, storytellers, and pickers featured a chili cookoff, songwriters showcase, and lots of storytelling around the many campfires. Go to http://www.larryjoetaylor.com/ for more information.

SAN ANTONIO: Fiesta San Antonio One of America's truly great festivals, Fiesta San Antonio is a ten-day celebration held for more than 100 years in April to honor the memory of the heroes of the Alamo and the Battle of San Jacinto and to celebrate San Antonio's rich and diverse cultures. One of the special parts of Fiesta is the multicultural conference. This year's conference will focus on the use of images by writers, photographers, artists, etc. to define a cultural and/or ethnic community. For more information call 1-877-SAFIESTA (723-4378) or go to http://www.fiesta-sa.org/default2.asp.

POTEET: Poteet Strawberry Festival This festival is recognized as the largest agricultural fete in Texas. The 95-acre site is located on Hwy. 16, 20 minutes south of San Antonio. The festival includes ten areas of continuous family entertainment, featuring concerts with nationally known country & western and tejano stars, dancers, gunslingers, clowns, puppets, regional bands, storytelling, various contests, and rodeo acts. Held annually during the second weekend in April. For info call (830) 742-8144.

JOHNSON CITY: Cowboy Songs and Poetry This annual gathering of cowboys at the Johnson Settlement presents lighter moments of the Old West. At the cabin where President Johnson's grandparents lived and ran a cattle business, modern cowboys meet to sing traditional songs, talk about the old days in poetry, and spin tales the equal of any that were told when the west was really wild. This is 1860s entertainment you can't afford to miss. Time: 1 p.m. to 4 p.m. Cost: free. Location: Lyndon B. Johnson National Historical Park, Johnson Settlement, Johnson City, Texas.

HARLINGEN: RioFest Fair Park will host RioFest's annual celebration of the arts, a 21st-century renaissance! RioFest has
been voted the "Best Family Festival" in Cameron County for
the past four years. RioFest is the premiere educational arts and
cultural event of the Rio Grande Valley and Northern Mexico.
As part of its air of festivity, the festival will provide a rich variety of performing arts, cultural arts, family and children's
activities. RioFest is held in Harlingen's 40-acre Fair Park. For
more information call (956) 425-2705. Held in April, usually the
2nd or 3rd weekend, depending on Easter.

HUMBLE: Good Oil Days Festival Festival blending art and oil,
entertainment and education, history and destiny into a
three-day celebration. A 50-acre site will depict Humble's oil
boomtown in the early 1900s, offering a view of the oil and gas
industry—its beginnings, its evolution, and its destiny in the
new millennium. Educational displays, exhibits, 400+ vendors,
a spectacular carnival, go-karts, live entertainment, auto shows,
beer pavilion, fireworks, and fabulous food. Location: one mile
east of Hwy. 59 on Will Clayton Blvd. For info call (281)
446-2128. Held annually in April.

WAXAHACHIE: Scarborough Faire, Renaissance Festival
Scarborough Faire is one of the largest and most popular
Renaissance Festivals in the nation, complete with entertainment, crafts, food, drink, games, and fun! Join the festivities as
hundreds of prominent entertainers perform, over 200 artisans
display and demonstrate their craft, and food and beverage vendors offer a delicious variety of over 60 menu items fit for a
king. For ticket information and directions refer to Scarbor-
oughRenFest.com.

**KERRVILLE: Annual Kerrville Easter Festival and Chili
Classic** Saturday events include a walkathon for youth,
cookoffs, 5K Easter Run, armadillo races, Easter egg hunt, chili

judging, 4x4 bed post derby. Other events include washer pitching tournament and children's activities. Location: Schreiner College Campus, Hwy 27E, Kerrville, TX. For more information call (830) 792-3535. Annual event held Easter weekend.

EULESS: Arbor Daze For fifteen years the city of Euless has sponsored this festival. Arbor Daze was selected as a White House Millennium Event, which receives special recognition from the president of the United States. Arbor Daze offers nightly musical entertainment from favorite oldies acts and has various opportunities during the day such as arts and crafts, business exposition, plant sale, tree giveaway, concerts, youth community stages, specialty foods and much more. The Arbor Daze Festival has won numerous awards (for a list check out their website). Location: Bear Creek Parkway and Fuller Wiser Road. For info call (817) 685-1821, or go to www.ci.euless.tx.us. Held annually the fourth weekend of April.

FREER: Freer Rattlesnake Round Up Join us at the Freer Cactus Corral, Freer, Texas, for the biggest party in Texas, featuring concerts with top artists. Fun for the whole family including carnival, parade, arts/crafts, stage shows, storytelling, daredevil snake show, fried rattlesnake meat, talent contest, and much more. For more info please call (512) 394-6891. Held annually the last weekend of April.

May

KERRVILLE: Cowboy Artists of America Roundup Annual "Art Stampede" show and sale. Cowboy Artists of America Museum. (830) 896-2553.

AUSTIN: Cinco de Mayo Festival: Lo Nuestro This event is a celebration of Hispanic culture featuring live country, tejano, mariachi, and conjunto music. Food, arts and crafts, game booths, plus the Mighty Thomas Carnival will provide family fun for everyone. Event location: Fiesta Gardens, 2101 Berg-man Ave., Austin. For more information: (512) 867-1999.

GRANBURY: Annual Old-Fashioned Fair Features pioneer demonstrations at the Hood County Senior Center. Call (817) 573-5548 or (800) 950-2212.

LAREDO: Annual Day Pow Wow Festival Features arts and crafts, inter-tribal dancing and more. Civic Center grounds. (956) 795-2080. Held annually on the second Saturday in May.

KERRVILLE: Kerrville Folk Festival Since 1972 the Kerrville Folk Festival has been held annually at the Quiet Valley Ranch, 9 miles south of Kerrville on Texas Hwy 16. Starting on the Thursday before Memorial Day at the end of May, the music and good times go on for 18 days with performances by more than 100 artists such as Peter Yarrow and Butch Hancock. Interspersed between weekends are other events including workshops in songwriting and booking and management for touring artists.

The annual **Kerrville New Folk songwriting competition** is held on the first weekend and draws some of the best of America's emerging songwriters. Award winners are recognized at a special concert on the second weekend. Bring your tent or RV and join us for as long as you can stay. The campgrounds abound with songwriters campfires, a favorite feature of the Kerrville Folk Festival since 1974. The Kerrville Folk Festival, P.O. Box 1466, Kerrville, TX 78029, (830) 257-3600 or email: info@kerrville-music.com.

FREDRICKSBURG: Founders Day Festival Mark your calendar and set your sites on beautiful Fredericksburg, Texas, as the Gillespie County Historical Society presents its annual Founders Festival. This festival celebrates the founding of Fredericksburg, May 1846. Focus of the festival is on local artisans, musicians, and vendors. There will be everything from sheep shearing, stone spitting, blacksmithing, and corn grinding to children's games, lots of great music, food, beer, and wine. This event coordinates with the Indian Pow Wow also going on in Fredericksburg the same weekend. For more info call (830) 997-2835 or e-mail gchs@ktc.com. Held annually on the second Saturday in May.

ATHENS: Uncle Fletch's Hamburger Cookoff and American Music Festival According to research by newspaper columnist and folk historian Frank X. Tolbert, the first hamburger was made by Fletcher Davis (known to Athenians as Uncle Fletch) at a cafe located on the square in downtown Athens. The people in Athens are proud of their history and celebrate this great occasion the second Saturday of May with a hamburger cookoff, food vendors, exhibits, a children's area, local artists, a battle of the bands, and an antique car show for an entertaining day. For more information contact the Athens Chamber of Commerce at (903)-675-5181 or e-mail Athenscc@flash.net. Held annually the second Saturday of May.

PASADENA: Annual Pasadena Strawberry Festival The Pasadena Strawberry Festival will celebrate its annual event at the Pasadena Fairgrounds, with continuous live entertainment, strawberries, arts & crafts, children's games, carnival rides, enormous variety of foods, beauty pageants, specialty acts, commercial exhibits, barbecue cookoff, demonstrations by various craftsmen, the State Mud Volleyball Championship Tournament, the "World's Largest Strawberry Shortcake," and MUCH, MUCH, MORE!! Proceeds from the festival funds scholarships, books for college libraries, and community projects that preserve and promote the study of Texas history. For more information, visit http://www.tourtexas.com/pasadena/strawberryfest.html or call (281) 991-9500. Held the third weekend in May.

MARSHALL: Stagecoach Days Festival Join us as we celebrate our history through home tours, parades, arts and crafts, and reenactments. For more information call Phyllis Prince at (903) 935-7868, or visit http://tourtexas.com/marshall/. Held annually the third weekend in May.

CEDAR PARK: Cedar Chopper Festival The Cedar Chopper Festival is in its 27th year. The festival is a one-day event held on the 3rd Saturday of May. Included in this year's events are: arts & crafts, three stages of music, storytelling and performing arts from around Texas, cedar carving demonstrations, Boy Scout Jamboree, Austin steam train rides, many kids rides and events, classic cars and motorcycles, and a health fair. The festival is alcohol free until 5 p.m. Beer sales begin at 5 p.m., with two bands playing blues and country until 12 midnight. For info call (512) 260-4260.

MCKINNEY: Mayfair Art Festival Join us on the historic downtown McKinney square. Fabulous parade kicks off Mayfair, Sat. 10 a.m. Fine artists pavilion hosts artists from three states. Maypole dancing like you've never seen. ArtCars on exhibit, two stages of entertainment, storytelling festival, carnival, over 100 vendors, great food, petting zoo, train rides, ponies, great fun for the entire family centered around the fine shopping of downtown McKinney. Event details and discount lodging, (972) 562-6880. For more information (972) 562-6880. Held annually the third weekend in May.

KOUNTZE: Southern Gospel & Bluegrass Gospel Singing Join the fun of singing the old southern gospel songs as you remember your parents and grandparents singing. We will start at 4 p.m. and end much later. Spend Memorial Day weekend with us and let's have a great time. For more information call (409) 246-2508.

June

SAN ANTONIO: Texas Folklife Festival For more than thirty years folks have gathered for the Texas Folklife Festival. The participants come from every corner of the state representing 43 cultural and ethnic groups, who will share their traditional dances, ethnic dishes, music, stories, and hand-made treasures, and exhibit products typical of the land from which their ancestors came.

The Festival is presented by the Institute of Texan Cultures as an extension of its role as a statewide educational center. For more festival information call (210) 458-2390 or check out their website at http://www.texancultures.utsa.edu/new/tff/tff-press.htm.

LOCKHART: Chisholm Trail Roundup & Kiwanis Rodeo For years folks have enjoyed this four days of fun for the whole family. Activities include two nights of professional rodeo, live entertainment, dances, a Kid's Fishing Derby, interactive outdoor displays, horseshoes, washers, carnival, arts, crafts, and food. Don't miss the Old Time Fiddlers contest and the Barbecue Capital of Texas Championship Cookoff and much more! Info: Lockhart Chamber of Commerce at (512) 398-2818, http://www.lockhart-tx.org/funstuff.html.

ARLINGTON: Texas Scottish Festival & Highland Games This is one of the largest ethnic festivals in North America. Featured are bagpipe bands, storytelling, athletics, children's events, food and drink, vendors, and crafts. Entertainment is continuous in the largest pub tent in the U.S.A. The all-weather festival site will once again be Maverick Stadium on The University of Texas at Arlington campus. For more information or for tickets, write to: Texas Scottish Festival & Highland Games: P.O. Box 151943, Arlington, TX 76015 or e-mail: TxScotFest@aol.com.

AMARILLO: Cowboy Roundup USA Annual celebration of cowboy and western heritage featuring the World Championship Chuckwagon Roundup and the Coors Ranch Rodeo. Kicks off with a cattle drive up downtown Amarillo's main street. Location: Tri-State Fairgrounds. For more information call the Amarillo Convention & Visitor Council at (806) 374-1497. Held annually the second week of June.

STANTON: Old Sorehead Trade Days Located halfway between Fort Worth and El Paso on I-20. Laid-back family atmosphere with entertainment, arts and crafts (400 vendors), antiques, historic tours, tradin' lot. Largest trade show in West Texas draws a crowd of 20,000. Free admission. For more information call (915) 756-2006.

FORT WORTH: Juneteenth Celebration This annual festival kicks off with a parade in downtown Fort Worth and day-long activities downtown, near the Fort Worth/Tarrant County Convention Center. For more information call: 1-800-433-5747.

LULING: Watermelon Thump Watermelon! It's fun. It's delicious. Some great storytellers always gather for this one. And it says, "summer!" like nothing else. Thousands enjoy this three-day outdoor festival honoring the nutritious, auspicious watermelon. Featuring a carnival, kiddie rides, arts & crafts, champion melon judging and auction, world champion seed spitting contest, rodeo, parade, car rally, melon eating contest, and more! Downtown Luling. For more information call (830) 875-3214.

EL PASO/JUAREZ: International Mariachi Festival El Paso Convention & Performing Arts Center, One Civic Center Plaza (downtown). The event is designed to capture the true identity of the Hispanic heritage and to promote mutual respect and understanding between cultures. The three-day event features mariachi groups, headline entertainment from Mexico, and excellent food and drink. It concludes with a Mariachi Mass. Call for times and admission: (915) 566-4066.

PECOS: Night In Old Pecos/Cantaloupe Festival A one-day event that takes place in the evening hours from 6 p.m. till midnight. The streets are blocked off and there is wide range of activities which include a street dance with live music and a variety of vendors. Cost: FREE. Location: downtown Pecos. For more info call (915) 445-2406. Held annually the last Saturday of June.

July

Tejas Storytellers Summer Conference
www.tejasstorytelling.com

STAMFORD: Texas Cowboy Reunion The classic events of the rodeo, including some unique to the TCR (wild cow milking, wild mare race) get underway nightly at the beautiful SMS ranch with the West Texas sunset playing backdrop to the authentic, rustic arena. Ranchers, cowboys, and those interested in western preservation return each year to the TCR Poetry Gathering to celebrate the history of the world's largest amateur rodeo and the unique qualities of the American cowboy. All of the material presented at the gathering must be authentic western verse presented by poets in authentic western attire. For information: Texas Cowboy Reunion, P.O. Box 928, Stamford, TX 79553 (915) 773-3614 or go to http://www.tcr-rodeo.com/index.htm.

SULPHUR SPRINGS: Independence Day Symphony on the Square Join us on the square in downtown Sulphur Springs for a celebration in old-fashioned style, a program of marches and patriotic favorites by the North East Texas Symphony Orchestra. When darkness falls the sky erupts in a blaze of colors as fireworks light up the sky over the historic Hopkins County Courthouse. Held annually the weekend of or just prior to

Independence Day. Admission: free; bring your lawn chair! For more info: (888) 300-6623.

LEVELLAND: Early Settlers Day Festival After more than 40 years, the Early Settlers Day Festival draws some 15,000 people to celebrate country, bluegrass, and tejano music performances, old settler activities, more than 50 food booths, games, horseshoes, activities for kids, and a parade that lasts an hour or more. Sponsored by the Levelland Area Chamber of Commerce. Location: Downtown Square, Avenue H. For more info call (806) 894-3157. Held annually the Saturday after July 4th.

McDADE: McDade Watermelon Festival This year McDade, Texas, will be celebrating its 55th annual McDade Watermelon Festival. Our community has approximately 300 residents and is located on Hwy. 290 East, 10 miles east of Elgin, Texas, and 30 miles east of Austin. Held annually every July.

EL PASO: VIVA! El Paso! Experience history in the picturesque outdoor McKelligan Canyon Amphitheater. In the top seven best attended outdoor dramas in the country, VIVA!'s legendary performances detail 400 years of Native American, Spanish, Mexican, and Western American peoples through traditional dance, original song, brilliant costumes, and stunning special effects. "If you go for no other reason, go to enjoy the superb costumes and choreography. It's simply dazzling." *Southern Living*, March 1999. Location: McKelligan Canyon Amphitheater, El Paso. For more information call (915) 565-6900. Outdoor musical performed annually from 1st weekend in June through August.

CLUTE: Great Texas Mosquito Festival Held the last weekend in July, this festival pays tribute to the Texas mosquito! Features include a mosquito legs lookalike contest, a mosquito calling contest, sharing of Texas mosquito stories, and any

number of excuses for a good time. Call (409) 265-8392 or go to
http://www.brazosport.cc.tx.us/~sbcvcb/Festivals.html.

UVALDE: Sahawe Indian Dancer's Summer Ceremonials The
Sahawe Indian Dancers, members of Boy Scout Troop and Ven-
ture Crew 181 from Uvalde, annually present their summer
ceremonials the last part of July. The fast moving colorful
dances of the Plains and Southwest Pueblo Indians are set
against a backdrop of teepees to set the mood for the performance. The 90-minute performances feature 16 to 18 different
dances that have thrilled audiences for almost 50 years. Location: Sahawe Outdoor Theater, one block south of U.S. 90. For
more information call (830) 278-2016. Held annually the last
weekend of July.

MEDINA: Texas International Apple Festival Held in Medina,
the Apple Capital of Texas, on Highway 16 on the banks of the
Medina River in a pecan orchard. We have great entertainment,
arts & crafts, food booths, clowns, children's area with a petting
zoo. We will have the San Antonio Chorale Society to sing, Jubilee Banjo Band, gospel stage, fiddlers contest, storytelling
stage, children's stage called the Johnny Appleseed Stage. For
more info call (830) 589-7224 or email mtdc@indian-creek.net.
Held annually the last weekend in July.

August

DALHART: XIT Rodeo and Reunion, Rita Blanca Park A
PRCA rodeo and a reunion for cowboys, most from the XIT
Ranch, which at one time was the largest ranch in Texas. Activities also include storytelling, dances, pony-express races, and
parades. Web site: http://www.dalhart.org/xitrodeo.html.

ROANOKE: Hawkwood Medieval Fantasy Faire Recreation of
a fictitious Medieval village based around the turn of the first
millennium (A.D. 1000). 100+ permanent shops. 10 stages with

continuous entertainment. Hundreds of village characters and entertainers. Real stunt show! Storytelling, music, dance, combat, comedy, drama, horse shows, games. We have both bawdy shows for the adults and play areas for the kids! Southeast corner of I-35W & SH 114, 20 miles north of Ft. Worth. For more information call 1-800-782-3629. Held annually, weekends mid-August through the end of September.

September

Voices in the Wind West Texas A&M University (Canyon, TX, just south of Amarillo) hosts "Voices in the Wind," a storytelling festival each September. The event includes special presentations for storytellers, teachers, librarians, parents, and children. Some of the events take place at the university, and others take place at the beautiful Palo Duro Canyon. For info contact West Texas A&M University, 2501 4th Avenue, Canyon, Texas 79016-0001, (806) 655-0675 or (806) 651-2000. Or email Douma at bluecorn_teller@hotmail.com.

WEST: Westfest A Czech folk festival with traditional storytelling, street dances, costumes and foods. Web site: http://www.westfest.com/westfest.html.

BANDERA: All American Cowboy Get-Together Come to Bandera—the Cowboy Capital of the World—and relive the Old West. Cowboy entertainers, poets, storytellers, chuck wagon cooks, and western vendors come together to create a true Old West experience. Trail ride and parade on Saturday morning. Cowboy Holy Eucharist on Sunday. Rodeo on Saturday evening. Location: Mansfield Park (three miles north of Bandera on Hwy. 16). For more information call (830) 796-3045 or (800) 364-3833. Held annually Saturday and Sunday of Labor Day weekend.

ARANSAS PASS: Official Shrimporee of Texas Great food (shrimp cooked in over 15 ways), continuous live entertainment (tejano, country & western, rock, and more). Over 150 arts and crafts booths, shrimp eating contest, carnival, parade, men's sexy legs contest, culinary tent including cooking demonstrations, children's entertainment, and much more. Location: Aransas Pass Community Park, Highway 361 and Johnson Ave. For more information call 1-800-633-3028. Annual event, generally held the second weekend in September.

ANAHUAC: Texas Gatorfest Held in Anahuac, the Alligator Capital of Texas, this truly unique festival combines the alligator, family, and good old-fashioned Texas two-stepping fun. A celebration of the alligator and its wetlands habitat, this festival has something for everyone. From the Great Texas Alligator Roundup to adult carnival and kiddie rides, arts and crafts, Texas artisans, and even airboat rides. Two stages of continuous entertainment along with street performers combined with over 25 food and drink booths serving a variety of fare including alligator prepared in an assortment of ways make for a bargain in family entertainment. Texas Gatorfest is located 45 miles east of Houston and 45 miles west of Beaumont, exit #810 off I-10 and travel 8 miles south on FM 563 to Fort Anahuac Park. For more information call (409) 267-4190. Held annually the weekend following the opening of alligator season, September 10.

DALLAS: State Fair of Texas Started in 1886, this event has something for everyone, fair, football game, exhibits, livestock show, and a great glimpse at Texas. Enjoy 24 days of nonstop food, fun, and entertainment. The State Fair is located in Fair Park in Dallas (about two miles east of downtown). For more information call (214) 565-9931, or visit the State Fair of Texas Homepage: www.bigtex.com or http://www.texfair.com.

October

FREDERICKSBURG: Oktoberfest Three big musical stages, 22 great German bands, 55 unique craft booths, and 18 tempting food vendors will greet visitors to the famous Oktoberfest this fall in Fredericksburg. Traditionally held the first weekend in October, this year's event gets underway on Marktplatz in downtown Fredericksburg. Music, food, and fun are the heart of this irresistible festival that celebrates Fredericksburg's German heritage. Oktoberfest is one event where the food and drink command center stage. Location: Downtown Market Square, Fredericksburg. For more info call (830) 997-4810.

TEMPLE: Early Day Tractor and Engine Association Annual Show The festival takes place on a 48-acre fairground near IH-35 in Temple. Watch as hundreds of antique tractors, engines, and farming implements demonstrate early day farming activities—from grain threshing to corn shelling, rope making, and water pumping. Enjoy delicious homemade ice cream, barbecue, and beans. Location: Exit 302 west on Nugent, right on Eberhardt. For more info call (254) 774-9988 or (254) 298-5720. Held annually the first full weekend in October.

REFUGIO: Refugio's Festival of the Flags Join us for a two-day festival celebrating our Native American culture on the downtown streets of Refugio. Enjoy a Native American pow wow, storytelling, demonstrations, art and craft booths, food booths, children's area, musical entertainment, volleyball and horseshoe tournaments, and historic homes tour (Sunday only for tour). No carnival or alcohol. For more info call (512) 526-2835.

ATHENS: Black-Eyed Pea Fall Harvest Events from the cookoff to the Miss Black-Eyed Pea Pageant, Miss Athens Pageant, and Little Miss Black-Eyed Pea Pageant. Gospel music, arts and crafts, square dancing, games for young and old, horseshoe tournament, a carnival, lots of food everywhere, participation sports including a joust, bass tournament, terrapin races, pea eatin' pea shellin', watermelon eatin', a pet show, and entertainment at the bandstand. Plus a lot more coming. For more information contact the Athens Chamber of Commerce at (903) 675-5181 or 1-800-755-7878.

KERRVILLE: Kerr County Fair Activities include chili and barbecue cookoff teams, stage entertainment featuring storytellers, bands, and performers, various contests including ugly hat and lovely legs, shoe box parade, pig scramble and goat milking, bull and barrel fest, team roping, petting zoo, carnival and midway, cowboy church, 5K run, talent contest, judged exhibits of crafts and skills, 75+ vendors selling wares and providing demonstrations, good food and plenty of beverages, judged livestock, scholarship pageant, classic car show, and a country auction. Located at the Hill Country Youth Exhibit Center on Hwy. 27 East adjoining the Guadalupe River, 60 miles northwest of San Antonio on IH-10. For more info call (830) 257-6833. Held annually the second weekend in October.

MARSHALL: Fire Ant Festival Our Fire Ant Festival is on the wild and wacky side, with its Rubber Chicken Chunking Contest, Fire Ant Calling (are you getting the feel for this one?), and other zany activities. For more information please call Phyllis Prince at (903) 935-7868, or visit http://tourtexas.com/marshall/. Held annually the second weekend in October.

GREENVILLE: Cotton Jubilee This annual festival salutes cotton, the fiber that weaves together our local history, and is a great weekend getaway filled with a variety of exciting events and activities for the entire family. Enjoy the arts & crafts show, business expo, health fair, Civil War encampment, cotton exhibits, children activities and entertainment, bike rally, bed races,

bingo, static displays, kids product show, 42 domino tournament, and live entertainment. Saturday's special event includes
a German Fest hosted by Knights of Columbus. Food and drink
concessions will be available all weekend. Free admission. Location: American Cotton Museum, located on the north frontage
road, off I-30, between exits 94 and 95. For more information
please contact the Greenville Chamber at (903) 455-1510, visit
http://www.greenville-chamber.org, or e-mail: jubilee@green-
ville-chamber.org. Held annually the third weekend in October.

PALESTINE: Hot Pepper Festival It's the hottest little festival
in Texas. Starts the day off with a parade and ends with a street
dance. In between enjoy arts and crafts and food booths, children's activities, classic car show entertainment on three
stages, quilt show, Macho Man pepper eating contest, chili
cookoff, salsa contest, Tour de Pepper bike tour and a whole lot
more. For more information please call 1-800-659-3484. Held
annually on the fourth Saturday in October.

FREDERICKSBURG: Fredericksburg Food & Wine Fest A
celebration of Texas food and wine. The Fredericksburg Food &
Wine Fest is in its 9th year. A full-course celebration of Texas
food, wine, music, arts & crafts, food court, and fun is expected.
Musical entertainment includes polka, jazz, blues, ethnic and
German oompah! Don't miss the grape stomping, cork tossing,
and other games that are also on the agenda, including the
Great Grape Toss and a fabulous auction. Location: downtown
Fredericksburg, on Market Square. For more information call
(830) 997-8515.

NEW BRAUNFELS: Wurstfest Bring the entire family to
Wurstfest because there's food and entertainment to suit every
taste! Enjoy sausage and strudel, pretzels and potato pancakes
served up by fun-loving folks; polka and waltz to good ol' fashioned oompah music performed by Myron Floren, Jimmy Sturr,

Alpenfest, The Seven Dutchmen, and more entertainment groups. See native attire like lederhosen and dirndls worn by friendly Texans who are proud of their German heritage. Admission $6. For more information call 1-800-221-4369.

November

GEORGE WEST: George West Storyfest The Storytelling Capital of Texas. This festival features cowboy poetry/music/storytelling. It is held at the Live Oak County Fairgrounds. www.georgewest.org/storyfest.htm.

Tellabration An annual event where storytelling takes place the world over at the same time. In the United States alone there are over 300 events in 42 states. Tellabration is traditionally held on the Saturday night before Thanksgiving. Some events, however, may be at an alternate time during the same weekend. This last year there were nine Texas events in Dallas, Austin, Houston, Burnet, Frankston, San Antonio, and Grapevine. Events are being added regularly, so please check out www.members.aol.com/tellabrate.

National Storytelling Week (NSW) is a long-range plan under development by the Program Committee of the National Storytelling Network (NSN) Board of Directors. Their goal is to promote NSW, which became part of the USA's official calendar last year, in conjunction with Tellabration.

TERLINGUA: Terlingua Annual Championship Chili Cookoff Held the first Saturday in November, the history is a little complicated. It started out as one festival in the late sixties and has broken up into several festivals. You can get the whole story by looking up http://www.bigbendquarterly.com/terlingua.htm. You will have plenty of good chili and fun listening to some great storytellers, cooks, and musicians. For more information go to

http://www.chili.org/terlingua.html, http://www.chili.org/
chili.html, or http://www.iitexas.com/gpages/terlinga.htm.

(Author's caution: Good advice for any Texas chili cookoff:
Never try any chili without having a cool drink handy, no matter
how much the cook assures you it's not hot!!! Most are wonderful, but I guarantee that, no matter how tough your mouth is,
some of them will blow your lips off!)

CRYSTAL CITY: Spinach Festival This South Texas town provides free live music all three days. Parade on Saturday.
Carnival all three days. All kinds of food booths, variety booths.
Softball tournament, car show, 5K run, walk-a-thon, basketball
tournament. For more information call (830) 374-3161 ask for
Mary. Location: downtown Crystal City. Held annually the second week in November.

HENDERSON: Heritage Syrup Festival Held in the Texas
piney woods, this festival features ribbon cane syrup making,
folk artist demonstrations, arts and crafts, music, food, and lots
of fun. Location: syrup making & folk artists at Depot Museum;
arts/crafts fair downtown Henderson. For more information call
(903) 657-4303. Held annually on the second Saturday in
November.

December

**STONEWALL: Christmas Tree Lighting and Evening Tours of
the LBJ Ranch** Join members of the Johnson family and enjoy
festive choir music and light a beautiful tree to usher in the
Christmas season. Then hop on a tour bus to see the Sauer-
Beckman Farm, all decked out for a German Christmas, circa
1915. The tour continues through the LBJ Ranch for lighting
displays around the historic buildings where Lyndon Johnson
was born, attended school, and had his "Texas White House."
Event begins at LBJ State Historical Park, one mile east of
Stonewall. For more information call (830) 644-2420.

Hill Country Regional Christmas Lighting Trail thru January 1 - Blanco, Bulverde, Burnet, Dripping Springs, Fredericksburg, Goldthwaite, Johnson City, Llano, Marble Falls, Mason, Round Mountain. Beginning Thanksgiving weekend, millions of lights will make miles of memories for families who follow the Hill Country's elaborate Regional Christmas Lighting Trail this holiday season. Eleven towns are set to dazzle visitors with breathtaking holiday extravaganza's between Thanksgiving and New Year's. Each of these charming and unique communities extends a heartfelt invitation to everyone to come view their wonderful seasonal displays. Santa parades, Christmas tree lightings, carriage rides, shopping, festivals, worship services, food, dances, and chorus concerts. Each community has something special to offer. write or call: Regional Christmas Headquarters, 703 N. Llano, Fredericksburg, TX 78624. For more information call (830)-997-8515.

Webliography

Storytelling Groups and Websites

Several years back I needed a word to describe this section. I couldn't find one, so I made up Webliography.

Mike Blakely's website Find out where Mike will be appearing, read excerpts from his books, and find pictures from his appearances. www.MikeBlakely.com

The Broken Spoke, Austin, TX Texas's most definitive dance hall, with the best honky-tonk music in Texas and serving the best chicken-fried steak in Texas. Keep track of who will be appearing and see loads of great pictures. www.lone-star.net/bspoke/

Bureau of Land Management, Wild Horse and Burro Program This website contains a number of references to publications dealing with horses and burros in the west. www.blm.gov/whb

Dyanne Fry Cortez *Hot Jams & Cold Showers: Scenes from the Kerrville Folk Festival*. A neat book by a neat lady. It's about what it's like to attend this wonderful festival over the years. Printed by Dos Puertas Publishing, 2000. http://www.dospuertas.com/

Dallas Storytelling Guild — The home page of the Dallas Storytelling Guild, telling web users about storytelling in general and about their guild, members, and activities in particular. http://geocities.com/SoHo/Study/1578/

The Digital Storytelling Festival is held in September, in Crested Butte, Colorado, to encourage thought, exchange ideas, and to ignite sparks for the creative application of digital technology and the Internet to the art of storytelling with a focus on art and innovation, education, and marketing and branding. It is an intimate gathering in a scenic location, which inspires our audience to leave with new connections and a better understanding of how the oldest art form of storytelling is moving into the new millennium. www.dstory.com/dsf5/home.html

East Texas Storytellers A group of storytellers and listeners who meet monthly for story sharing. We are an affiliate guild of Tejas Storytelling Association. We strive to provide a supportive network for tellers in our area. We help produce the Squatty Pines Storytelling Festival, a very special three days held on the shores of Lake Tyler, near Tyler, Texas. www.homestead.com/EastTexasTellers

Folklife Sourcebook, A Directory of Folklife Resources in the United States lcweb.loc.gov/folklife/source/sourcebk.html

Steven Fromholz website, gives you all the current information on where Steven is playing, and lots of neat pictures, lyrics, and more. www.StevenFromholz.com

George West Storyfest, held in the Storytelling Capital of Texas http://www.georgewest.org/storyfest.htm

Jim Gramon's website Find out where Jim will be appearing, order books, and find loads of great pictures. www.JimGramon.com

The Handbook of Texas Online, provided as a joint effort of the Texas State Historical Society and the University of Texas. I heartily recommend it as an excellent resource on many aspects of Texas. www.tsha.utexas.edu/handbook/online/articles/view/

Houston Storytellers Guild One of the most active and vital local storytelling organizations in the nation sponsors a Liar's Contest the first weekend in April. Membership is open to anyone interested in storytelling and oral traditions. For more info go to http://www.houstonstorytellers.org, write to them at Box 130801, Houston, TX 77219-1644, or phone (713) 827-2620.

Houston Storytelling Circles:
Northeast Circle, Second Tuesday Storytelling Circle
http://users.aol.com/drroff/SecondTuesday.html
Meeting Dates: Second Tuesday of each month at 7:00 P.M.
Site: Jacinto City Library, Jacinto City, Texas

For more info contact James H. Ford Jr. at 11811 I-10 East, Suite 185A, Houston, TX 77029, or call (713) 455-1707 or e-mail drroff@aol.com

1960 *Area Storytelling Circle* Box 131644, Houston, TX 77219-1644, (713) 523-3289 Maryanne Miller (contact)

Bay Area Storytelling Circle Box 131644, Houston, Texas 77219-1644, (713) 523-3289 Charlotte Byrn (contact)

Ft. Bend Storytelling Circle Box 131644, Houston, Texas 77219-1644, (713) 523-3289 Tom Burger (contact)

The Institute of Texan Cultures at the University of Texas at San Antonio http://www.utsa.edu/

International Folk Culture Center — San Antonio has information and links dealing with folklore, folk dances, and folk music. http://www.n-link.com/~ifccsa/

Kerrville Folk Festival Schedules, music, pictures, merchandise, and more at www.Kerrville-Music.com

Kinky Friedman's Websites, get the real skinny about what Kinky is up to. Find out all the latest on where he will be appearing, new books and CDs.

http://www.kinkyfriedman.com/ or http://www.kinkajou-records.com/

La Pena, Latino Arts in Austin, La Peña is a community-based organization dedicated to the preservation, development, and promotion of Latino artistic expression in all its forms. The board of directors and staff of La Peña believe that cultural expression and knowledge is crucial to the survival of the community. www.hyperweb.com/LaPena

Luckenbach, Texas, a must for every Texan's favorites list. Keep track of all the fun doings in this wonderful town. www.LuckenbachTexas.com

Lone Star Spirits is a website devoted to things related to the supernatural and paranormal in Texas. This includes a section on tales relating to those topics. http://www.lonestarspirits.org/

The National Storytellers Network (NSN), also known as StoryNet, is the website for the National Storytelling Association, described below. www.storynet.org/index2.htm

The National Storytelling Association is the largest organization of its kind in the United States. It has been probably the greatest single influence on the revival of storytelling as a professional art form. It offers a great many benefits for members and non-members interested in storytelling. www.storynet.org/index2.htm

The Rio Grande Folklore Archive, situated in The University of Texas-Pan American Library, is one of the largest collections of Mexican American folklore. It is the major depository for the folklore of the Lower Rio Grande Valley of Texas and Northern Tamaulipas, Mexico. This archive's holdings include over 99,000 items, which represent the major genres of folklore. Data for the Rio Grande Folklore Archive is collected on the basis of genre specific collection forms. For example, "The Folktale Collection Form" is specifically designed to collect folktales. Demographic and contextual information is also collected for all genres of folklore. www.panam.edu/dept/folklore/

StoryNet, also known as the National Storytellers Network (NSN)is the website for the National Storytelling Association, described above. www.storynet.org/index2.htm

STORYTELL is an information source sponsored by the School of Library and Information Studies at Texas Woman's University in Denton, Texas, and is a forum for discussion about storytelling. It can serve as a source for information on conferences, workshops, and events or a place to ask (and answer) questions about derivations of stories, intellectual freedom concerns, or organization of storytelling events. www.twu.edu/cope/slis/storytell.htm

The Storytelling Ring (a series of websites that include a wide variety of storytelling areas. www.tiac.net/users/papajoe/ring.htm

The Storytelling Round Table is sponsored by the Texas Library Association to promote an appreciation of the art and tradition of storytelling, particularly its uses in the library setting; exposes TLA members to storytelling through education and performance; and encourages TLA members to share stories and storytelling. www.txla.org/groups/story/storyrt.html

Tejas Storytellers Association Their mission is to foster the appreciation of storytelling as an oral tradition and a performing art. Their goal is to influence the values of the citizens of our region by promoting and supporting the art, craft, and history of storytelling so as to ensure the continuation of the tradition. www.tejasstorytelling.com

Texas Folklife Resources website This site maintains links to a variety of folklore links. www.main.org/tfr/links.htm

Texas State Government Information website, another official state site. Information here focuses on doing business, traveling, and which government agencies perform which functions and how to contact them. There is also info about all of the state symbols. http://www.texas.gov/TEXAS_homepage.html

Texas State Official website, this site is the central site for the state. One area of particular interest is Texas Information, including a Texas History area, as well as information on the census, courthouses, state symbols, legends, and landmarks. http://www.state.tx.us/

Texas Travel - @Texas, this is a great website, offering valuable information about a wide variety of destinations and attractions taking place in the Lone Star State. This site is jointly sponsored by the Texas Festivals & Events Association, Texas Travel Industry Association, and @ction Travel Group. http://www.tourtexas.com/

@round Texas — Clicking on this icon will take you to a section of this site quite handy for locating upcoming events. It offers three different ways to search their database of events. You can search by Date, by geographic Region, or by Type of Event. http://www.tourtexas.com/@roundtexas.html

Texas State Historical Association Organized on March 2, 1897, the Texas State Historical Association is the oldest learned society in the state. Its mission is to foster the appreciation, understanding, and teaching of the rich and unique history of Texas and by example and through programs and activities encourage and promote research, preservation, and publication of historical material affecting the state of Texas. www.tsha.utexas.edu/.

University of Texas Friends of the Library Calendar of Events This site lists a number of events throughout Texas, many of which relate to folklore and storytelling. www.lib.utexas.edu/About/friends/friends.calendar.html

VirtualTexan.com is a site devoted to the state of Texas. It is sponsored by the *Fort Worth Star-Telegram* and occasionally has Texas storytelling related items. www.virtualtexan.com

Rusty Wier's website Keep up with where Rusty will be appearing, pictures, and more at www.RustyWier.com.

Writers' League of Texas This website hosts a wide variety of activities that can help aspiring or experienced storytellers improve their skills and meet others with common interests. www.WritersLeague.org

www.jfordetc.com/Storytellerorganizations.html This website maintains a great list of links to storytelling websites.

Texas Groups Associated with the National Storytelling Network

Austin Storytellers meets each Monday at Koffee and Ice Kream, 6700 Middle Fiskville Rd. (512) 892-2296

Bluebonnet Scops Storytelling Guild meets 1st Saturday. For location: (254) 729-5104

Central Texas Storytelling Guild meeting: 2nd Tuesday of each month at Barnes & Noble, 701 Capital of Texas in S. Westlake. Contact: Reba Ott (512) 258-3345

Dallas Storytelling Guild meeting: 2nd Wednesday of the month at Half Price Books, NW Hwy. and Shady Brook in Dallas, and the 4th Wed. at a site TBA. Contact: Julia Gibson (214) 331-4559

Denton County Storytellers meeting: 3rd Tuesday of the month in member's home. Contact: J.B. Keith (940) 320-1154

East Fork Storytellers and Aficionados meeting: 3rd Monday of each month. Contact: Jerry Young (972) 279-0991

East Texas Storytellers meets the last Saturday at 9:30 a.m. at Times Square Cafe, Tyler. Contact: Pam Pipkin (903) 084-0420

Hill Country Storytelling Guild meets at the Herman Brown Free Library in Burnet most months (512) 756-2328

Houston Storytellers Guild meets the last Wednesday of each month at The River Cafe, 3615 Montrose Blvd. Performances at 8:00 p.m. Information line (713) 466-4438 or contact vschill@stic.lib.tx.us

The Houston Storytellers Guild meets at 7 p.m. on the third Wednesday of each month at the Houston Center for the Arts, 3201 Allen Pkwy. Guests are always welcome and there is never a charge. The guild's professional arm, the Official Guild Storytellers, produces storytelling concerts on the last Wednesday of each month at the River Café, 3615 Montrose Blvd. Performances are at 8:00 p.m. $5 at the door ($3 for members). For more information, call (713) 827-2620, log on to http://www.houstonstorytellers.org/. Send email to hsginfo@hern.org, or write to HSG, Box 131644, Houston, Texas 77219-1644.

Houston's Millennium Storytelling Circle meets at 7 p.m. on the first Tuesday of each month at the Freed-Montrose Branch Library, 4100 Montrose Blvd. The small, informal meetings provide a safe environment for tellers to work on their stories and discuss the craft. Contact: Tom Burger at (281) 530-0930 or send email to tom@houstonstorytelling.com

McKinney Storytelling Guild meeting: 4th Monday of the month in the Foote Chapel in Heritage Square in McKinney. Contact: Waynetta Ausmus (972) 569-9424

Mesquite Storytellers of Abilene meeting: 3rd Tuesday of the month at the Abilene Public Library. Contact: Naomi Huff (915) 893-4362

Oak Valley Storytelling Guild meeting: 3rd Thursday of the month at Oak Valley City Hall. Contact: Gayle Horton (903) 874-7877

Richardson/Plano Storytelling Guild meeting: 3rd Tuesday of each month at the Senior Citizens Center in Richardson. Contact: Doris Brown (972) 661-3923

The Rio Grande Valley Storytellers Guild Contact: Nicole Cruz (956) 584-0316 or (956) 584-1948

San Antonio Storytellers Association meeting and story swapping: third Tuesday 6:30-9:00 at the third floor meeting room of the San Antonio Central Library, 600 Soledad. Contact: Mary Grace Ketner, (210) 271-0628 mketner@lonestar.utsa.edu

San Antonio Stories Galore storyswap: 2nd Sunday 7-9 p.m. at Riverwalk Inn. Contact Mary Grace Ketner (210) 458-2253 mketner@lonestar.utsa.edu

Storytellers of the High Plains meeting: Every other month at the American Indian Cultural Center, Amarillo and monthly performance at different locations. Contact: djsorenson@msn.com

Tarrant Area Guild of Storytellers meeting: 1st Monday of the month at the Center for Change, Development and Support in Arlington. Also the 3rd Monday at Barnes & Noble in Hurst. Contact: Tsagoi (817) 833-3703

Weatherford Storyteller's Guild meets at its library (817) 594-4880

Bibliography

Adams, Florene Chapman. *Hopkins County and Our Heritage*. Sulphur Springs, Texas: 1974.

Abernethy, Francis Edward. *J. Frank Dobie* (Vol. I of the Southwest Writers Series). Austin: Steck-Vaughan Company, 1967.

Armadillo World Headquarters Archives, Barker Texas History Center, University of Texas at Austin.

Austin American-Statesman, April 10, 1990.

Barnstone, Howard. *The Galveston That Was*. New York: Macmillan, 1966.

Bedichek, Roy. *Adventures with a Texas Naturalist*. Austin: University of Texas Press, 1961.

_____. *Letters of Roy Bedichek*, ed. William A. Owens and Lyman Grant. Austin: University of Texas Press, 1985.

Biggers, Don Hampton. *German Pioneers in Texas*. Fredericksburg, Texas: Fredericksburg Publishing, 1925.

Boatright, Mody C. *Folk Laughter on the American Frontier*. New York: The Macmillan Company, 1949.

_____. *Folklore of the Oil Industry*. Dallas: Southern Methodist University Press, 1963.

Bode, Winston. *J. Frank Dobie: A Portrait of Pancho*. Austin: Steck-Vaughn Co., 1968.

Bosque County History Book Committee. *Bosque County, Texas, Land and People: History of Bosque County, Texas*. Dallas: Curtis Media, 1985.

Brown, John Henry. *Indian Wars and Pioneers of Texas*. Austin: Daniell, 1880; reprod., Easley, South Carolina: Southern Historical Press, 1978.

Burton, Michael C. *John Henry Faulk: The Making of a Liberated Mind*. Austin: Eakin Press, 1993.

Cortez, Dyanne Fry. *Hot Jams & Cold Showers: Scenes from the Kerrville Folk Festival*. Austin: Dos Puertas Publishing, 2000. http://www.dospuertas.com/

Cumberland, Charles C. "The Confederate Loss and Recapture of Galveston, 1862-1863." *Southwestern Historical Quarterly* 51 (October 1947).

Davidson, John. "The Man Who Dreamed Up Luckenbach." *Texas Monthly*, July 1984.

Dickey, Dan W. "Tejano Troubadours." *Texas Observer*. July 16, 1976.

_____. *The Kennedy Corridos: A Study of the Ballads of a Mexican American Hero*. Austin: Center for Mexican-American Studies, University of Texas at Austin, 1978.

Dugger, Ronnie (editor). *Three Men in Texas: Bedichek, Webb, and Dobie; Essays By Their Friends in the Texas Observer.* Austin: University of Texas Press, 1967.

_____. "Dobie, Bedichek, Webb: Workers in the Culture." *The Texas Observer*, August 19, 1983.

John Henry Faulk Papers. Barker Texas History Center, University of Texas at Austin. Andie Tucher, ed.

Fehrenbach, T. R. *Lone Star: A History of Texas and Texans*. New York: American Legacy Press, 1983.

Frantz, Joe. *The Forty-Acre Follies*. Austin: Texas Monthly Press, 1983.

_____. "Remembering Walter Prescott Webb." *Southwestern Historical Quarterly*, Vol. 92 (July 1988).

Furman, Necah Stewart. *Walter Prescott Webb: His Life and Impact*. Albuquerque: University of New Mexico Press, 1976.

Germann, John J. and Myron Janzen. *Texas Post Offices by County* (1986).

Gillespie County Historical Society. *Pioneers in God's Hills* (2 vols.). Austin: Von Boeckmann-Jones, 1960, 1974.

Handbook of Texas: A Supplement. Vol. 3. Austin: Texas State Historical Association, 1976.

The Handbook of Texas Online. I heartily recommend it as an excellent resource on many aspects of Texas. www.tsha.utexas.edu/handbook/online/articles/view/

Harrigan, Stephen. "Worked to Death." *Texas Monthly*, October 1988.

Hayes, Charles Waldo. *Galveston: History of the Island and the City* (2 vols.). Austin: Jenkins Garrett, 1974.

Henderson, Tim. *Sweeping Up Dreams, Lyrics As Poetry*. Wimberley, Texas: Sun Country Publications, 1996.

Jackson, Bruce, Michael Taft, and Harvey S. Axelrod, eds. *The Centennial Index: One Hundred Years of the Journal of American Folkore*. Washington, D.C.: American Folklore Society, 1988.

James, Eleanor. *Roy Bedichek*. Austin: Steck-Vaughn, 1970.

McComb, David G. *Galveston: A History*. Austin: University of Texas Press, 1986.

McLeRoy, Sherrie S. *First in the Lone Star State, a Texas Brag Book*. Plano: Republic of Texas Press, 1997.

McMurtry, Larry. *In a Narrow Grave*. (The chapter "Southwestern Literature?") Austin: Encino Press, 1968.

Menconi, David L. "Music, Media, and the Metropolis: The Case of Austin's Armadillo World Headquarters." M.A. thesis, University of Texas at Austin, 1985.

Mendoza, Vicente T. *El corrido mexicano*. Mexico City: Fondo de Cultura Económica, 1954.

Moyers, Bill. *A World of Ideas II: Public Opinions from Private Citizens*. New York: Doubleday, 1990.

Ornish, Natalie. *Pioneer Jewish Texans*. Dallas: Texas Heritage, 1989.

Orren, C. G. "The History of Hopkins County." M.A. thesis, East Texas State Teachers College, 1938. *Texas Magazine*, February 1911.

Owens, William A. *Three Friends: Roy Bedichek, J. Frank Dobie, Walter Prescott Webb*. Garden City, New York: Doubleday, 1969.

Paredes, Américo. "Ballads of the Lower Border." M.A. thesis, University of Texas, 1953.

_____. "El Corrido de Gregorio Cortez: A Ballad of Border Conflict." Ph.D. dissertation, University of Texas, 1956.

_____. *A Texas-Mexican Cancionero: Folksongs of the Lower Border*. Urbana: University of Illinois Press, 1976.

_____. *With His Pistol in His Hand: A Border Ballad and Its Hero*. Austin: University of Texas Press, 1958.

Patman, Wright. *A History of Post Offices and Communities: First Congressional District of Texas*. Texarkana: Wright Patman, 1968.

Patoski, Joe Nick. "Lookin' Back, TX." *Texas Monthly*, December 1990.

Patterson, Becky Crouch. *Hondo, My Father*. Austin: Shoal Creek Publishers, 1979.

William C. Pool. "Bosque Territory." Kyle, Texas: *Chaparral*, 1964.

Powell, Lawrence Clark. *Books in My Baggage: Adventures in Reading and Collecting*. (The chapter "Mr. Southwest") Cleveland: World Pub. Co., 1960.

Ragsdale, Kenneth B. *Quicksilver: Terlingua and the Chisos Mining Company*. College Station: Texas A&M University Press, 1976.

Reid, Jan. *The Improbable Rise of Redneck Rock*. New York: Da Capo Press, 1974. Vertical Files, Barker Texas History Center, University of Texas at Austin.

Ryan, Bryan, ed. *Hispanic writers: A Selection of Sketches from Contemporary Authors.* Detroit: Gale Research, 1991.

Simmons, Merle. *The Mexican Corrido as a Source of an Interpretive Study of Modern Mexico, 1870-1950.* Bloomington: University of Indiana Press, 1957.

Stowers, Carlton. "Hondo Crouch and His Backwoods Camelot." *Texas Almanac,* Millennium Edition. *The Dallas Morning News,* 1999.

Texas Observer, June 27, 1959.

Tinkle, Lon. *An American Original: The Life of J. Frank Dobie.* Boston: Little, Brown, 1978.

Vertical Files, Barker Texas History Center, University of Texas at Austin.

Webb, Walter Prescott. *The Great Plains.* Boston: Ginn and Company, 1931.

_____. *The Texas Rangers: A Century of Frontier Defense.* Boston, New York: Houghton Mifflin Company, 1935.

_____. *Divided We Stand: The Crisis of a Frontierless Democracy.* New York, Toronto: Farrar & Rinehart, Inc., 1937.

_____. *The Great Frontier.* Boston: Houghton Mifflin, 1952.

_____. *The Handbook of Texas.* Austin: Texas State Historical Association, 1952-76.

_____. *More Water for Texas: The Problem and the Plan.* Austin: University of Texas Press, 1954.

_____. *An Honest Preface, and Other Essays.* Boston: Houghton Mifflin, 1959.

West, John O. *Mexican-American Folklore.* Little Rock: August House, 1988.

Woolley, Bryan. *Mythic Texas.* Plano: Republic of Texas Press, 2000.

A Word From the Author

I live at Shady Slope, in the heart of scenic downtown San Leanna, Texas. There I write books, articles, poetry, and songs. I also do freelance writing and photography for a number of firms. Since I program in 14 computer languages, I often do freelance technical writing for firms that want their documentation to be understood by nonprogrammers.

Texas Co-Op Power Magazine (850,000 readers) carries my monthly column about special Texas festivals or events. (Few folks remember the name but know it as the colorful little magazine that goes out to everyone getting electricity from an electric cooperative.)

I'm currently working on four books that will be out over the next two years. These include another Texas storytellers book, one about Texas musicians, and I'm working with Aaron Allan on Aaron's biography. About Christmas 2002, I will be finishing the manuscript for the first book of a new literary genre, the Texas techno-thriller.

This fast-paced adventure will be complete with bad guys (and gals), computer crimes, murders, espionage, and of course, lots of down-home Texas characters. (Yes, there will be some musicians that you will recognize; the hero owns a Texas honky-tonk.) And of course there will be a good ol' Texas boy trying to solve the mysteries and getting help from famous "totally fictitious" detective friends like Kinky Friedman.

I regularly do tours, emceeing, storytelling, and signing books at events and festivals. You can keep track by checking www.JimGramon.com.

If you are interested in having me emcee an event, do a storytelling, or do some freelance writing, you can reach me at Jim@JimGramon.com or at P.O. Box 2100, Manchaca, TX 78652-2100.

Index